28/3/2013

Slough L **KT-462-220**

Please return this book on or before the date shown on your receipt.

To renew go to:
Website: **www.slough.gov.uk/libraries**
Phone: **03031 230035**

LIB/6198   0466

Katie Fforde was born and brought up in London but has lived in Gloucestershire with her family for the last thirty years. Her first novel, *Living Dangerously*, went on to be chosen as part of the WHSmith Fresh Talent Promotion. There have been over eighteen novels since, as well as some grandchildren. Her hobbies, when she has time for them, are singing in a choir and flamenco dancing. She also enjoys exploring a different profession or background for each of her books, and has conducted her research by working as a porter in an auction house, trying her hand at pottery, refurbishing furniture, delving behind the scenes of a dating website, and even going on a Ray Mears survival course. Currently she is President of the Romantic Novelists' Association.

You can discover more about the author at www.katiefforde.com

A SECRET GARDEN

Lorna is a talented gardener and Philly is a plantswoman. Together they work on the grounds of a beautiful manor house in the Cotswolds. They enjoy their jobs and are surrounded by family and friends. But for them both, the door to true love remains resolutely closed. So when Lorna is introduced to Jack at a dinner party, and Lucien catches Philly's eye at the local market, it seems that dreams really can come true and happy endings lie just around the corner. But do they? Troublesome parents, the unexpected arrival of someone from Lorna's past, and the discovery of an old and secret garden mean their lives are about to become a lot more complicated . . .

Books by Katie Fforde
Published by Ulverscroft:

LIVING DANGEROUSLY
THE ROSE REVIVED
WILD DESIGNS
STATELY PURSUITS
LIFE SKILLS
THYME OUT
HIGHLAND FLING
ARTISTIC LICENCE
PARADISE FIELDS
RESTORING GRACE
FLORA'S LOT
PRACTICALLY PERFECT
GOING DUTCH
WEDDING SEASON
LOVE LETTERS
A PERFECT PROPOSAL
SUMMER OF LOVE
RECIPE FOR LOVE
A FRENCH AFFAIR
THE PERFECT MATCH
A SUMMER AT SEA

KATIE FFORDE

A SECRET GARDEN

Complete and Unabridged

CHARNWOOD
Leicester

First published in Great Britain in 2017 by
Century
part of the Penguin Random House group
London

First Charnwood Edition
published 2018
by arrangement with
Penguin Random House UK
London

A catalogue record for this book is available
from the British Library.

ISBN 978–1–4448–3534–2

Published by
F. A. Thorpe (Publishing)
Anstey, Leicestershire
Set by Words & Graphics Ltd.
Anstey, Leicestershire
Printed and bound in Great Britain by
T. J. International Ltd., Padstow, Cornwall

This book is printed on acid-free paper

To women who garden, everywhere.

Acknowledgements

As always, it takes almost as many people to create a book as it does patches to make a double-size quilt, and inevitably I will forget some of these people and get things wrong. I fervently apologise for both these things. I don't do it on purpose; I do it because I am very forgetful! But below are the people I haven't forgotten, and I thank them most sincerely for their help and inspiration.

To everyone, past and present, who is involved in the Rodborough Real Gardens and Sculpture Trail. Of course we had to appear in a book!

Alan Ford, who introduced me to the heroic and inspirational Pascal Mychalysin, Master Mason of Gloucester Cathedral.

Marion Mako and Tim Mowl, garden historians and extremely entertaining lunch companions.

Ori Hellerstein, artisan baker, who told me about three-phase electricity amongst more bread-based things.

Sarah Watts, garden designer and wonderful source of information.

Tim Hancock and Rebecca Flint of Tortworth Plants, and Deny Watkins of Special Plants Nursery.

Sue Devine, guide at Gloucester Cathedral, whose knowledge could fill several books.

Richard Davis, brother of the wonderful writer and friend Jo Thomas, who knows an awful lot about betting and how sometimes people do win!

Dr Annie Grey and her team for the wonderful programme *Victorian Bakers*, which was part of the inspiration for this book.

All my wonderful team at Century — Selina Walker, Georgina Hawtrey-Woore, Asian Byrne, Chris Turner and Sarah Ridley, and Charlotte Bush and her team.

My wonderful agent Bill Hamilton. Crème de la crème of agents.

Richenda Todd, copy-editor worth double her weight in rubies.

To all my writer friends who keep me going, thank you.

1

Philly pulled at the gaffer tape with her teeth, failed to tear it and groaned. 'Hand me those secateurs, Grand,' she said. Wind found its way up the sleeves of her coat, far colder than wind in April ought to be, in Philly's opinion. If it weren't for the primroses in the hedgerows and the trays of forced bulbs in her greenhouse, it could have been February.

Her grandfather shook his head. 'You need scissors, or a knife. Here.' He took out the Swiss Army knife he was never without and cut the tape.

Philly applied it to the rip in the polytunnel and then looked carefully for more potential holes. 'If we get the weather that's forecast, I need to be sure the wind can't get in.'

'Child dear!' said her grandfather. 'A new polytunnel is what you need. Why won't you let me buy you one?'

Philly, satisfied the tunnel was as windproof as it could be, handed him back his knife. 'Grand? Do we have to have this conversation every day? Wouldn't once a week be enough?'

'C'mon now. There's a storm brewing that might tear this old thing down. What would happen to your precious salvias then?'

Philly nodded. 'They might all be blown to bits, I realise that. But it's too late for a new polytunnel now.' She smiled at him, knowing he

1

couldn't win this argument.

'But it's not too late for the next gale. You know they say 'April is the cruellest month'. It could quite easily produce a hurricane for you.' He was as stubborn as she was.

She put her hand on his arm. 'Grand, dear, I owe you enough already and I don't want to get into more debt with you. I'll make do with this tunnel until I make enough money for a new one.'

Her grandfather tutted but didn't argue any more. He wasn't giving up the battle, just retrenching. 'Come away in and have some tea. There's cake.'

Philly brightened. 'So what's wrong with it? Did you leave the walnuts out of a coffee and walnut?'

'It's a trifle overbaked,' he said. 'Or burnt as we said in the olden days.'

Philly was surprised. 'What, actual burnt, burnt?'

'Indeed no! But it's not of merchantable quality.'

Philly laughed. 'That's OK then. But if you wouldn't mind hanging on, I need to do my posies and check which bulbs are advanced enough for me to bring to the stall. It won't take long. I've all my material picked and ready. Then it'll be time for the phone call. You remember they're all off to a party on Sunday so they brought it forward? Could we have tea after that?'

'Of course we could. I'll put the potatoes in for supper. The cake can be pudding.'

'Perfect!' She kissed his cheek and took his arm as they set off. Philly headed for one of the outbuildings, her grandfather for the house. She was rather dreading the phone call. She had nothing new to tell her parents, nothing that would make them stop worrying, and therefore nagging for her to come home to Ireland, even if that meant leaving her grandfather here in England.

She had no desire to abandon the adventure she and her grandfather had set out on, three years ago, when her grandfather had happened to see a small-holding online and something about it appealed to him although he'd been after a house with a few garages. She had gone with him to see it. When she'd seen it, she'd fallen in love with it too. It had a few acres, lots of outbuildings and even a couple of old poly tunnels. It was perfect for her to grow plants in and see if her life-long dream to be a plantswoman would withstand real-life experience.

The house was a tumbledown money pit, no doubt about it, but Philly and her grandfather didn't mind living in the big old farmhouse kitchen and shutting off other rooms in winter. And what had completely sold it to her grandfather was the mouldering old Alvis in one of the garages. He would have gone to England all on his own, desperately needing a new project and to get away from his family, to distract him from loneliness after his wife died — but when Philly, who had just gone to keep him company at the viewing, had said she wanted to come too, it had all seemed too perfect not to pursue.

How such a property had stayed out of the hands of developers was a great big hunk of Irish luck. It had an agricultural covenant on it that meant no one could turn the outbuildings into dwellings, even holiday lets. The seller had made sure his property wouldn't get into what he felt were the wrong hands.

Also, when Philly and her grandfather had come to see it, the elderly seller had taken a shine to them. He invited them into his mouldering house, gave them tea out of stained mugs and insisted they sat down. As there was no alternative they sank into a sofa that had the consistency of a bog. While they were unable to move without assistance, he grilled them about their plans. When they admitted that they were both running away from a well-meaning but overbearing and conventional family, he decided theirs was the offer he'd accept. Even if it wasn't the highest. (He told them this at the time.) He was going to take the money for the property and end his days on a narrow boat.

He had asked if they wouldn't gentrify the house too much and they had agreed. They had no trouble consenting to this although there was nothing legally binding — just no chance of there being any spare money for anything beyond keeping out the worst of the weather.

Now, three years later, things weren't much different. But in spite of the hard work and the discomfort ('utter squalor', as Philly's horrified mother described it) they both still had their dreams intact.

It didn't take Philly long to make twenty or so posies, all in makeshift containers: jam jars, tin cans or yoghurt pots. The containers, although rustic, had had a bit of a facelift — a lick of paint or a good scrub — something to make them look fresh and not as if they'd been salvaged from a huge pile of rubbish found at the house. (Which was where they had all come from.) A bit of oasis, some greenery (she loved the fresh acidity of new spring foliage), several different tulips, dark velvet polyanthus, a few sprigs of blossom and she had informal arrangements that people loved. Then she gathered several pots of growing bulbs, scillas, white and blue grape hyacinths and some late miniature daffodils, and she had something that would grace anyone's table. Her offerings were very popular with people headed for dinner parties. Philly also bunched together larger sprays of hedgerow plants and small trees that were beloved of flower arrangers. As Philly was sometimes roped in to do the flowers in church, she knew how hard it was to find enough suitable greenery if you had a tidy garden and so she provided it. This all supplemented the containers of bulbs that she sold officially but which, she reflected now, weren't quite such good earners. The posies and greenery bunches represented 100 per cent profit.

When she'd created enough to make her stall look attractive and make an extra fifty pounds or so, she went back to the house, looking forward to warming up. Then she'd talk to her mother.

Dead on six o'clock, the phone rang.

'Well, darling, how are you?' said Marion Doyle, unable as ever to conceal her anxiety about her youngest child.

'I'm fine, Ma, really. How are the boys?' Philly had two older brothers who fitted in better with what Marion considered proper.

'They're fine. Working hard. Now tell me about you.'

Philly always felt a bit put on the spot when her mother asked this. 'Well, I've got lots of things to sell at tomorrow's market. And now it's spring, there'll be loads of tourists and second-homers wanting to brighten up their gardens.'

'And your grandfather? Is he still — you know — baking?' In Philly's mother's world, men didn't bake.

'He is — he's brilliant at it. You should be proud of him.'

'It's not that I'm not proud, it's just I find it a bit odd. I blame you, Philomena. You introduced him to that programme.'

Philly laughed, refusing to be apologetic. 'I admit I never thought Grand would take up baking just because of *Bake Off* but he's brilliant at it! People depend on him being at the stall on Saturday mornings. He even takes commissions,' she added proudly.

Her mother sighed. 'Well, I suppose it beats messing around with that old car, but it's hardly a manly activity, is it?'

'It's perfectly manly,' said Philly, knowing her mother would never accept this. 'And it is better for him in winter, anyway. It's far warmer in the kitchen.'

'But the kitchen, darling! Is it even hygienic, baking in there?'

'Ma, you haven't been over to visit us since that first time. You haven't seen all we've done to the kitchen to bring it up to professional standards of hygiene.'

Marion didn't comment. Philly could tell she was holding herself back from saying, yet again, that however much they might have done to the kitchen, the house was still unfit to live in, especially for a man of Seamus's age. Knowing this would create bad feeling she said instead, 'Well now, have you got a boyfriend yet?'

Although Philly was relieved that her mother wasn't telling her yet again that her grandfather shouldn't live in such a cold house, she wasn't awfully pleased with this topic of conversation. 'No, Ma! I didn't have one last week either!'

Her mother sighed. 'But are you even meeting any young men who might become boyfriends, stuck out there in the middle of nowhere?' Marion didn't think much to the very pleasant little town that was less than three miles away from the smallholding.

'Not at the moment.' Here was where Philly and her mother were in agreement. Meeting a few boys of her own age would be nice. One even. There was a boy who worked on the cheese counter opposite them when they did the market, but she felt so shy if they needed cheese she managed to always get her grandfather to buy it. She wasn't going to admit this to her mother though. 'I'm thinking of asking the pub if they need any bar staff,' she went on. 'That would be a good way to meet young people.'

Marion tsked but didn't comment. She had another little arrow to fling at Philly before she commented on what she thought about her daughter working in a pub. She didn't really approve that Philly worked as a waitress from time to time, to a very upmarket caterer. 'Well, don't forget there's a lovely boy waiting for you here.'

'Ma, he's not waiting for me. He's got a lovely girlfriend.' This boy was sweet and had been a great childhood sweetheart but he wasn't much of a one for adventure and risk and had a good safe job in his parents' stationery business.

'He'd leave her for you if you came home.'

'Well, what sort of a boyfriend would that make him? Anyway, you and the da OK?'

'We're fine. Just worrying about you two tear-aways.'

Philly laughed. 'Well, there's no need. And you can hardly describe us as tearaways. Grand is a respectable man in his seventies and I'm over the age of consent.'

'You're twenty-three! That's hardly the most responsible age.'

'How old were you when you and Da got married?' As she knew the answer to this Philly felt she'd scored the winning goal.

'OK, so I was only nineteen but I was a very mature nineteen and you were only twenty when — '

'We're going to be all right, Ma,' said Philly,

8

interrupting. 'I know we are. I'll make a go of my plants and Grand is happy. What more can you ask for?'

'For you both to be back home in Ireland! But I know that's a vain hope.' Marion sighed. 'I'm glad you're both happy. And don't leave it too long before coming to see us again.'

* * *

The market the following day was even more hectic than usual. It took over the centre of the town once a week, in front of the old, picturesque buildings that included an ancient abbey, used as the parish church, which was almost as big as a cathedral. Currently outside it was a despondent thermometer displaying how much more money they needed to raise in order to repair parts of building but it was still beautiful.

Now spring was here — according to the calendar if not the weather currently — holiday-home owners, who had stayed in London over the winter, were beginning to come down to their little places in the country and wanted to beautify them. The market was also somewhere they could bring visiting friends and as you could buy almost everything you needed for a weekend's entertaining in an enjoyably green and environmentally sound way, it was bustling. Having a second home was more acceptable if you supported local businesses, Philly assumed was their thinking. As she and her grandfather benefited she had no complaints. They were busy almost to the end. The boy with the floppy hair whom she liked was on the cheese stall. They were doing a roaring trade too.

They were just about to pack up when a tall, attractive, middle-aged woman with dark red hair cut stylishly in a wavy bob came over.

'Caught you!' she said. 'I am desperate for cake. And posies.'

'Hello, Lorna,' said Philly. 'I'll wrap the posies for you.'

Lorna rummaged in her purse. 'How much for them?'

'I'm giving them to you,' said Philly firmly, 'if I can have the jars back. The flowers cost nothing, you know that, and as my best customer for the nursery, you get them free.'

'Oh,' said Lorna. 'I feel I shouldn't have asked now.'

'Of course you should. Now, Grand, how much are you going to charge Lorna for the cake?'

'Is a fiver too much?' he asked.

'A fiver is an absolute steal, but I'll take it,' said Lorna.

'If you don't mind my saying so, you don't look to be the sort of woman who eats a lot of cake,' he said, putting it in a bag.

'I do! Well, I have a bit now and again. The rest I cut into slices and freeze. Then when I want a gorgeous pudding I put it in the microwave, heat it up and then serve with ice cream. It's delicious.'

'It does sound good,' said Philly. 'We must try that, Grand.'

10

'Well, in exchange for a recipe, you must tell me why you call your grandfather 'Grand'. It's not in the normal range of grandfather names and I've wanted to know for ages but never dared ask.'

'It's short for Grandiloquent,' said Philly after a short pause.

'I never cared for any of those 'Grandpa' sort of names,' said Seamus. 'I came across 'grandiloquent' and thought it was a fine sort of a word. I suggested the little ones call me it, but it only stuck with Philly.'

'My mother encouraged it,' Philly explained. 'She said that Grand was pretty much a delinquent in many ways, although we do know it's not the same word really.'

Lorna laughed. 'Well, thank you for that. And how are my salvias coming along?'

'Fine, I think. And will you be wanting more tubs of delphiniums this year?'

'Oh, I should think so. They were beautiful last year, really made an impression. I'll be sending you a list of things I need soon. I know I should have done it before but you know how things go.'

'It's a shame more people don't get to see your garden,' said Philly.

'It's not my garden, thank God,' said Lorna, 'but you're right, it should be seen more. Perhaps when it's a little further along in its restoration we'll think about opening it. It is still very early days.'

When Lorna had taken her cake and her posies and moved away, Seamus said, 'That is a fine figure of a woman.'

'She is,' Philly agreed. 'But she's a bit young for you.'

'Indeed,' said her grandfather.

Philly carried on packing up the stall. Maybe, instead of asking her about her love life every week, her mother should have been considering that of her father-in-law.

2

The following Monday morning, Lorna's boss handed her a cup of tea and then sat down on the step next to her. In front of them was a bumpy bit of turf that would one day (Lorna fervently hoped) be a fine lawn. Behind them were the tall columns of a graceful Palladian frontage. By mansion standards, Burthen House was on the small side, but by those of any normal home, it was enormous. Built of the honey-coloured stone common in the area, it needed a bit of work to make it truly elegant but Lorna liked its rather decayed beauty. One day, she knew, it would be fully restored but she preferred it now, really.

'So,' Lorna asked. 'How did Friday night's date go?'

Peter, lord of all he surveyed and the house, all of which was currently under restoration, sighed. 'Well, actually — ' He stopped, gulped and said, 'It was amazing.'

Lorna's heart fluttered a little. 'Oh?' Peter was an optimistic online dater, pursuing women at least two decades younger than his fifty-seven years. But because he still had a lot of good hair and teeth, not to mention a stately home, he had plenty to choose from. Most of his dates were disastrous, causing him and Lorna to laugh a lot when he told her about them later. So far, none of them had caused him to gulp. And while this went on, Lorna's dreams were still intact.

He nodded. 'Yes. Apart from being absolutely gorgeous, she was really intelligent, asked all the right questions.' He sipped his coffee and then fumbled in his pocket for a packet of biscuits. He handed them to Lorna.

Lorna took one. She liked it when his dates had gone badly; she was waiting patiently for him to realise that he'd do much better with a woman his own age, i.e. her. They'd met as children, spent most of their lives apart, but here they both were, single, in the same location and yet not an item. 'So go on,' she said. 'She didn't just want to know about the size of your estate? In other words, check out if you were really rich or just bigging yourself up on the website?'

'You're cynical, you know that, Lorna?'

'It's how I stay healthy,' she said and stretched out her leg in front of her. There were perfectly good benches they could have sat on but somehow they always sat on the steps of Burthen House, as if they were still children.

'Well, you'd be pleased!' Peter went on. 'She wanted to hear about the garden and not just about old masters and stuccoed ceilings.'

'That is a good sign. A woman with the right priorities.'

'I told her you were restoring this for me and she wanted to know all about your plans.'

'And you could tell her all about them, could you?' Lorna smiled up at him, knowing full well that his interest in the garden was very superficial. He very much liked the idea of living

14

in a stately home but wasn't all that interested in the practicalities.

'I just told her what I knew,' he said, slightly on the defensive. 'That you'd been restoring them for a couple of years and eventually hoped to get them back to how they had been.'

' 'Eventually' is about the right timescale,' said Lorna. 'I need more help in the gardens if we're really going to make a difference.' She realised she was talking about the garden to stop him telling her about his wonderful date.

But Peter wasn't cooperating. 'Go on then. You have my permission to take on more staff, but let me tell you more about Kirstie.'

Lorna decided she had to be content with the thought of extra staff. If Peter hadn't noticed she was the perfect wife for him by now, he probably never would. 'So, what makes her better than the other young lovelies you've been out with?'

'She has a brain. She's a freelance events organiser. She'd heard of the Beatles, laughed at my jokes, was generally — well, brilliant. And so pretty.'

Lorna smiled to hide her sigh. 'I can't wait to meet her.'

She'd felt sarcastic when she said it but he didn't pick it up. 'Well, isn't that perfect? You are going to meet her.'

'Am I? When?'

'As soon as I can arrange it. I'm going to have a dinner party, invite Mother, too.' He frowned ever so slightly, his brows drawing together above his aristocratic nose. 'I think she should meet

Mother sooner rather than later or it'll be difficult.'

'Would it?'

He flapped his hand. 'Of course it would! You know what she's like. A horrendous snob and can be quite spiky with people she doesn't like.'

Lorna did know what she was like. Peter's mother, Lady Anthea Leonard-Stanley, was a friend of hers. Anthea and Lorna's mother had been great friends and Lorna had always got on with her too. It was through Anthea that Lorna had got the job of garden designer and restorer (and, mostly, weeder and digger) for Burthen House. She was very kind-hearted but didn't suffer fools. Lorna didn't think she was always a snob but could be snippy about her son's unsuitable girlfriends.

'But you'd invite other people? It wouldn't just be you and Kirstie, and me and Anthea?' The thought was horrifying.

It obviously horrified Peter too. 'Good God, no! We're going to invite several people. Kirstie knows someone who can cater it. Although we might need to find someone who could help serve.'

Lorna frowned. 'Peter? You've been on one date and you're already saying 'we' and giving a dinner party together. Aren't you rushing things a bit?'

He looked at Lorna and Lorna looked back, wishing she didn't find him so attractive. She'd had a crush on him when she was seven and although most of the intervening years had been spent apart, both with spouses for at least some

16

of the time, she still felt the same.

He looked distracted. 'Lorna, after our date was over and I'd seen her home safely, I rang her, just to say goodnight and — well, we talked almost all night.'

Lorna's fluttering heart descended to her Hunter wellies and stayed there. This was serious. She could remember those times when you first meet and don't want to stop talking.

'And then we spent the whole weekend together. Reg drove her home for me on Sunday night.'

Reg was Peter's driver. 'I see. You're in love then.' She tried to sound upbeat and felt she'd managed quite well.

'Yes!' He looked at her properly for the first time that day. 'You are pleased for me, aren't you?'

Lorna took a sip of coffee to give herself an extra moment to compose herself. 'If she's really right for you, and you both really love each other in a way that will last forever, then of course I'm happy for you. How could I be otherwise?'

'I'm so glad, because I sometimes wondered — you know — ' He stopped.

As Lorna knew him so well she knew perfectly well what was in his mind: did she have romantic feelings for him? Well, she had to put that idea out of his head, especially because it was true.

She laughed, praying it sounded amused and not desperately embarrassed. 'Peter! I admit I did quite fancy you when I was seven but that was a long time ago.'

'So you're really, really happy for me?'

'Of course!' And in time she would be. One of the things about loving people was that you did, on the whole, want the best for them.

'It's just I know my mother always wanted us to get together and she'll never forgive me if I've broken your heart.'

This time her laugh was a little less strained. She had always wondered if Anthea knew how she felt about Peter. 'Would you like me to go and see her and assure her you haven't?'

'Would you? I'd be so grateful. It's going to be hard enough getting her on side without her thinking that Kirstie has cut you out in some way.'

'I can see that.' She hesitated. 'Have you a date for this dinner party?' She wanted to ask if they'd been too busy exchanging life histories and love-making to get down to the practicalities but held back. Nothing she said must even hint that he'd been right about her feelings.

'We thought maybe Saturday week? Are you free?'

Lorna got out her phone and checked her diary although she knew perfectly well she was free, 'Seems to be OK.'

'And you can find someone to wait at table?'

'Have you thought of taking on a personal assistant? You can afford it and it would make your life — and mine too, come to that — so much easier.'

He blinked. 'Why employ an assistant when you can have a lovely new wife to do it all for you?'

She smiled, acknowledging she recognised that

he was joking. 'She could be an interim measure, until you get a lovely new wife?'

He shook his head. 'Not necessary, I'm positive. Kirstie is the one. I can't wait for you to meet her. I know you'll get on.'

3

Leaving Burthen House, Lorna walked home across the park that once had deer roaming in it, and would one day, she hoped, have some rare-breed sheep. She'd heard Peter being enthusiastic about girlfriends before but this was different. He was obviously besotted. And if Kirstie felt the same, then there was no point in her keeping her little flame of hope alive. She'd better just try and get over it.

'Lorna!' said Anthea, opening her front door wide. 'How wonderful to see someone civilised. And it means I can have coffee.'

Lorna slipped her feet out of her boots. Peter's mother lived in the Dower House. The fact that there was such a handsome one as part of the estate had been one of the reasons he'd bought it, that and the fact he had to do something with the obscene amount of money he earned.

Anthea was a firm friend to Lorna and she followed into her kitchen.

'And have you heard?' Anthea went on. 'Peter is officially in love!' She managed to make this state sound unspeakably vulgar.

'He does seem very happy.' Glad that she didn't have to break this news, Lorna kept her tone neutral.

'He sounds deranged.' Anthea slapped the kettle on to her ancient Aga. 'He's just been on the telephone. Told me about this dinner party.

To be honest, Lorna darling, I'd find it easier if he wasn't so ecstatic. I mean, has he lost all his critical faculties? He's nearly sixty, for God's sake.'

'Speaking as someone who's getting on that way I don't think it necessarily makes you any wiser.'

'Well, no,' Anthea agreed. 'But when it's one's son involved, one does rather hope it might.' The kettle having now boiled, Anthea filled a coffee pot with water to warm it and then set about finding beans, grinding them and eventually putting two pots on the table, one with coffee, the other with hot milk. 'I always have instant when I'm on my own so it's nice to have an excuse to make proper coffee.'

Lorna, who had seated herself at the table, breathed in the smell. 'I think you make the best coffee of anyone I know.'

Anthea put down two bone-china mugs — a compromise between her really preferring cups and saucers and yet appreciating mugs didn't need topping up so often. 'Thank you.' She began pouring. 'So you don't think Peter's gone entirely mad? Meeting this girl one night and practically moving her in the next?'

'Is she moving in?' This was news and a shock.

'No, I don't think so. But this dinner party — apparently she's asking lots of her friends who have to stay the night. What the poor staff will do about proper bedlinen I don't know.' She frowned. 'It's just it's all so sudden. And I'll have to do flowers.'

'I thought you loved doing flowers. I thought

21

that was your thing.'

'It is, but I'm on church flower duty that week and won't want to be up at the house trying to hide the damp patches behind the arrangements.' Anthea took a comforting sip of coffee.

'I could ask Philly to do them,' Lorna suggested. 'I'm already going to ask her to wait at table. Apparently Kirstie knows a good caterer but he needs a waiter. Possibly a kitchen assistant too. Philly could do both. If she's not too busy with her market stall.'

'Is Philly the one who raises plants for you? Nice girl. Although she always looks at me as if I'm going to eat her.' Anthea frowned. 'Maybe it would be better if I didn't try and smile. It's the smile that terrifies them.'

Lorna laughed. 'She is shy but very efficient. I'll ask her to help out but we have to get Peter to pay her properly.'

'Hmm. The trouble with Peter is he's always been so charming he expects to get everything for nothing. I'll get him to pay her a hundred pounds. Is that enough? I mean, it sounds like a small fortune to me but I'm still living in the Dark Ages.'

'It would be generous but appropriate,' said Lorna, glad to think Philly would get a reasonable sum out of it. 'I just hope she can help.'

'I'm sure for a hundred pounds she'll be able to,' said Anthea. 'Did you want a biscuit? Toast?' When Lorna had shaken her head, she went on: 'So what do we think about this Kirstie?'

'Without having met her, it's hard to say, but

Peter is obviously enraptured.'

'Doesn't sound a good thing at his age.'

'I think it's lovely. Don't we all want to be swept off our feet?'

'Absolutely not! Didn't want it when I was a girl, don't want it now' Anthea sounded so appalled and so vehement, she obviously shocked herself. 'Of course I was in love with my husband, but it was an emotion that grew as we got to know each other. It wasn't a *coup de foudre*. I distrust passionate emotions that come out of nowhere.'

'Well, I see your point,' said Lorna, whose loyalties were stretched in both directions. She would have enjoyed having an old-fashioned bitch about this unknown woman but also wanted to support Peter. If this was the real thing, she had to go along with it. 'But judging by what he's told me about her, she seems nice. Interested in the gardens, which makes me inclined to like her.'

'You don't think she's just after him for his money, do you?'

'I shouldn't think so. I mean, the house needs a lot of doing up. He doesn't flaunt his wealth. She may not know he's rich.'

'He's mean, you mean.'

Lorna laughed. 'Not really! I mean, I know he's careful — probably how he got to be so rich — but he doesn't have a flashy car — if you overlook having a driver.' She paused. 'Actually, him having a driver will tell her exactly how rich he is. But let's give her the benefit of the doubt. At least until we've met her.'

'Very well then. We'll be on our best behaviour and tear her apart afterwards.'

'But only if she holds her knife like a pen,' said Lorna.

Anthea laughed. 'I do wish it could have been you, Lorna. We've always understood each other.'

'Well, if it's not meant, it's not. We'll always be friends anyway. And I hope he's very happy.'

'Very magnanimous of you, dear. Personally I'd want that outrageous fortune for myself!'

'To be honest, being happy in my work, which I am, having a nice house, which — thanks to you and Peter's estate — I have, and being healthy is pretty much enough.' It wasn't *absolutely* enough but Lorna wasn't going to share that. 'And having my son also well and happy and in work, which I'm pleased to tell you is currently the situation, is almost perfect.'

'How very wise you are, my dear,' said Anthea.

Wishing she felt as wise as the impression she had given Anthea, Lorna went home to get her car and then drove to Philly's.

★ ★ ★

Philly was in the greenhouse, checking her plants. She jumped when she heard someone behind her. 'Oh, Lorna, it's you. How nice.'

'I found Seamus and he told me you were here. He said you wouldn't mind if I came and found you. Please don't let me stop you working.'

'Did you come to see what I'm growing for

24

this season? I'd just decided that I've chosen all the wrong stuff and none of it will sell.'

Lorna laughed. 'You said that last year and everything went.'

'Because you bought it!' Philly was never sure if basing a business on only one client was sensible. It meant there wasn't any wastage but she knew her parents would say it was putting all her eggs in one basket.

'You grew what I wanted. But I'm not here about that. I have a job for you.' Lorna frowned slightly. 'Maybe if you're ready to stop we could talk about it in the house?'

'That sounds mysterious, but I'm more than happy to stop.'

Philly led the way to the house wondering what Lorna was looking awkward about. She made them both tea and found some cake.

'This is why I came, really,' said Lorna. She was seated at the kitchen table, looking enthusiastic as Philly cut into the chocolate confection.

'This is what my grandfather calls 'gattox',' said Philly. 'He won't be told that only works if there's more than one of them.'

'I'm going to call it gattox myself now you've told me,' said Lorna.

'So,' said Philly. 'What can I do for you?'

Lorna frowned again. 'Well, it's two things and I'm not sure you're going to be keen because it's on a Saturday and I know you're busy at the market on Saturdays.'

'Is it a waitressing job? That's OK, it'll be in the evening.'

25

'It is a waitressing job but they also want you to do the flowers. It's for Peter and . . . ' Lorna paused just for a second. 'Kirstie. He has a new girlfriend and they're having a dinner party so he can show her off to people — his mother, me, etc.'

'Oh.' Philly had always suspected that Lorna had a soft spot for Peter herself, although she'd never said anything. 'What's she like? Have you met her?'

'No. The dinner party will be the first time. She's got a caterer but he wants a waiter and maybe some prepping help. And Anthea wants you to do the flowers.'

'It would be a long day but I expect it'll be OK. Do they want me to provide flowers as well?'

'I think they expect you to just cut a few branches from the grounds. There are some trees just coming into leaf, some winter-flowering things still doing their thing, and lots and lots of bulbs.'

'That is the sort of flower arranging I like,' said Philly.

'That's what I thought. And I've managed to get you a hundred pounds. But that includes the waitressing.'

'That sounds OK,' said Philly, having done a quick sum. 'Better than the minimum wage anyway. I wonder if they'd mind if I did the flowers the day before?'

'I'm sure they wouldn't. I'll tell Doreen — you know? The housekeeper? I'll be there too, to make sure you get given the best vases. Some of them are tucked away in rooms that aren't used.'

'I must say, it would be nice if more of the house was in use, wouldn't it? It's such a huge place, with a massive garden and currently it's just Peter and the staff.'

Lorna gave a tiny sigh. 'Yes, it would be nice if it were used more. Maybe Kirstie will open it all up and there'll be weekend house parties and things.'

'Weekend house parties are very good for the market,' said Philly. 'Lots of new money circulating.'

'It would be good for the town generally actually. The fact that the house is within walking distance of the town means they probably would shop a bit and go to the pub . . . ' Lorna fell silent at the thought of Kirstie presiding over social events at Peter's side.

'You don't sound terribly pleased about it though,' said Philly.

4

Philly was pleased to see Lorna already by the back door when she arrived at the house on the Friday before the dinner party. She was a bit anxious about the job but as a hundred pounds represented a good chunk of polytunnel money she couldn't have turned it down.

'Hi, Philly!' said Lorna. 'I can't remember if you know Doreen? She's found all the big vases for you and I've had a good old prune and cut a lot of material. It's all in the stable. Will you be all right in there? The light isn't brilliant, I'm afraid.'

'The vases are there too,' said Doreen. 'I thought three big arrangements each for the dining room and drawing room — that's always what her ladyship does.'

Philly nodded, unsure if Anthea was really a lady, or if 'her ladyship' was a nickname. 'I'm sure if that's what she does — '

'And a big one for the hall table too,' said Doreen. 'Just as well you came today it's a lot of work.'

Lorna looked discomforted. 'I'll see if I can get you some more money. If it's two days' work you're doing, it should be more than just a hundred.'

Doreen pursed her lips. 'Good luck with that. I suggested the guest bathrooms all needed new shower curtains and he said, 'Can't you wash them?' Well, of course I can, but is that the best use of my time when we're expecting a houseful of visitors? No, is what I said.' She paused. 'I'll send Reg down to B&Q and add the cost to the grocery bill. Anyway, if you're OK here, I'll get back to finding half-decent sheets. Thank goodness they're all going to the pub for a meal.' She looked at her watch. 'They'll start arriving after six, Peter thought. Just hope I'm ready.'

'Do you know how many are expected?' said Philly as she and Lorna walked to the stable.

'I don't know exactly because I don't know how many locals are being invited,' said Lorna. 'But there are three couples staying, so that's six. Me and Anthea, eight, plus, presumably, men for us to talk to, which would be ten.' She paused. 'Quite a lot.'

'I'll keep it big and simple,' said Philly, excited at the prospect, 'and then maybe, if there's the right material, I'll do posies for the guest bedrooms.'

'That would have you in Doreen's good books forever!' said Lorna. 'Here we are.' She opened the door to the stable in which there was a long table, covered in flowering branches of various trees and shrubs. 'I've gone big — you don't want to be fiddling around too much.'

'They smell heavenly!' said Philly. She picked up a branch of something that looked like pink blossom. 'Is this New Dawn?' she asked.

'Probably,' said Lorna. 'I didn't plant it. It could be another variety of *bodnantense*. We're lucky it's still out. Where would we be without the jolly old virbunums?'

29

'A bit stuck for colour in the winter, not that we need to worry about it now,' said Philly. 'Oh, magnolia! How extravagant to have branches of it!'

'It needed hacking back. And it's where no one sees it, so if it suffers a setback next year, it won't matter.'

Philly picked up another branch, covered in coral-pink flowers this time. 'Oh, and I love this pink *Chaenomeles* — what Grand calls japonica. I could just put this in a vase on its own if there's something faintly Japanesy — and it'll look wonderful.' She saw Lorna looking at the heap of plant material. 'I'll be fine here, Lorna. I expect you want to get on with something.'

Lorna shrugged. 'I haven't much on, if you'd like me to give you a hand.' She looked faintly embarrassed. 'I asked Peter for some more money, as you were doing the flowers as well as waitressing and he gave that bewildered look as if I'd suggested there might be Martians landing in the park. I thought I'd get Anthea to ask him.'

'No need, a hundred is fine.'

'Well, I'm going to help you. I can go out and cut anything you're short of. Oh, and there are masses of tulips. I didn't pick any because sometimes they go flop.'

Philly picked up one of the vases. 'Although they'd be OK in here. At least, they should be. It's deep enough.'

Together, they got the flowers done, both women enjoying the process. They ended up with some wonderfully dramatic arrangements and enough small posies for the guest rooms and

30

their bathrooms. When Doreen saw them, she nodded. 'Flowers will do a lot to disguise the general shabbiness.'

'Isn't it called shabby chic these days?' said Philly.

Doreen snorted. 'I think plain 'shabby' covers it.'

★ ★ ★

The following evening, Philly turned up earlier than necessary at Burthen House, in case any of the flower arrangements had dropped in the night. She found her way through several back passages and reached the kitchen. She opened the door and was instantly reminded of one that might feature in a period drama set in the thirties, when it would have been full of maids with lacy headbands over their eyes and men in tail coats. It seemed to have made no concessions to the twenty-first century, and not that many to the twentieth.

At the same time as she took in the antiquation of the kitchen, she realised that the chef, currently looking wild-eyed and more than a little demented, was the floppy-haired boy from the cheese stall.

His hair wasn't floppy now; it was literally standing on end, as if desperate fingers had pulled it upwards countless times. As she crossed the room towards him he looked at her with eyes that seemed unable to take in anything.

'Hello?' she said. 'I'm Philly. I'm here to serve at table and do a bit of washing up.'

31

He took in that he was looking at a fellow human being and frowned. 'Aren't you the girl on the flower stall?'

Colour flooded Philly's cheeks — she could feel it. 'Yes, but I do waitressing as well as flowers.'

He put a damp hand into hers. 'Lucien. I'm supposed to be the chef but it's already a disaster.'

'I'm sure we'll work something out,' said Philly, hoping she sounded as if she really could help.

'Don't think so. The f — bloody oven's broken.'

Philly was touched that he held back on the expletive he really wanted to use. 'That's bad.'

'A disaster,' he repeated.

Some part of Philly noted that when he said this, Lucien sounded just a little bit like Craig from *Strictly Come Dancing*, only Lucien's voice was even posher than Craig's.

Just then a woman came into the kitchen. She was medium height with an hour-glass figure. She was very well made-up but her head was supporting a set of rollers the size of baked-bean cans.

'Hi!' said the woman. 'Excuse the rollers. I've just come down to make sure everything's OK and you've got everything you need? You're Lucien? My friend said you were amazing, so I really hope you are! I'm Kirstie, by the way.' She found his hand and shook it.

Lucien frowned. 'I'm afraid I have to tell you that the oven has broken down.'

Kirstie bit her lip. 'Oh no. What a nightmare! Are you sure we can't get it going?'

Philly noted that Kirstie seemed naturally optimistic, someone who wouldn't accept that an oven really could be broken down.

'I'm afraid not.' Lucien seemed calmer now, Philly thought.

'Oh God, I should have hired one,' said Kirstie. 'Or got in outside caterers who cook it all off-site.' Then Kirstie looked at Lucien. 'Although my friend said you were so brilliant, and just starting out — '

Doreen came into the room, carrying a large cobwebby box. 'I found this in the staff flat,' she said. 'It's an electric hob.'

'You're not going to manage on just one of those,' said Kirstie, who seemed to be accepting reality now.

'We've got one at home,' said Philly. 'Ours has got two plates.' Everyone looked at her and she blushed again. 'I could ring my grandfather and get him to bring it over.'

Lucien looked at her again and Philly dropped her gaze. She really wasn't embarrassed — she just couldn't help blushing. 'That would be great. But we really need an oven.'

'Can't we — you — light that?' Kirstie pointed to an ancient range. 'We've got a few hours, after all.'

'Not me,' said Doreen firmly.

'Nor me,' said Lucien. 'My parents have an Aga but it's gas-fuelled.'

'Shame,' said Kirstie, sounding despondent for the first time. 'I don't suppose Peter could do it.'

33

Doreen laughed and then stifled it with a hand.

'I could have a go,' said Philly.

'You?' said Kirstie. 'I'm not being rude or anything — or at least I hope I'm not — but you must be too young to know about fires. Or could you get your grandfather to do it? I mean, it is really old.'

'No, actually, I'm better at fires than my grandfather.' Aware everyone was looking at her, she carried on. 'When we moved into our house — my grandfather and me — we had one of those. It was all there was to cook on for a couple of weeks, before we managed to get Calor gas organised and bought a big four-oven cooker.'

'You are a saviour!' declared Kirstie.

'I might not be!' protested Philly. 'It's vital to have really dry wood. Or coal.'

'We haven't got coal — have we, Doreen?'

Doreen shook her head firmly.

'But we have got masses and masses of dry logs,' said Kirstie. 'Peter showed me this vast shed full of it. He told me it was years old, from when several trees came down. It was here when he bought the house.'

'OK,' said Philly. 'I'll have a go. And of course, if I got the oven going, the top would get hot too.' She looked at Doreen. 'I don't suppose you've got a spare apron? I don't want to get filthy — I've got to serve dinner later.'

'I'll get you one,' said Doreen. 'And I'll ask Reg to bring in some logs.'

'So, should I ask my grandfather to bring the

electric hob?' Philly asked Kirstie and Lucien.

'Yes please,' they said in unison.

Philly went to find her phone.

An hour later, the range was roaring and three electric hot plates were in use.

'Really cool that you knew how to do that,' said Lucien while Philly finished assembling the canapés. 'Thanks.'

At least the warmth of the kitchen meant she was already a bit pink. 'Pleasure. Glad I could help.'

5

Lorna dressed carefully for the dinner party. Her pride was at stake. She was never going to be able to compete with a beautiful woman in her mid thirties but she didn't want to look like a hag.

She'd given her naturally red hair a bit of help — because, the box assured her, she was worth it — and it had come out a pleasingly rich, dark colour. Then she had manipulated her curls with tongs until they had looked deliberate and not just there by chance. She decided she would wear her favourite outfit, never in fashion but never quite out of it either. It was a black, fitted jacket with a high collar and a peplum. She put it with a dark gold scoop-neck top and a long dark green skirt and flat boots. By the time she'd put on her favourite amber necklace, large beads surrounded by silver, with earrings that vaguely matched, she was relatively satisfied with her appearance. It was an outfit she'd been wearing with various changes on and off for years and she always felt good in it. When she looked at herself, standing well back from her favourite, badly lit mirror that was at the end of the hall, she felt she looked OK. She knew proper lighting would ruin this illusion and didn't risk it.

She felt she'd already contributed enough to the success of the evening for it to be unnecessary for her to bring a gift. Peter's wine cellar was one of his hobbies and she had helped Philly with the floral arrangements. She would just go and be her charming self.

At eight o'clock she put on her ancient black alpaca coat, still as glamorous now as it had been when she'd first bought it from a second-hand shop about ten years ago, and set off across the park to the house.

Lorna had been single most of her adult life, married only long enough to give her son his father's name — he wasn't giving away a lot else — and although there had been partners on and off she mostly attended parties on her own. Yet she'd never quite got used to walking into a room full of chattering people and having to look round, hoping to find someone she knew.

She usually did find someone and if she didn't, she'd hit on the shyest-looking person and introduce herself. It was always fine after the first ten minutes or so.

This time was different. This time she was going to meet the woman who had stolen her man, even if the man in question had never seen her as more than a friend and confidante.

The front door was ajar and she let herself in, leaving her coat on the sofa in the hall, hoping the fire was going well and she wasn't going to be cold. Then she opened the door to the drawing room and went in.

She knew the dinner party was for ten people but hadn't planned to be the last guest to arrive. She remembered belatedly that two couples were staying with Peter and she now felt late.

'Oh, here you are, Lorna,' said Peter, rising

from the arm of the sofa where he'd been perched next to a very pretty woman easily identifiable as Kirstie. 'Come and meet the people you don't know. This is Kirstie.'

He spoke proudly, as if she were a prize-winning racehorse that he had personally bred. Lorna couldn't blame him. She was lovely. She smiled warmly at Lorna.

'Hello! I've been dying to meet you. I've heard so much about you and have been all over your garden. And I gather you told us about Philly, who has been a *lifesaver*.'

She said this with so much emphasis that Lorna wondered, if unbeknownst to her, Philly was a trained first aider who'd been required to do CPR in the kitchen. 'Oh?'

Kirstie nodded. 'Bloody cooker broke down. Not only did Philly's grandfather supply a double electric hob — Doreen found a single — but Philly knew how to get the old Rayburn going so we've got an oven.'

'All right, sweetie,' said Peter, patting Kirstie's arm, 'I've promised we'll get a new one, a top-of-the-range range, with at least eight burners and a wok setting. Whatever you want.'

Lorna had to laugh. Peter's notorious meanness was going to be seriously challenged. She would probably have put up with the idiosyncratic central heating, the lack of insulation or any modern convenience. If a broken cooker was pushing things too far, she'd probably have only asked for a simple four-burner budget model. 'Well, I'm very pleased about both those things, first that Philly is such a star — although I did know that — and second that this house is going to get a few mod cons.'

'And your garden!' went on Kirstie. 'It's going to be fabulous.'

'Well, technically, it's Peter's garden.'

'Oh, I know that, but much to my disappointment he doesn't seem very interested in it,' said Kirstie, taking Lorna's hand and squeezing it.

Peter leant over and kissed Lorna's cheek. The whiff of Acqua di Parma that always worked for her added piquancy to the exchange.

'Hello, Peter.' Anthea, Peter's mother, crossed the room towards the group in the middle. 'You look delightful, dear,' she said, kissing Lorna. 'Do you know Bob? He's the mayor. I expect you recognise him because he's in every single issue of the local paper.'

'That's not quite true, Anthea,' said Bob, who obviously didn't know Anthea well enough to be completely relaxed in her company. 'But I am the mayor.'

He looked like a mayor, Lorna thought, shaking his hand and smiling. He looked at home in his dinner jacket and she was a bit disappointed not to see medals on his chest.

Kirstie put a hand on her arm. 'If you'll excuse us, Anthea, Bob, there are a couple of artists I'd like Lorna to meet.'

Wondering why, Lorna followed her to where two couples were sitting round a table, chatting. A man, separate from the group, was inspecting the paintings. Lorna hoped the one he was looking at gained his approval as it was one she had persuaded Peter to buy when they'd been to an exhibition together.

'This is Jamie, married to my old friend Nat — so they're Natalie and Jamie Chambers. Rosalind and Christopher Bloom. Oh, and that's Jack.' She indicated the man who had moved on to the next painting, also one Lorna had endorsed. 'This is Lorna Buckthorn,' Kirstie went on. 'She's restoring the garden for Peter, and doing a whole lot else besides.'

Lorna smiled at the group, thinking that Peter must indeed have told Kirstie a lot about her and that if she'd met Kirstie in any other circumstances she'd have liked her instantly. It was a shame she couldn't entirely commit to liking her now.

'Jack,' said Kirstie. 'Come and say hello.'

The man obliged. 'And this is Jack Garnet,' said Kirstie.

Lorna smiled at him. He was a few years younger than her but seemed pleasant. He looked at her and frowned a little. 'Sorry,' he said. 'Kirstie, who is this?'

'Not paying attention, Jack? This is Lorna Buckthorn.'

'Oh,' he said, 'you must think me very rude but I thought I recognised you.' He took her hand and squeezed it.

'Hello,' said Lorna, suddenly feeling scrutinised.

At that moment Philly came up with a tray of champagne. 'Oh, Philly,' said Lorna. 'How lovely, just what I need. How's it all going? I gather you've averted catastrophe downstairs.'

40

Philly, who did look slightly strained, smiled. 'Well, the cooker breaking down was a bit of a disaster.'

Jack took a glass of champagne too. 'I've got a another glass somewhere,' he said.

'Oh, it's OK,' said Philly. 'We've got plenty of glasses. I'll be round with the bottle to top you up now I'm sure everyone's got something to drink out of.'

'Philly's here under false pretences,' said Lorna. 'She's acting as a waitress but really she's a wonderful plantswoman. She raises plants for the garden here.'

'Whatever she does as a day job, she's been an absolute star for us,' said Kirstie. 'If she's as good at raising plants she must be brilliant.'

'I'll go and get some more canapés. I'm not quite sure when we'll be serving dinner,' said Philly after a quick glance at her watch.

'Well, the canapés are fabulous,' said Natalie. 'I'm afraid we scarfed down the first lot in record time.'

'And if dinner is late, it's not the chef's fault,' said Kirstie. 'Although I would say that. I recommended him.'

Peter came up to join the group and Lorna couldn't help noticing how sweet he was with Kirstie. He didn't claim her with an arm round her waist or anything obvious, he just touched her arm and smiled down fondly at her.

Lorna looked away to spare herself and found she was still being studied by Jack. Rather than watch Peter and Kirstie, she went over to him. 'Are you still trying to remember where you've

41

seen me? I've probably got a doppelgänger or something.'

He smiled and his severe features were hugely improved. 'I'll work it out. In the meantime, tell me about you?'

Lorna didn't awfully like talking about herself but she brought out her prepared patter. 'I'm a garden designer — and restorer. I've been working on Peter's garden for about three years but we've know each other since we were children.'

'Is that why you got the job?'

Lorna laughed. 'No, that was because I'm also friends with Peter's mother, Anthea. Have you met her?'

'We haven't been introduced but going by what I've seen, she's a formidable woman.'

Lorna nodded. 'When she told Peter I was the one to get his garden into order he was obliged to agree.' She paused. 'So what do you do?'

'I'm a stonemason. Also a sculptor.'

Philly appeared with a tray of things to eat. 'So, how's it going down there?' Lorna asked, taking a blini.

'Put it like this: it's just as well there are plenty of canapés. Fill up,' she suggested. 'Dinner will be a while.'

Lorna sipped her champagne. She knew there would be plenty of drink and she hoped everyone wouldn't be rip-roaring drunk before they sat down to eat. And champagne, though delicious at the time, could give one the most monumental hangover.

Jack's voice broke into her rather gloomy

thoughts. 'I think I've worked out where I've seen you, but I'll have to check at home,' he said. 'Do you live locally?'

'Yes, pretty much. I can walk home from here, so I can drink. Which is just as well. Peter always has lovely wine and masses of it. It's funny because in some ways — ' She stopped, aware she was about to tell a complete stranger that their host was mean. That would have been disloyal.

'I've only just met him but he seems nice enough.'

Lorna was grateful that he'd overlooked her stumble. 'Nice enough for Kirstie do you mean? As I'm a friend of Peter, I'm checking that Kirstie is nice enough for *him*. And I think she is, as far as I can tell.'

'I don't really know her. We only met a couple of weeks ago. But she has a reputation of being a mover and shaker. My friends told me that once she has taken on a project, nothing will stop her seeing it through. And of course, it's always exciting to be invited to the Big House for dinner.'

In that instant Lorna realised that Peter probably needed someone dynamic. While he had been a dynamic businessman, in his private life he was too laid-back and lazy. He needed shaking up, needed to be made to spend his money where it was required and not save unnecessarily. She, Lorna, would have let him bumble on in his own sweet way and put up with it. 'So how did you meet Kirstie?'

'It was at an Open View. She's friends with

some other friends of mine. Artists.' He frowned. 'I'm not quite sure why she asked me.'

Nothing to do with you being an attractive, apparently single, man, thought Lorna. Out loud she said, 'So are you a sculptor first and then a stonemason, or the other way round?'

'I don't really separate them. But what about you? Are you an artist as well as a gardener?'

'Well, actually I was. I went to art school but when I knew I was going to be a mother I changed to gardening. It satisfies my artistic needs and is a much more reliable way of earning a living.'

'So what does your husband do?' Jack seemed stern all of a sudden.

Lorna shrugged. 'I really don't know. We separated soon after my son was born. Nowadays we wouldn't have got married just because I was pregnant but then it seemed the thing to do. Even if we were both artists and supposedly more Bohemian.' She paused. 'So how about you? Married? Children?'

'I haven't any children. I was with someone for some years but there were no babies.' He smiled, a little melancholy. 'Maybe it was just as well.'

'So now you're single? Maybe you should try the website that brought Kirstie and Peter together.' She stopped suddenly, wondering if how they had got together was a secret and certain that she shouldn't have said that to someone she'd only just met.

'I don't think so,' said Jack, not appearing surprised or offended at what Lorna had said. 'I think I like meeting people in real life better.'

'Me too,' said Lorna. But privately she wondered how she should go about this. Perhaps the only option was to try and find a boyfriend online. Otherwise she'd just have to look at Peter and Kirstie being in love all the time, which would be depressing. However, she didn't much like the idea and dismissed it.

Anthea came up, without her consort. 'Well, Lorna, who's this? I don't think I know you, young man.'

Lorna made the introductions and watched with amusement as Anthea studied Jack rather in the way that Jack had studied her. But before Anthea could say anything outrageous, Kirstie clapped her hands for everyone's attention.

'Before we go into dinner, folks, I just want to tell you all why we're here. It's not only so Peter's family can meet me' — Kirstie's sweep of a smile included Lorna as family — 'and you can meet some of my friends, it's because this town has a battle on its hands and I think we should join forces to win it!'

'Hmm,' muttered Anthea to Lorna. 'I thought there was more to this dinner party than just sociability.'

'What battle?' asked Bob, the mayor. 'If it's about the supermarket on the ring road — '

'Much more important than that!' declared Kirstie. 'I know I'm not local. I don't come from round here, and perhaps that's why I see things with a new perspective.'

'So if it's not the supermarket, what is it?' asked Anthea, slightly irritably.

45

'It's the cathedral!' declared Kirstie.

There was a silence. Then: 'It's not a cathedral,' said Bob, 'it's a very large abbey.'

'And does that make any difference?' demanded Kirstie. 'There's a thermometer outside that 'very large abbey' which, if you look at it closely, shows there has been no money raised for two years! It's deplorable. It's a national monument and you're — we're — letting it fall apart! Jack, tell us who you are and what's going on in the church.'

'I could have done with a bit of warning,' said Jack, 'but Kirstie's right. We do need an awful lot of money.'

'Sorry,' said Bob, 'who are you?'

'I'm the mason attached to the church. Jack Garnet.'

'Oh, sorry,' said Bob. 'I do know your name, but not your face.'

'My fault, I should have introduced him better,' said Kirstie. 'But the thing is, I have an idea for fundraising.'

'What, marrying Peter?' muttered Anthea so only Lorna could hear.

'Currently it's only one event but I think there should be a chain of events for fundraising, which would benefit artists as well as the church.' Kirstie smiled in the direction of her artist friends. 'And the event is — opening Peter's garden to the public!'

Lorna choked and had to take a gulp of champagne. 'What? It's nowhere near ready!'

'No, I know it's not ready now,' said Kirstie. 'But it's still beautiful and my idea is to have an outside sculpture exhibition, in the garden — probably at the end of May. The last weekend. It'll be an opportunity for artists to show off really large pieces, which hardly ever get shown to the public. We'd charge admission, do teas, maybe have a concert, a whole weekend of amazing events, right here in Peter's garden.'

Lorna looked at Peter, expecting him to have blanched, fainted even, at this prospect. But he looked perfectly sanguine.

'Are you all right with this?' Anthea demanded of her son, obviously expecting the same reaction as Lorna had.

'Kirstie has convinced me it's a brilliant idea,' he said, beaming down at Kirstie. 'It'll inspire us to get the garden looking good.' He caught Lorna staring at him and possibly noticed her pursed lips and raised eyebrows. 'Lorna's been doing a great job since we've been here, but she's been desperately under-resourced. She's been virtually single-handed and needs a couple of assistants. And Reg would like a bigger ride-on mower.'

'I think you'd like that too, Peter,' said his mother.

'Well, yes,' he agreed. 'And I do think it's time I got more involved. Now I live here permanently — and may be no longer alone' — he gave Kirstie a very fond glance — 'I'd like to do something for the community.'

'Good for you,' said Lorna. 'While obviously I'm very daunted at the prospect of getting the garden ready for the public — even if they will be distracted by enormous reclining nudes or

47

whatever, I do think the town will be delighted and grateful to see you taking an interest in local matters.'

'You could stand for the council if you liked. They'd welcome you with open arms, a businessman like you,' said Bob.

'I'd rather stick to fundraising,' said Peter. 'And getting the house back in full working order.'

'Well, I think it's a brilliant idea,' said one of the male artists. 'I like to do large work and there are very few opportunities to show non-commissioned work. And while I probably shouldn't do non-commissioned work, I yearn to do bigger stuff than I usually get asked for.'

'Are you up for it, Lorna?' asked Peter, moving towards her. 'I know it's putting a big responsibility on to you.'

'Give me the resources,' she said, 'and I'm up for it.' She gave him a warm smile, wanting to make sure he knew she was completely happy about Kirstie and her plans. She wasn't completely happy at all. The torch she had carried for him for so long would take a lot more extinguishing, but she was withdrawing gracefully. She wouldn't take on Kirstie. If she couldn't get Peter when there was no competition she wouldn't get him now he'd fallen in love with a dynamo like Kirstie.

But she was glad when Doreen appeared, looking unfamiliar in a black dress. 'Ladies and gentlemen,' she said grandly. 'Dinner is served.'

'Only about an hour late so we're not completely drunk,' said Anthea, sotto voce. 'And if they've got the temperature of the dining room up above freezing, it may not be total torture. Come on, Bob.'

★ ★ ★

Lorna, who was escorted by Jack, thought someone — probably Philly — had done wonders with the usually arctic dining room. There was a roaring fire in the grate, a large number of candles, both on the table and anywhere else that could support them, and the floral arrangements were dramatically simple. There was just a hint of smoke in the air which intimated that the fire might have smoked when first lit. Possibly the many candles were there to disguise the smell.

'Not as dingy as I'd feared,' said Anthea, more loudly this time. 'And maybe the food will be edible, if the chef our hostess has been boasting about is any good. Possibly I was wrong to have an omelette before I came.'

Kirstie obviously heard this and Lorna saw that a tiny frown flashed across her features; she even thought she heard a little sigh.

One of the female artists — Lorna remembered was called Natalie — obviously overheard Anthea. 'I've had Lucien's food before. He's amazing. Really talented. So unless you're a really big eater, I should think it was definitely a mistake to have an omelette first.' She accompanied this with a glaring smile.

Now Kirstie looked panicked. She wouldn't want her new man's mother offended when she'd gone to so much trouble to get in her good books.

However, Anthea took this in her stride. 'You're probably right but when you're as old as I am your stomach rumbles rather loudly if you don't eat regularly. I wouldn't hear it — deaf as a post — but embarrassing to you younger people.'

Everyone laughed.

'Well, do find your places and sit down,' said Kirstie.

'Oh, you've done a *placement*,' said Anthea, using the French word. 'How sensible. And unusual these days. But I'll need my reading glasses.'

'You're here,' said Bob, 'next to me.'

'And you're next to me,' said Jack to Lorna.

Lorna found her place and smiled to her other neighbour, Natalie's husband, Jamie. Disappointingly, he gave her a smile that was perfectly polite, but that dismissed her as a woman of a certain age who could be in no way interesting to him. She decided to prod him a little. 'So, if you could afford to buy any sculpture in the world, which one would it be and why?'

Jamie looked startled. 'Well, I don't know — '

'I'll allow you to have a house or garden big enough to accommodate anything, so don't restrict your choice because of size.'

'I still don't know,' said Jamie.

'I know what I'd have,' said Jack. 'I'd have Elizabeth Frink's *Early Horse*.'

Lorna looked at him quickly. 'That's what I'd choose!' she said. 'What a coincidence.'

'Somehow I'm not surprised,' said Jack. And

he gave Lorna a look that made her start.

Jamie might have dismissed her as an older woman, but Jack was obviously beyond seeing women only as sexual objects. He could see they might have interesting things to say, too.

6

Downstairs in the kitchen, Philly at last felt able to take off her apron. 'Is it all right if I go now?'

She didn't quite know if she should ask Lucien or Doreen, so she said it into the room and hoped that someone would say 'yes'.

'Of course, dear,' said Doreen. 'You've worked like a trooper. I wish I could ask you to come in tomorrow and help me with the breakfast. I wasn't taken on as a cook. I shouldn't be asked to cook breakfasts for guests.'

'I could do breakfast,' said Lucien. 'You could ask Kirstie if it would be OK.' He paused. 'It's not that I need permission exactly, but I'd want to get paid.'

Doreen looked at him thoughtfully. 'I must say it would be great for me if you could do it. I can't boil an egg, let alone poach one!'

'Why don't you go and ask Kirstie now?' suggested Lucien. 'Then maybe Philly will get her wages, too.'

'Very well. They're past the stage of wanting more coffee or green tea or whatever gnat's piss they drink,' said Doreen. 'I'll go up.'

She came down a few minutes later with Kirstie. 'Darlings! You were amazing! Everyone was so impressed. Even Peter's terrifying mother thought it was good.'

Philly didn't say anything but she felt a flash of

connection with Kirstie. She thought Anthea was terrifying too.

'That's great,' said Lucien. 'Considering the conditions we had to work in — '

'I know! Next time you come I promise you we'll have a proper cooker.'

Lucien smiled, and scooped his hair off his face. He had taken off the chef's cap he had been wearing and his fringe had fallen back over his eyes. 'Maybe not the next time. Doreen would like it if I stayed on and cooked breakfast for your party.'

Kirstie's eyes widened, first with joy and then with disappointment. 'Oh, Lucien, that's a brilliant idea, but where would you stay? There are lots of bedrooms but all the ones that actually function are occupied.'

'It's OK. I'll sleep in the van.'

'You can't do that!' Kirstie was horrified.

'Yes I can. I do it all the time.' He grinned. 'I've got it all set up so I can do overnight stays. Fixed it myself.'

'Well, that's wonderful. I knew Doreen wasn't keen.' She flashed Doreen a smile that told Philly she was desperately anxious to keep in with Peter's family retainers. 'I don't blame her. Right, Philly — let me give you some money' She took out a stash of bank notes from the pocket of her dress. 'We said a hundred but I'm going to make it two. You were so brilliant with the stove.'

'Really?' said Philly. 'That's amazingly generous. I wasn't — ' She stalled. She liked Kirstie; she didn't want to put her off Peter by telling her how mean he was.

53

'I know. Peter is a bit careful, but he totally agreed we shouldn't skimp on this dinner party. It's so important in so many ways. Right, I'd better get back to my guests. By the way, Doreen? Did we buy a bottle of Bailey's the other day?'

'I don't think so, madam,' said Doreen, horrified at the thought.

'Pity. Never mind. I'll have to put them all off wanting flaming sambucas some other way.'

★   ★   ★

Philly was feeling very happy as she walked across the yard to where her car was parked. She was dead on her feet and prayed there would be enough hot water for a shower, if not a lovely bath, when she got home, but she had two hundred pounds in her bag. That represented a polytunnel and possibly some other things.

She was progressing slowly along the dark and muddy lanes when she saw a car pulled over. And she was fairly sure she knew who was in it.

It took a bit of courage to pull up behind and go and see the driver, just in case an opportunist axe murderer was hoping for someone like her to appear, but she took her torch and went to investigate.

'Bloody stupid vehicle!' said Anthea when she saw Philly. 'You're the girl who grows plants for Lorna, aren't you?'

Grateful and surprised that this starchy old woman hadn't referred to her as 'the waitress' she agreed she was. 'What can I do to help? I've got my phone if you need to call the AA or anything?'

'Not a member. And I have a phone of my own but don't know whom to ring.'

'Well, my grandfather used to be a garage mechanic. We could ring him? Or I could drive you home in my car and let him sort it out in the morning?'

Anthea let out a long sigh. 'I really hate being reliant on people. I value my independence.'

'Having a lift home if your car's broken down isn't being dependent. It's being sensible.' Somehow, Anthea didn't seem so daunting now. 'What do you think your grandfather can do?'

'Well, if he can't sort it out himself he could tow it to a garage or something. He's got a tow truck.' She paused. 'Wouldn't you like me to drive you home?'

'It sounds silly, I know, but I don't like to abandon my old warhorse. Why don't you go home and tell your grandfather where I am and if he wouldn't mind coming out so late — '

'I can't abandon you here,' said Philly. 'And it is late. My grandfather might prefer to look at the car in daylight.'

'Will he have gone to bed?'

'No. He always waits up for me. He doesn't really believe I'm old enough to go out to work in the evening.'

'He has a point. You are very young.'

'But I have got a reliable car.'

Anthea laughed. 'I think the current expression is 'that's me told'. Perhaps you'd be kind enough to drive me to your home? Then I can

55

discuss the matter with your grandfather myself?'

'Of course.' She considered for a second. 'But I'll ring him, so he'll expect us.' She didn't want her grandfather opening the door wearing his coffee-stained Pogues T-shirt. He'd die of embarrassment.

'Grand?' she said when he picked up the phone, moments after the first ring. 'I'm with — ' She froze as she realised she didn't know Anthea's proper title. 'One of the dinner guests. Her car has broken down. I'm bringing her home with me so she can talk to you about it.'

'Right you are. I'll get out my tool box and jump leads. It may be the battery. What kind of car is it?'

Philly asked Anthea. 'It's a Volvo,' she said. 'It's practically pre-War.'

Philly related this word for word.

'Ah!' said her grandfather. 'It'll be an old Amazon. Go on for years. Very simple to fix.'

As Philly disconnected she couldn't help smiling. Her grandfather sounded thrilled to be called after midnight about a broken-down car. His two favourite things in the world were helping people and fixing old cars.

He had obviously scrubbed up a bit, Philly realised when he opened the door wearing a proper shirt and trousers with a waistcoat and a neckerchief. It did give him a slightly 'Irish traveller' look, but none the worse for that.

'Come away in,' said Seamus, holding the door wide. 'Philly will put the kettle on and you can tell me about your car. I expect you're very fond of it. And why not? Who's to say they're not sentient beings, after all?'

Philly inwardly sighed and went to do as she was bid. Not only did her grandfather look like someone off *My Big Fat Gypsy Wedding*, he sounded as if he were away with the fairies. Or the 'little people' as he'd have put it. But still, he was doing Anthea a favour, not trying to win her over. She only wished she could remember Anthea's proper title. She never called her anything herself, but Doreen had described her as 'her ladyship'. Was this a proper title, or just a slightly disrespectful way of describing your boss's mother?

Anthea and Seamus followed Philly into the kitchen, which was a good decision. It was fairly untidy but it was the only room that was warm. The glacial (and also untidy) sitting room was no place to be at this time of night.

'Sit down, woman dear,' said Seamus to Anthea, who duly sat. 'And tell me what happened?'

'Well, a red light came on as soon as I set off so I parked in the lane so I could go down the hill if it wouldn't start.' She paused. 'It wouldn't.'

'Sounds like the alternator or the battery. I'll take a spare fan belt and my jump leads. Will you stay here in the warm while I go and see what the problem is?'

Philly, warming the pot for tea, mentally started. The thought of having to make conversation with this terrifying woman (although she did seem slightly less daunting currently) for an unspecified length of time was hideous. Apart from anything, she was dead on her feet.

'I'd rather come with you,' said Anthea. 'I'd really like to get home.'

'There's no worry about that. I can drive you home,' said Seamus.

'I don't want to leave my old car lying in a ditch, and have to worry about getting it back in the morning,' said Anthea.

'Well, fair enough. Now . . . ' To Philly's ears her grandfather sounded more and more Irish with every word. 'Will you be happy to come along in my van with me? Or would you like young Philly here to drive you?'

'Oh no,' said Anthea. 'Philly must be exhausted. She's been running up and down stairs all evening looking after my son's guests. I'm perfectly happy to travel in a van. It wouldn't be for the first time.'

Philly saw them off a few minutes later, when the tea had been hastily swallowed. Then she went to bed. Her grandfather would be fine, and if he wasn't, he'd ring her.

★　★　★

Having said her goodbyes, Lorna found her coat and put it on, aware that she'd enjoyed herself far more than she'd expected to. It was due to Kirstie being an excellent hostess and Jack being such an entertaining dinner companion. A man who was interested in what she had to say had always been rare, but now she was well past child-bearing age, it had become rarer. It was sad to think she had completely lost her sex appeal

58

but she had accepted it, particularly when Peter had failed to notice her and only treated her as a confidante and gardener. But Jack had made her feel interesting to talk to.

She had opened the front door and was halfway through it when he appeared. 'I'll walk you home.'

She smiled. 'Really there's no need. It's only across the park. There won't be muggers and any ghosts there may be won't bother me.'

'I'll still walk you home. It's on my way.' He took her arm.

'It's in the opposite direction! If you live in town you're the other side to the park. There's a good path — '

'I know about the good path — I took it on my way here. But I want to see you home safe.'

As she found it extremely pleasant to have a very firm arm supporting her — even if she didn't need support — she didn't argue any further.

They didn't speak as they crossed the park via a less-used and so slightly muddy track. It didn't seem long before they arrived at Lorna's cottage door.

'I would ask you in — ' she began, feeling obliged.

'No, no. It's late.' He looked down at her, his face illuminated by the light outside the porch. 'I'm so glad to have met you.'

Lorna nodded in agreement. 'Well, goodnight then.'

There came the awkward moment when she had to decide whether to kiss him or not. She

59

had merrily kissed all the other guests, but somehow this felt different.

He made the decision for her. He leant forward and kissed her cheek. 'Goodnight.'

7

Annoyingly, Lorna pinged awake at six the following morning. In spite of going to bed later than usual, being tired and having told herself firmly there was no reason she couldn't sleep in, her internal alarm went off and she was awake.

She put the radio on and tried to go back to sleep but gave it up after a few moments. If she was awake, she might as well get up. But as a gesture to her lie-in, after a quick shower she put her pyjamas and dressing gown back on and went downstairs to make tea.

She knew what had made it difficult to sleep in. It was the effect of a bit too much to drink and the fact that her life had changed somewhat since the dinner party. Meeting Kirstie, finding her impossible to dislike, but also being forced to accept that what she and Peter had looked genuine, was a reality check. Peter would never look at her now he'd managed to find a lovely young woman like Kirstie.

But she hadn't had a miserable evening — far from it. She had really enjoyed her long conversation with an interesting new acquaintance — who happened to be a man. She had relived the chatter in her sleep, dinner guests getting muddled and changing places, and now, as she waited for the kettle to boil, she thought she really should get out more.

Although the sun was coming through, it was

a bit chilly. As she should still be asleep in bed, she decided to spoil herself by lighting her wood-burner and pulling a blanket over her on the sofa before reaching for her laptop and catching up on her emails and social media.

She couldn't help thinking about Kirstie, particularly her plan to have a sculpture show in the gardens of Burthen House.

It could be brilliant. Although only a fairly small proportion of the formal sections of the garden were properly in order, there were plenty of wilder bits that could really set off large pieces. And people would come, she was sure of it. Burthen House was a great source of curiosity to the locals. Whenever she was in company with people new to the town, they all asked her about the house, about Peter, and when, if ever, they would be allowed in to see it.

Just how much money it could raise remained to be seen, but although she would have to work very hard herself, and train the assistants Peter had told her she could have, she was keen to do it. To have Peter, encouraged and cajoled by Kirstie, actually interested in the garden would be great.

But while there was a lot to be positive about, the flicker of hope that Peter would look at her as a prospective partner had died. She had to accept that.

She put her laptop down and closed her eyes, forcing her mind away from Peter and on to the garden. What plants would she need? What was the quickest way of getting it into order?

She was awoken by a knocking at the door.

Still half-asleep she threw off the blanket and went to open it. It was Jack.

If there was anyone in the world she would not have wanted to see her when her face was a make-up-free zone, it was Jack. Peter had seen her without make-up before (and didn't appear to notice) but Jack was a new friend. She didn't want him to see her as the older woman she was. She'd have liked him to go on thinking about her as the interesting woman who didn't look too bad by candlelight. It was all she could do to smile.

'Oh!' he said. 'Is it horrendously early? I couldn't sleep. I suppose I didn't notice the time.'

Lorna looked at her watch. 'It's a quarter to nine.'

'God! I'm so sorry. Far too early to call on someone on a Sunday. I'll go away and come back later.'

His discomfiture made her relax. 'Why don't you come in? I haven't had breakfast yet. Could you manage a piece of toast?'

The relief on his face made her courage worth it. 'Now you say 'toast' I realise I haven't had any breakfast either. But I'm still so sorry to have woken you up.'

Lorna closed the door behind him.

'I like your house,' he said, following her into the kitchen.

'I rent it, very cheaply, because I work on the estate. Very feudal. But I like it too. It's small but it suits me. And it's quiet but not completely isolated. Although the other cottages are holiday lets, they are occupied quite a lot of the time.' She paused briefly, aware that her cottage had been due to become a holiday let and it was only Anthea's intervention that stopped it, insisting that the gardener should have accommodation. 'Tea or coffee? I'll put the kettle on and then run up and get dressed.'

'Coffee, please. Would you like me to make it?'

'Oh — yes,' said Lorna. 'There's the grinder, the beans are in that jar, and then there are filter papers and a jug.'

Having shown him where everything was, she went to get dressed. Finding some trousers and a nice V-necked jumper was easy, what was harder was the question of how much make-up she should put on. She put on enough to make her feel half-decent but not as much as she'd worn the night before. Adding a string of coloured beads helped her feel presentable.

The smell of coffee reached her as she went downstairs. He had found a saucepan and was heating milk. 'I hope you don't mind,' he said. 'I just think hot milk in coffee makes it more a Sunday thing than a quick cup you might have during the week.'

She acknowledged this with a nod. 'I don't often bother to heat the milk during the week, it's true. So it does make it more special. Now, toast? Or I could make porridge? I have eggs but no bacon — '

'Toast would be great.'

'Good. I have home-made marmalade to go with it. I didn't make it,' she added hurriedly. 'Anthea did. You remember? From last night?'

'I couldn't forget her. A wonderful woman.'

'She is. Now I must just put a log on the wood-burner — '

'I'll do it. I should make myself useful as I seem to have invited myself for breakfast.'

'Go on then. I'll put this lot on a tray and we can eat at the table in there and enjoy the fire.'

As she loaded the tray she realised she was enjoying the prospect of breakfast with Jack. It was a very easy way to entertain, once she'd got over the shock of opening the door to an attractive man in her dressing gown.

'So,' said Lorna after they'd eaten their first piece of toast. 'What brought you to my door so early?'

'Oh — I am so sorry about that. But — well — it's a bit awkward — '

Lorna didn't speak but waited expectantly.

'It's about this sculpture thing. I wanted to have a look round the gardens so I could think about what I might exhibit.'

'There won't be time to make anything that's site-specific,' said Lorna. 'It's only a few weeks away now.'

'No, but I have a few pieces that might be appropriate and a couple of the lads might have suitable things. Presumably you'll need quite a lot of work?'

'I expect so. It's Kirstie's gig. In fact, you should have gone to see her really You could go after breakfast. It'll be a good time to call. The other guests will be having drinks, I should imagine.'

He crunched his way through his last

mouthful of toast. 'I was really hoping you'd show me round.'

'You don't need anyone to show you round —'

'No, but I'd like it. The more I can understand about the gardens the better able I will be to choose.' He took a sip of coffee. 'It's terribly short notice, after all. I don't think Kirstie really understands what's involved.'

Lorna realised that she wanted to go with Jack very much but felt obliged to check her conscience for any reason why she shouldn't. There didn't seem to be any.

'Well, I've nothing particular to do today and it would be a good idea to walk around making notes so we could go together. I'll find my boots and notebook.'

He held her hand while she poked her feet into her boots, his grasp reassuringly solid. He was, she decided, a very physical person. Tall, very fit and well muscled. She supposed that working lifting stone and using his hands had developed the muscles over the years. Peter was tall but willowy.

He released her hand when she was in her boots and didn't take it again. After she'd locked the door and put the key in her pocket she realised she rather wished he'd hung on to her. She'd enjoyed the feel of his arm when they walked back from the party the previous evening.

They walked up the path to the house. Last night, going downhill, it had seemed a short walk but now it seemed longer, possibly because they kept stopping to look at various vistas.

'Do you think anyone would come this far down if they were looking at sculpture in the garden?' asked Jack. 'I've a pair of wrestlers that would look wonderful in that dip but getting them there would be massively expensive and very hard work. I wouldn't want to do it if no one would see them.'

'I don't know what Kirstie has in mind,' said Lorna, 'but I would imagine she'll be quite organised and arrange a proper trail for people to follow. We're only about five minutes from the house, after all.' She frowned. 'There isn't time to plant anything, but do you think this bit would look better mown?'

'My wrestlers would prefer the grass to be long. It would make their fight look more natural.'

She smiled. 'Do you know who wins?'

He shook his head. 'Currently it could go either way.'

They had reached the house, which looked particularly lovely in the spring sunshine. From this angle its proportions were perfect, set above the gardens and park; and from here, the parts that needed restoring were out of sight. Lorna always took a moment to admire it and be grateful that Peter had bought it, and so brought her to the area that she now loved.

Now she said, 'The formal gardens are this way — '

At that moment the French doors that overlooked the parterre opened and Kirstie called out to them: 'We're just having coffee, do you want to join us?'

'Thank you, but we'll pass,' said Jack. 'Lorna is showing me round and I want to find the best sites before anyone else sees them. I may not be able to get her on my own again so I'm taking advantage.'

'Well, why not come for lunch when you've finished? We've still got Lucien and he's working miracles with the leg of pork.'

After the briefest possible glance at Lorna, Jack went on, 'Tempting as that sounds, I've already asked Lorna to come with me to the pub.'

'Fair enough,' said Kirstie and went back into the house.

'I'm terribly sorry,' said Jack before Lorna could speak. 'If you want to go and have roast pork with everyone we can, but I'd prefer — '

'We can just have a tour, we can both make notes and then I can go home. You don't have to worry about my lunch,' said Lorna. She wasn't quite sure how she felt about him being what seemed to be a bit proprietorial. She felt a bit confused. It had been a long time since she'd been in male company on her own. She'd probably forgotten the conventions.

'I'd be made up if you came to the pub with me. It's really very good and I'm sure it does roast pork if that's what you're longing for. What do you think?'

Lorna laughed. 'I think it's far too soon after breakfast to be thinking about lunch, but if the offer is still open when we're finished, I'll probably be delighted to go to the pub.'

He seemed relieved. 'I'm glad. I didn't want to

rush you into anything, and it is selfish of me to want you all to myself.'

He didn't enlarge on this statement and Lorna wondered why he wanted her to himself. They'd have been round the garden by lunchtime — surely he would have all the information he'd need by then?

'I'm going to have two lists,' said Lorna, half an hour later. 'A 'must do' list, and a 'do if time' list. Peter has promised me assistants but I wonder who I could get who I could trust to work on their own? Although I suppose if I had a good planting plan, and the plants . . . ' She stopped, suddenly overwhelmed with the hugeness of the challenge. 'I'm not sure if it's doable, frankly. I think I might suggest to Kirstie that we keep the garden out of it, and just have sculpture in the park.'

'That would be a shame,' stated Jack. 'It may not all be as perfect as you'd like it, but what you've done is a credit to you.'

She was pleased. 'There was a fair bit here already, when I came.'

'Was that patch of blue under the trees here?'

'The grape hyacinths? Well, no. They'd completely taken over several of the beds so I heaved them all out and put them there. I like to think they look like a lake, when the sun is shining in the right direction.'

'They do look like a lake, although when the sky is grey it's odd to have a blue lake.'

'I prefer blue lakes, on the whole,' she said seriously.

He laughed. 'So do I!'

★ ★ ★

'Much of what I can plant now would be out in time for the show,' said Lorna an hour or so later. 'I'll just have to rely on what I've done the past couple of years. Although I could probably track down some bits and pieces already in flower.'

'I'm sure it'll be fine,' said Jack. 'And as for help, didn't someone tell me that the girl who waited on us last night had something to do with plants? Couldn't she help you? She seems very efficient.'

'That's a genius idea! Why didn't I think of it? I know she has to do other jobs to keep herself going. She'd probably be quite happy to do gardening rather than waitressing. I'll have to find out how much Peter will pay. But that could be at least part of the answer.'

Jack smiled. 'Now, have we done enough work? Can I take you to the pub? Or do you want to go home and write up your notes?'

Lorna made a face. 'Of course that's exactly what I should do, but it is Sunday and I can just about read my handwriting. I can write up my notes this afternoon.' She grimaced. 'If I don't doze off, that is.'

'Didn't you sleep well?' said Jack. 'I didn't either. Come on.'

Lorna allowed herself to be taken by the arm and towed to the pub, speculating as she went what *his* excuses for a bad night were.

70

8

Saturday came round again far too quickly in Philly's opinion. The previous week she had been about to serve at a dinner party, this Saturday she was behind a stall slightly lacking in cake.

It was just as well that she had extra bowls of bulbs to sell. A patch of warm weather had brought things along nicely and Grand had managed to knock up a few jam sponges (the very best seller). But he'd spent a lot of his week fixing Lady Anthea's ancient Volvo (Philly had checked with Lorna that this was the correct way to refer to her). And it was making him very happy so she didn't comment. It was only when he saw her getting out bags of flour and looking anxiously at the KitchenAid that he scoured his hands and did some baking himself. Philly thought her cakes were fine, but they were not up to her grandfather's standards and weren't allowed on the stall.

She had only just finished setting up (her grandfather was joining her a bit later) when Lucien came over from the cheese stall.

'Hi,' he said. 'Good to see you again.'

Philly hoped the stiff breeze would either disguise her blush or prevent it. 'Hi. Have you recovered? It was pretty full on last week.'

'It was OK. I did breakfast and their Sunday lunch in the end. Nice little earner.' He paused. 'On your own today?'

71

'Not for long. My grandfather is repairing Lady Anthea's Volvo. He's delivering it today. She's either going to give him a lift here, or he'll borrow the Mini her son lent her while her car was out of action.'

Lucien seemed to have lost interest in Lady Anthea's Volvo. 'The cake looks OK but why don't you have any bread?'

'Um, well, my grandfather has a very light hand with a sponge but he can't seem to get the hang of bread.' She frowned. 'Aren't there other stalls doing bread?' She looked around and discovered that there weren't. 'Well, you can buy all sorts of loaves from the supermarket.'

'Yes, but wouldn't this crowd' — he indicated the shoppers who were beginning to appear — 'rather buy really good artisan bread?'

Philly regarded the people, many of them obviously down from London for the weekend if they hadn't yet moved down here permanently. 'I suppose they would.'

'You're missing such a trick here,' he said.

'But Grand — my grandfather can't do bread. Why don't you do it?'

'Because I haven't got access to an oven.'

'What — no sort of oven at all?'

He shook his head. 'My accommodation doesn't have one.' He grinned suddenly. 'I'd better get back to the cheese. You should come over later. At the end I'm sometimes allowed to buy the off-cuts cheap. I don't always have a use for them. You could have them.'

'That's kind.'

He shrugged and went back to his stall.

Philly's heart gave a little skip of happiness. It wasn't that Lucien had declared undying love, or even asked her out, but he had recognised her and come over specially. Even if it was to complain about the lack of bread.

Her grandfather arrived shortly afterwards, looking very pleased with himself.

'Hello, Philly, how's it hangin'?'

Philly grimaced. 'Grand! Where do you get these expressions? And why are you looking so smug? Did Lady Anthea pay you in used, non-denominational tenners?'

He looked slightly embarrassed. 'She would have done, but I didn't let her. It was such a pleasure to work on that old Volvo I did it for the love of the thing.'

'Really?' Her grandfather knew the state of their finances as well as she did and while he had his pension and some savings the general fund always needed anything extra that could be scrounged. A week's work (it seemed to have taken up a lot of his time) for nothing wasn't the way forward. Because she was a bit cross with him, she went on, 'Lucien — he was the chef at the dinner party — said we should do bread.'

'I can't do bread,' said Seamus.

'I told him. But he said this crowd would really appreciate some artisan loaves.'

Her grandfather frowned. 'I might go across and have a word with that young man.'

Philly wanted to stop him. She didn't want her grandfather to tell Lucien off for stating the obvious, but a customer came and she couldn't.

Lorna arrived shortly afterwards and bought a

73

cake. 'No chocolate ones this week? Not that I don't really like a Victoria sponge but — '

'I know, I'm sorry Grand has spent all week mending Lady Anthea's car so hasn't had much time for baking — and he did it for nothing!' She realised she should have kept this to herself, but her annoyance broke through her discretion.

'That's very kind of him. Anthea told me she broke down after the dinner party and your grandfather did the knight-in-shining-armour thing.'

'Yes. But I didn't expect him to do it for nothing.'

'Nor did she.' Lorna changed the subject. 'Did you enjoy the dinner party Philly or were you working too hard for that? How was it for you lot in the kitchen?'

Philly smiled. 'Actually I loved it. You're right about it being hard work but I liked swooping in and being the heroine and lighting the range. Very good money too. And a massive tip. I think that was down to you.'

Lorna shook her head. 'Not really. I mean, I did tell people you needed to be paid properly, but I think Kirstie was responsible for the massive tip.'

Philly sighed as she rearranged the stall slightly, having wrapped Lorna's Victoria sponge. 'It's a shame I earn so much more for my waitressing jobs than I do for raising plants, which is so much more skilled.'

'It's all wrong, isn't it?' Lorna dallied at the stall. 'Philly if I was allowed to take on a full-time assistant, would you be up for it? It

74

might not be permanent, although goodness knows I need someone, but just to get the garden in shape for this sculpture show?'

'Oh! I heard about that. At least, Lady Anthea told Grand, who told me. And I'd certainly like to think about it.'

'It needn't be absolutely full time — just a few hours a day. But I think between us we could really make an impression.'

'That could be perfect for me. As long as I have some hours for my plants. Hey — my new polytunnel has arrived and we're hoping to get it up this afternoon. I'm so excited!'

'I bet you are. Let me know if you need a hand. I've got nothing much on later.'

'How kind. Can I say yes please? These things are always easier with extra hands to hold things down.'

'Let me know when you're ready and I'll be over.'

'I will.' As a potential customer arrived at that moment Lorna slipped away. Philly smiled. 'What can I get for you?'

★ ★ ★

Grand rejoined her a little later. 'I've invited your man there to come over after the market. I think he might be able to add something to our offering, if he really can make bread.'

'Today? We've got the polytunnel to put up this afternoon.'

'I know, but putting it up needn't take long. We could ask him to help with it.'

75

'Lorna's already offered,' said Philly. 'And I said yes.'

'Well, no one ever said 'too many hands don't make light work!'' her grandfather objected.

'They did say 'too many cooks spoil the broth'.'

'Come on now. No need to panic.'

Philly had rather hoped her panic hadn't been noticeable. She sighed. 'So when's he coming?' she asked, inclining her head in the direction of the cheese stall.

'I said, after the market. When he's finished, at about one. I said we'd give him a spot of lunch.' He regarded her expression. 'Now what have I done? It's no bother to knock up a bit of lunch, is it? We'll have to eat ourselves, anyway.'

'Grand! He's a trained chef! What we do for ourselves is not — well, it's not what trained chefs do.'

Seamus shrugged. 'But I'm sure you'll find it's what they eat when they're not on duty.'

Philly had to acknowledge the sense of this but was still racking her brains for something to give him that was not too shaming as they packed up the stall and went home.

Once through the door, she had starting chopping onions before she'd taken her coat off, so anxious was she to have something made before Lucien arrived.

'What are you doing?' said Seamus. 'Girl dear, take your outdoor things off before you start cooking. What are you making?'

'Soup. There's bound to be some vegetables I can put in it, and you taught me soup is almost always the best choice for lunch.'

Seamus seemed surprised. 'Well, I'm glad to think I've taught you something. Will I peel you a couple of potatoes?'

'That would be amazing.' She found some moderately fresh chicken fat in the fridge and emptied it into a pan. Then she added the onions. 'It'll be OK. Now, I could make a frittata or something — '

'No,' said her grandfather firmly. 'We'll have soup and bread and cheese. I know the bread is from the supermarket but it's posh bread, and the cheese comes from the stall where he works. That will be quite good enough for your young man.'

'He's not my young man!' Philly shrieked.

'Then why are you making so much fuss?'

'Because he's a chef,' Philly went on more calmly.

'He's a hungry boy. Whatever you put in front of him will be grand.'

Only half an hour later, Lucien came with a large package of cheese. Thank goodness the soup was now simmering away, thought Philly as she accepted the package.

'Thank you so much for this. As we're only having bread and cheese for lunch, and some soup, this will add some variety.' She paused. 'You're probably fed up with cheese.' Philly wished she didn't sound so apologetic even though she was apologising.

'Never,' said Lucien. 'I love cheese. It's one of the many reasons I work at the cheese stall.'

The men were sitting round the hastily cleared

kitchen table, although Seamus's idea of a clear table meant the newspapers were in a neat pile up one end, while Philly put soup into bowls, none of which matched.

'And what's one of the other reasons for working on a cheese stall?' asked Seamus a little later, when the first few spoonfuls had gone down.

Lucien grinned. 'They offered me a job. This is great soup,' he went on. 'Bags of flavour. I bet you didn't get that from a stock cube.'

'A couple of stock cubes,' Philly admitted. 'But I fried the onions in the chicken fat from last Sunday's roast.'

He nodded. 'Lots of flavour in fat.'

Philly realised her grandfather was right. Lucien was very hungry and ate with enthusiasm.

'So,' said her grandfather, 'tell us a bit about yourself, Lucien.'

'Grand!' said Philly 'Don't interrogate the poor man.'

'Sure, I'm not interrogating him. I'm just interested. If he's going to be putting his home-made bread on our stall, I have to make sure he's up to it,' said Seamus calmly.

To be fair (and Philly did try to be fair), Lucien didn't seem that put out by her grandfather's questions.

'Well, I'm a trained chef, but I'm really interested in baking. Not cakes so much but bread.'

'So did you train right out of school?' asked Seamus. 'And didn't your parents want you to go to university?'

Lucien smiled again. He had a slightly crooked smile but very straight teeth. Philly decided he'd probably had a brace when he was growing up, to have teeth that even. 'How did you guess?'

'The way you speak,' said Seamus. 'And how do they feel about you being a chef? Did you go to college to train or learn on the job?'

'Bit of both,' said Lucien. 'I sort of left home when they were so angry with me for not going to uni. I had good A levels and they thought they'd be wasted in a kitchen.'

Seamus and Philly exchanged glances. 'I sort of left home, too,' said Philly. 'My parents had different ideas from mine about what would make me happy.'

'But Seamus is your grandfather, isn't he? How is that leaving home?'

Lucien seemed more confused than critical although Philly did feel embarrassed. To cover this, she said, 'Oh, when I left home I took the precaution of taking my grandfather with me.'

'I left home too,' said Seamus. 'We're a pair of runaways.'

'Although we do go home for Christmas if it's not our turn to have the family here,' said Philly

Lucien found this very amusing. 'Well, I did it properly! I had a little money my godfather had given me for my eighteenth birthday and I managed to draw it out before they could put it in another account I didn't have access to. I bought my van with it and drove until I found someone who'd give me a job. I worked as a washer-up for a few weeks but I pretty soon realised I needed qualifications or it would take me ages to work my way up.'

'And qualifications cost money,' said Seamus.

'Yup. Fortunately I still had just enough to pay for a short pro cookery course if I worked in the evenings and at weekends. I got my qualification. It meant I could apply for better jobs in restaurants. But although I was learning a lot I wasn't earning enough to keep myself, really.'

'I understand that,' said Philly. 'You work appallingly hard and you still don't earn enough to eat. I'd be sunk if it wasn't for Grand — my grandfather here.'

'And the fact you do other jobs,' Seamus put in.

'You were great the other night,' said Lucien. 'You have valuable skills.'

Philly, who was beginning to relax, laughed. 'Because I could get the old range going? It was easy! There was about a ton of really dry wood. I couldn't go wrong. Really.'

'She has a way with fire,' said Seamus. 'It comes from being just a bit of a pyromaniac.'

'Not at all,' said Philly. 'So, what did you do next?'

'I set up as a private chef. I got — still do, really — most of my work through friends, or friends of friends. But although the pay is better, I don't get enough work.' He sighed.

'Hard to pay the rent?' asked Seamus.

'Oh — no.' Lucien smiled. 'The rent isn't a problem. I don't pay rent.'

Seamus frowned, which gave Philly a stab of anxiety. He was quite capable of asking Lucien if he was 'living off the earnings of a high-born lady' or some such. She stepped in. 'Oh? Do you always get live-in jobs? Or do your friends put you up after you've cooked for them?'

He smiled. 'If they did, I'd be homeless a lot of the time. No, I live in my van. I just have to find somewhere safe to park up. It's perfect. I never have to drive home late. On the other hand, it's sometimes hard to get a shower. If I'm working for friends I can ask for one though, so mostly I don't smell.'

'We didn't think you did,' said Philly. 'At least — you do, but of some quite nice aftershave.'

'Very expensive aftershave,' he confirmed. 'Floris. A friend of my mother gave it to me one Christmas before I left home. I didn't use it then but something told me it would be a good thing to pack.'

'So where are you living now? Still in the van?' asked Seamus.

'Yup.'

Seamus plunged right in. 'Well, we've plenty of room here. If you'd like a proper bed and more or less regular hot water, you could live with us. Couldn't he, Philly?'

Philly appreciated her grandfather's kind heart, she really did, but she sometimes wished it wouldn't get the better of him and allow him to make rash offers without consulting her.

'I don't suppose Lucien would like that,' she said. 'He's obviously a free spirit. And our spare room is desperate. It needs completely redecorating,' she added, in case Lucien didn't understand exactly what 'desperate' meant in this instance.

'Tell you what,' said Lucien. 'I could help you redecorate if you let me stay. And when I'm not working or baking, I could do other jobs around the house.' He paused. 'In lieu of rent,' he said, sounding embarrassed. 'I can work hard, but I can't afford rent. Just at the moment.'

'We don't need rent money,' said Seamus. 'But we could certainly do with a hand about the place. And never mind about redecorating, Philly has a polytunnel she needs to get up this afternoon. You could be just the man to help us.'

Philly cleared her throat. She was the youngest present but someone needed to be sensible. 'I think it could be great having you here, Lucien. But for all our sakes, I suggest we should have a trial period.' She smiled, she hoped politely, and not in a rabbit-in-the-headlights way. 'Just to make sure we all get on. Grand and I are a bit — well, we may not be the easiest to live with.'

Lucien nodded. 'Tell you what, you seem to have plenty of outdoor space. If I could just park my van here, and maybe use the facilities, I wouldn't have to live in the house.'

'We couldn't leave you out in the cold . . . ' said Philly, wishing she'd kept her mouth shut and just let the men reorder all their lives.

'It's not cold, it's spring. And I have a really great sleeping bag.' He grinned again. 'The advantage to having been born a posh boy is that when I'm living rough, I have high-quality camping gear.'

Among the general laughter, Philly's anxieties faded a little.

'There's more soup — ' she said.

'Yes please,' said Lucien. 'People should eat more soup.'

9

Lorna was just about to set off to help erect Philly's polytunnel when she saw Jack pull up outside her house. 'Oh, hello. Were you coming to see me?'

He half got out of his car. 'Yes. I've got some pictures of my work. I'd like your advice on what would work best — '

Lorna frowned slightly. Surely he, as the artist, would know what would work best in the garden? 'Well, as you can see, I'm on my way out. Philly has asked me to give her a hand putting up a polytunnel. To raise plants in. You know she has a nursery?'

He got fully out of his car. 'Are you an expert on polytunnels?'

Lorna laughed. She was pleased to see Jack even if his reason for coming seemed spurious. 'Far from it! I'm only going to hold things and prop bits up when asked. They've got the foundations all done. I gather the more helpers the better for the rest.'

'I'll come too, then,' he said. 'I can provide a certain amount of heft. Which you can't.'

His eyes skated down her body as he said this, making Lorna feel slightly awkward. Also a bit flattered. Why would he be looking at her like that? 'Well, follow me then.'

'Can't we travel together? I could drive you?'

Lorna scanned her brain for reasons why she

should refuse and couldn't come up with any. 'Oh, OK. I suppose that would make fewer cars to find room for at the other end. Lucien, who cooked for us the other night, has his van there.'

'He's got roped in too, then?'

Lorna shrugged. 'I gathered from Philly that he roped himself in. Or maybe Seamus asked him. Have you met Philly's grandfather? No, of course, why would you? But he's a real character.' She took her bag from her car and then locked it.

She settled herself into Jack's car which bore all the signs of a working man. 'Sorry it's such a mess,' he said as she did up her seat belt.

'It's fine. My own car isn't tidy. I can keep my house looking nice, because I live there and I don't want to be surrounded by mess. But cleaning out the car just seems a job too far.'

'That's exactly how I look at it.' Jack sounded pleased, as if not liking to clean out one's car was an important bond.

'I suppose we're both working people who use our cars to carry things that aren't always very clean,' said Lorna. Then she settled back. 'If you go along the Beckworth Road towards Wychester, I'll tell you when to turn.'

★ ★ ★

'Ah ha!' said Seamus when he saw Lorna and Jack approaching. 'The army of helpers has arrived!'

'Hardly an army,' said Lorna. 'But Jack happened by just as I was leaving so I brought

85

him along.' She introduced them.

When he had crushed Jack's hand in his, Seamus said, 'Great to have someone else who's strong. Young Lucien is struggling.'

'Maybe a stepladder would help?' suggested Jack.

'It would indeed, if only I could find the blessed thing. And to be honest, I'm not even sure I brought it over from Ireland.'

After a couple of minutes' thought, Jack said, 'Well, if it would help, I'll pop home and get mine.'

'That would be a real kindness, and there'll be a cake in it for you. In fact, I'll put the oven on now when I go inside to fetch the laptop.'

'The laptop?' said Lorna.

Seamus nodded. 'According to Lucien, anything you need to know, including how to put up a polytunnel, will be on YouTube.'

★ ★ ★

Putting up the polytunnel took a lot longer than YouTube led everyone to expect. It was nearly eight o'clock and dark when Seamus called a halt.

'We'll finish it in the morning — my stomach thinks my throat is cut.'

'That means he's hungry,' explained Philly. Several voices were raised in agreement.

'Let's go inside into the warm,' said Seamus. 'Maybe it's time for a wee drop of something.'

'Maybe it's time for supper,' said Philly.

'Hell, yes,' said Lucien. 'I don't mind cooking.'

The group moved off towards the house.

'There's not a lot to cook,' said Philly, sounding a bit anxious at the thought of having to feed five people at very short notice.

'There's bound to be something,' said Lucien. 'I bet I can find the makings of a half-decent meal if you give me a chance.'

Jack cleared his throat. 'Why don't Lorna and I go out and get fish and chips for everyone? Then if Lucien can't produce a meal out of thin air and Philly's store cupboard, we can still eat?'

The agreement was deafening and it took a little while to find out what everyone wanted but eventually, Lorna was sitting in the front of Jack's car with a list.

'Well, that was fun if exhausting,' said Lorna. 'Who knew polytunnels were such hard work? Though personally I can't put up a tent on my own. At least, not a real tent.'

'What do you mean?' Jack started the engine. 'A real tent?'

'I mean a two-way tent. One that you can take down as well as put up. Didn't work for me and my pop-up tent. Putting it up was easy but I broke it when I tried to take it down.'

'Do you like camping?' He sounded curious.

'I do, actually, in very particular circumstances.'

'Which are?'

'I have to feel very safe, confident no one is going to attack me in the night.' She laughed. 'But I love feeling very close to nature and waking up early and seeing the dew on the grass.' She sighed in reminiscence. 'It reminds me of the time, years ago, when I slept rough for charity.'

'Lorna?' Now he was shocked.

'Oh, it's all right. As I explained it to my son and his friend who happened to be there when I was getting ready, it was to raise awareness about homelessness. I said that we were all going to be given a cardboard box which we'd sleep in, like a homeless person, but that people would stay up all night and watch over us so it was completely safe.' She laughed at the memory. 'The friend said, "So not all like a homeless person, then."' She paused. 'He was right. It wasn't a cold night, I had a good sleeping bag and I felt completely safe. I loved it.'

'I'll take you camping one day, where you feel safe and can see the dew on the grass and all that. I know just the spot.'

'Jack! Why would you want to do that?' Why would any man want to take a random older woman camping? she asked herself. It didn't make sense.

He shrugged and turned on to the road that led to the fish-and-chip shop. 'I think it would be fun.' He glanced at her quickly. 'I was planning to take you out to dinner after the polytunnel but it felt mean abandoning the others.'

Lorna laughed loudly. 'Even before the polytunnel I wasn't dressed for going out. Now I'm hardly clean enough to go into a fish-and-chip shop!' Only when her amusement was spent did she query why he would have wanted to take her out to dinner. He'd only just taken her out for lunch. Annoyingly she couldn't ask. But she wondered about it in her head while out loud she wondered why there was such a huge queue for fish and chips. Apparently they'd only just opened.

They were still in the queue when Lorna's phone went. It was Philly. 'Hi!' She sounded a bit stressed. 'Lucien wants to make tartar sauce. Is there any chance you could pop into the supermarket and get some capers?'

'Or I could get some ready-made from the chip shop? I'm still in the queue. Or buy it from the supermarket if you have a preferred brand.'

'No. It has to be capers themselves. And if you can get them in oil rather than brine, that would be brilliant.' She paused and Lorna could hear her walking out of the room. 'It's Lucien. He's a chef. They're not like ordinary people, I've just found out.'

Lorna laughed. 'Ooh, must be tough having one in your house.'

'In my kitchen and all my cupboards!' said Philly.

'I'll ask Jack to go for the capers. I can't lose my place in the queue now.'

'I might try and have a snack without Lucien knowing,' said Philly 'I'm starving!'

★   ★   ★

Although he'd gone along with the plan, Lucien was not entirely happy with the fish-and-chips idea.

'The chips are always soggy,' he said. 'I hate that.'

89

'I don't mind chip-shop chips,' said Philly. 'Especially between slices of white bread and butter. Plenty of butter. No vinegar.' The thought of those things, when she was so hungry, made it hurt just behind her ears.

'Interesting,' said Lucien. 'Have you tried with balsamic?'

Philly laughed. A few hours ago, if anyone had told her she'd have felt relaxed enough to laugh at the posh-boy chef with floppy hair she'd have put money on that never happening. But after several hours struggling with aluminium tubing and plastic she'd lost a lot of her inhibitions. 'No. And I'm going to grab a quick shower now, unless you want one?'

Lucien shook his head. 'I'm going to sort out the kitchen.'

'But we're having fish and chips!'

'Food is always important, Philly,' he said solemnly. But then laughed.

Philly ran up the stairs feeling happy. It was scary having him in the house but it was also fun.

She was slightly less thrilled when she came down again, feeling wonderfully clean, and found that he'd taken their kitchen apart. He had also found their guilty secret, a deep fat fryer, bought by Seamus at a car boot sale and seldom used.

'This kitchen is a mess!' declared Lucien.

'It was OK before you attacked it!' said Philly, offended.

'I don't mean it was untidy — although it was — I mean it was incredibly badly organised!'

Philly opened her mouth, puffed up with

indignation, ready to give him a blast. But he hadn't finished.

'But don't worry, I'll sort it. You go and have a drink. Your grandfather is looking for cooking oil and beer.'

'Oh. I'd better help him.' She really hoped there was cooking oil. She didn't want to have to ring Lorna again.

She found her grandfather in one of the outhouses. It was a place where they stored extra groceries and alcohol. They called it 'the caboosh'. Philly wasn't sure why, but her grandfather was full of odd expressions and she just accepted it.

'I've found oil and beer and a bottle of whisky left over from last Christmas. Forgot it was there!' He seemed delighted.

'Grand, Lucien has trashed our kitchen!'

'Oh God, has he? When I left him he was just tearing into the cupboards. What has he done now?'

Some of Philly's indignation faded. 'He's — well — tearing into the cupboards. He says the kitchen is untidy and disorganised. Who is he to come here and say that?'

'He's a boy who's spent all day helping you get your polytunnel up and was willing to cook supper for us. And who doesn't think chips from the chip shop are crisp enough.' He paused. 'Let him be, child dear. There's no harm in him.'

Carrying a bottle of oil so big it needed both hands, Philly walked back to the house with her grandfather. She was very glad that Grand liked Lucien. It made it OK for her to like him, although the attack on her kitchen, even if it wasn't only hers, still stung a bit.

She put the bottle of oil down on the now perfectly clear work surface. Quite how Lucien had sorted everything out and put it back in the cupboards she could only guess, but he'd managed it.

'There won't be time to heat the oil,' she grumbled, watching him take the bottle and tip a huge amount of it into the deep fat fryer.

'Well, we'll have to wait. How's the fire going in the sitting room? Your grandfather was having trouble lighting it earlier.'

Although it was ridiculous, Lucien rather reminded her of her grandfather. He seemed to have her best interests at heart (although obviously not in a romantic way) and distracted her in the same way her grandfather did, by giving her a job. But she went to the sitting room willingly enough. If there wasn't a blaze of flame and a good lot of crackling, she felt she'd failed. Seamus didn't have her way with logs.

★　★　★

'I am so sorry we were so long!' said Lorna, putting plastic bags on the table. 'The queue was enormous. Apparently they'd only just opened and the oil wasn't hot but it means they're really lovely and crispy.' She looked around. 'Why what have I said?'

Lucien took the bags and rummaged through them. 'They may be crispy by some people's standards, but — '

Philly, who'd been persuaded to have 'a drop of the crater' by which her grandfather meant whisky and was feeling better, interrupted: 'But they'll be crisper than ever after Lucien's had his wicked way with them. He's made some crostini to keep us going while we wait for the fish and chips.' She offered the plate of tiny circles of toast with chopped-up tomatoes and basil on them. 'He made some pesto, too. Only with some sunflower seeds and wild garlic we've got growing in the wood, where it's really sheltered. It's actually delicious.'

'Good Lord!' said Jack, who, unlike Lorna who'd accepted a large whisky with gratitude, was drinking ginger beer. 'I've never seen anyone turn a fish-and-chip supper into a three-course meal before.'

'You've never met me before,' said Lucien, proudly tipping the first batch of chips into the boiling oil.

'Actually I was at the dinner you did for Burthen House,' said Jack.

Lucien groaned. 'Oh God. Bloody nightmare! Still, thanks to Philly here, it was sort of OK in the end.'

Philly took another tiny sip of whisky to conceal both her embarrassment and her pleasure.

'So what did Philly do to save the day?' asked Jack.

'She got the old range going,' said Lucien. 'The oven had broken down. She's got a way with fire.'

'Anyone has a way with fire if the wood is dry,'

said Philly. 'And that wood must have been in the wood shed for at least five years.'

'Well, it's not her only skill,' said Lorna. 'So I think we should toast her new polytunnel.'

Before anyone could, Philly broke in. 'And I propose a toast to you all, who got it up for me. I promise to give you all plants when it's productive. Are those chips ready yet?'

'Any minute now,' said Lucien.

'Actually,' said Lorna a few minutes later, with her mouth full, 'these chips are really amazing.'

'Told you!' said Lucien happily.

'It may just be the effect of the whisky,' Lorna said, teasing.

10

'Well,' said Jack a while later, as he and Lorna walked towards his car having said their goodbyes to Philly, 'considering that wasn't at all what I'd planned for the evening, it was surprisingly good fun.'

Lorna decided to ignore the reminder he'd wanted to take her out to dinner. 'Yes it was. I hope Philly isn't going to be driven mad by Lucien. I rather gathered Seamus has invited him to lodge with them.'

'I think it will be fine. He's a good lad and a very hard worker. I see quite a lot of young men in my work and they're not all grafters by any stretch.'

'He's a bit unexpected, isn't he?' said Lorna. 'I do like him but he's a bit of a force of nature and I hope . . . ' She paused.

'What?'

She had been going to say she hoped Lucien didn't break Philly's heart but had suddenly realised she didn't really know Jack. People had been treating them as a couple, and in a way they'd been behaving like one, but they were hardly even friends. More acquaintances really. 'Oh, nothing.'

He opened the car door for her and when he'd got in but not started the engine, he said, 'Would you like to see what I do? As a day job? When I'm not being an artist?'

'That would be fascinating!' said Lorna and then had a reality check and tried to backtrack. 'I mean, I would really like to know what a mason does in a church but I'm very busy. This open-garden thing is terribly short notice. I don't think Kirstie can have any idea of how much work getting a garden ready for public scrutiny entails.'

He put his hand on hers, just for a second. 'Come on, I'm sure you can have some time off.'

'After dark,' Lorna agreed.

'After dark is no good for me.' He thought for a moment. 'Tell you what, I'll let you have a good go at the garden — I might even come and help you at weekends — and then, when you're fed up and need a change of scene you can let me know and get the tour.'

'That sounds lovely,' said Lorna, glad that the perfect solution had been found. The ball had been left in her court; she didn't have to pick it up and serve.

'But you won't let me know, will you?'

Quite how he'd worked this out when he really didn't know her at all, she couldn't guess. 'Well — '

'You don't get me, do you?'

'What do you mean?' She was flustered. She certainly didn't get him! She liked him — a lot — but she had no idea why he seemed so keen to be friends with her.

'You know perfectly well what I mean,' he said calmly. 'But I won't push it. Now. I will when I think the time is right, though.'

It was odd, sitting in the dark, in the car, not

96

looking at each other, but it encouraged Lorna to ask something she'd wondered about since he'd first mentioned it. 'Tell me, you said you'd worked out where you knew me from. So where was it? I'm sure I'd have remembered if I'd met you before.' She realised this was a bit revealing, but it didn't seem to matter.

'I will tell you that too, but not yet.' He started the car and they set off.

'I wish you'd tell me now! It's so annoying not knowing. I keep racking my brains trying to think where we might have come across each other and never come up with anything.'

He laughed gently. 'Sorry about that. But I can't tell you until the time feels right.'

Lorna punished this stubbornness by not making any more conversation on the way home. She was worrying about the kissing thing again. She'd kiss any other friend on the cheek when she said goodbye but somehow with Jack she felt awkward.

He obviously didn't share her awkwardness. He got out of the car, waited until her key was in the lock and, when the door was open, said, 'Goodnight, Lorna. It was a lovely day. Thank you.' Then he kissed her firmly on the cheek and watched until she'd gone in.

'Er — goodnight, Jack,' she said, and went quickly through her front door, keen for the awkwardness to be over and feeling very odd.

By the time the kettle had boiled for a soothing mug of camomile tea she concluded that the oddness was because it had been a long time since she'd been near any man apart from

97

Peter and he wasn't much given to friendly pecks on the cheek. And somehow this kiss was different from when he'd kissed her after the dinner party.

It wasn't good, she decided, taking the tea upstairs into the bathroom where it could cool while she had a shower. Once again she reflected that she had to get out more, as the saying went. But how?

Internet dating. Maybe she had to think about it seriously. Hot water poured over her and she revelled in it for a moment. But was it really her thing? If anyone else had suggested this, she'd say: Don't knock it till you've tried it; but having listened to so many tales from Peter about totally unsuitable matches she was wary. Although — she wrapped herself in a warm towel and sipped the tea — he had now met Kirstie thought the internet. And that seemed to be going really well.

As she padded through to her bedroom she examined her feelings. How *did* she feel about Peter, the man she'd always thought of as the love of her life, finding love with a much younger woman? It ought to matter to her a lot, she realised. But somehow it didn't hurt any more. Her pride was still a bit bruised, but her heart? No.

So what had cured her? Surely it wasn't Kirstie. You weren't cured of longing and pining by the appearance of an attractive younger woman at the side of your love-object. It must be something else.

But although her mind refused to accept it,

her thoughts kept returning to Jack. Jack was a nice man. Good-looking, a sculptor. Practically perfect in every way, as Mary Poppins might have said. Except he wasn't perfect. He was too young for her.

★　★　★

After she had seen off Lorna and Jack, Philly went back into the house to find that Lucien had removed all traces of the party. The dishwasher was chugging away and the table cleared.

'Gosh! That was quick,' said Philly, a bit stunned. 'I've only been out of the room about five minutes.'

'I'm a professional kitchen tidier,' said Lucien, wringing out a cloth so hard Philly expected it to beg for mercy. 'If you don't clear up quickly, you never get home. Talking of which, I'll get out of your hair — '

'No!' said Philly urgently. 'I mean, God, after all you've done, the least we can do is give you a proper bed.'

'No, really — '

'We had the family over at Christmas. You can have the room my parents slept in. It's the best of the bedrooms.' She paused. 'This is a four-bedroom house, and it's good for the rooms to be used, otherwise' — she lowered her voice, embarrassed — 'they just get filled up with junk.'

Seamus came in. 'Goodness me. Has the Kitchen Fairy been?'

Philly giggled. 'I don't think Lucien would like to be described as a fairy.'

99

'Certainly not. Shall I make tea?'

'I could murder a cup of tea,' said Seamus. 'There's some cake in the tin.'

Feeling that she didn't really want to be there while Lucien ate what wasn't good enough for the stall, Philly said, 'I'm going to make up the spare room for Lucien, Grand. I think he deserves a proper bed after all he's done.'

'Indeed. Will you have a cup of tea when you come back?'

Philly was tempted but decided she was really tired and had to be up early in the morning. 'I won't, thanks. I'll do the bed and pop down to say goodnight.'

As she burrowed in the linen cupboard for the sheets they'd bought specially for her parents she wondered what on earth she'd say about Lucien when they had their next catch-up call. Knowing her mother, this would make her nag them even harder about using Skype, something she and Grand had resisted as she knew her mother would demand a tour of the house. If she knew there was a boy involved she'd become an irresistible force. Maybe Lucien would have gone by Sunday night and she needn't worry.

She came down a bit later to find Seamus and Lucien deep in conversation about bread.

'Maybe you can have a go tomorrow?' Seamus was saying.

'I'd love to,' said Lucien, 'but we've got to finish Philly's polytunnel first. Mind you, I could get it going and do the polytunnel while it's rising. Maybe we could start a sourdough mother?'

'What's one of those when it's at home?' asked Seamus.

'It's when you mix flour and water — could be wine or beer even — and allow it to catch the wild yeasts in the air. You can call it a starter.'

Philly frowned. 'I prefer that name. I think one mother is enough, thank you very much. But if you want to make another one — ' Then she remembered that he'd run away from home and felt her joke might have been out of place. 'Sorry,' she added.

Lucien looked at her, confused for a second, and then, obviously deciding he didn't understand why she was apologising, went on: 'It's supposed to be quite easy.'

'We'll never have the ingredients. Where would you buy them?' asked her grandfather. 'Some specialist bakery place, no doubt?'

'Nope. Flour and water should do it.'

'Well, we've plenty of that,' said her grandfather. 'Philly! He liked the cake. He thought using ground hazelnuts instead of almonds worked well with the chocolate.'

'Good,' said Philly. 'Now, if you don't mind, I'm going to bed.' Biting her tongue on the words, 'Don't stay up too late, you two,' she went to her room.

Having had a shower she didn't really need to do much more than brush her teeth and fall into bed, but instead she found some cream her mother had given her (to stop her getting those dreadful broken veins people who work outdoors always get) and applied it carefully.

She was aware of feeling very happy.

101

Downstairs was a boy — young man? She didn't know how she thought of him — who was not only very easy on the eye but was also getting on really well with her grandfather. But she knew enough not to get over-excited. He probably wouldn't stay long and even if he did, he would most likely think of her as an annoying younger sister, or even a non-annoying one. But he was there and she was determined to enjoy his company even if he did shake up their cosy lives more than somewhat. In fact, he already had.

11

'Oh! Marion!' said Seamus, saying hello to his daughter-in-law. 'You'll be pleased with us this time! Philly's met a young man!'

It was the weekly Sunday-evening phone call from her parents and now Philly groaned, cursing herself for not telling her grandfather about her plans to say nothing about Lucien even being in the house. And to say she'd 'met a young man' implied all sorts of things. Her mother would leap to conclusions like a salmon to the fly.

Philly didn't actually need to be able to hear her mother to know exactly what she was saying: partly from experience and partly from what her grandfather was saying. The trouble was, Philly knew, that although her mother was desperate for her to find a husband and have children and go back to Ireland where her mother could take them over, she had no faith in Philly's ability to pick out her own mate.

Seamus held out the phone. 'She wants to speak to you.'

Philly took the phone and sat down, glad that Lucien was out. He'd had a call from someone he knew who ran a pub and needed someone to knock up bar meals at short notice.

'Hiya — ' Philly began but wasn't given time to say more.

'Well, darling, tell me all about this young man

then. What does he do for a living?'

'He's a chef but, Mam — '

'Is that a stable job, do you think?'

'No, not at all, but it doesn't matter — '

'Of course it matters, darling! You need — every woman needs — a man who can keep them, at least when they're raising children!'

Philly didn't know where to start with this. 'I meant it doesn't matter because Lucien is only staying with us. He's not anything to do with me personally.' She was proud of this; it sounded very detached.

'Oh, come on now, you can't tell me two young people living in the same house won't have feelings for each other! I didn't come down in the last shower.'

'No! Really and truly! It was Grand. He heard Lucien was — ' At the last moment she stopped herself saying the word 'homeless' because then her mother would think Lucien was a tramp. 'Had nowhere to stay, and said he could stay with us for a few days while he got himself settled in the area. It may only be for a couple of nights.'

'Oh,' said her mother, deflated.

Philly felt guilty. She had lied to her mother for very good reasons but hearing the disappointment in her voice made her sad that there wasn't a boyfriend for her mother to worry about. 'He is very good-looking though,' she said, by way of reparation.

'Ah!'

Philly could imagine her mother sitting up straight in her chair, head on one side, straining to hear a subtext that might mean her daughter was interested in a young man. 'But don't get excited. I'm sure he wouldn't ever be interested in me but he is a very good lodger — '

'Lodger? I thought it was just for a couple of nights?'

'What I meant was, he's very helpful, clears up and cooks great food.'

'You know a lot about someone you say you're not interested in.'

'We met because he was cooking at a dinner party. I told you. I tasted the food; it was great. He cares about food a lot which is why he and Grand get on so well.' This at least was true.

'Well, you just watch yourself. You don't want to get involved with a handsome devil.'

Philly laughed. 'Would you rather I got involved with an ugly one?'

'You know what I mean, Philomena,' said her mother.

★ ★ ★

A few hours later, Lucien came back to find Philly still up. She had her laptop open and the kitchen table was covered with gardening books.

'Hey,' she said. 'Would you like a cup of tea or something? Or there's a beer?'

Lucien smiled and shook his head. 'I'm good, thanks. What are you up to?'

'I'm trying to work out what I can grow in time to make the Burthen garden spectacular.'

He nodded. 'Seamus gone to bed, then?'

'No, actually, he's still out.' She frowned. 'It's

105

partly why I'm still up.'

Lucien frowned now. 'You're worried about him? What can have happened? Where did he go?'

'He's gone to Lady Anthea's. She rang him to say she had a problem with a tap. He shot round there before I could blink. And yet a dripping tap is hardly an urgent problem.'

Lucien shrugged. 'I suppose it could have caused a flood, gone through a ceiling or something.'

Philly suddenly clutched the table and got up. 'That's the van! He's home. He mustn't know I waited up for him.'

'No! Wait! Philly — '

She hesitated and then it was too late: she'd never get out of the room and up the stairs before her grandfather came in. She sat down quickly.

Feeling guilty she looked down at the mess of paper and books in front of her.

'Oh, hello, Grand,' she said as he appeared in the kitchen.

'Hello! You two still up? Not waiting for me, were you?'

'Of course not,' said Philly, crossing her fingers under the table. 'I've been working and Lucien's just got in. How did you get on with the tap?'

Seamus looked confused for a moment. 'Oh! Well, I fixed it. And then stayed on for a nightcap.' He looked at his granddaughter. 'It was herbal tea.'

Philly snorted. 'Herbal tea? You, Grand?

You've always said it tasted of gnat's piss before.'

'It depends on the herbal tea,' he said sniffily. 'Now I think I'll get to bed. It's late. And I suggest you two do the same.'

Lucien and Philly looked at each other. 'Well, that's us told,' said Philly. 'But why was he so grumpy about it?'

'He looked caught out,' said Lucien. 'As if drinking herbal tea with an old lady was something to feel guilty about.'

Philly bit her lip. 'It's crazy. It's not as if — well — '

'You mean, if they had a thing going?'

Philly was horrified. 'Surely not! They're both so old!'

Lucien shrugged. 'It's possible.'

'No! She's such a snob. Even Lorna, who's her friend, says that.'

'So what's wrong with your grandfather?'

'Lucien, you know as well as I do. You're a posh boy. My grandfather is a car mechanic with an Irish accent. Lady Anthea isn't going to . . . ' She shuddered. 'I can't even let my mind go there.'

Lucien chuckled. 'You're right, I am a posh boy, although I do hope I'm not only that. And I can't imagine my grandmother ever fancying — '

'Please don't use that word.'

' — a car mechanic with an Irish accent, but, well, people differ.'

Philly sighed deeply. 'I'm sure it's impossible. Now I've got to have a nightcap. Do you want hot chocolate?'

'Oh, cool! I'll make it. Have you got any

107

chocolate we can grate? High cocoa solids if possible.'

Philly wasn't in the mood for Lucien's cheffy notions of what hot chocolate should be. 'No. I'll make it. With bog-standard drinking chocolate. OK?'

Lucien held up his hands. 'Whatever! I'll make you proper hot chocolate with vanilla bean or star anise some other time.'

As Philly whisked chocolate powder into hot milk she realised that she'd lost her shyness of Lucien. She'd told him off quite sharply. And the sky had not fallen in. Good!

As Lucien sat at the kitchen table, obviously not, as Philly had been going to do, planning to take his hot chocolate upstairs, she sat down too.

'You must think my cheffy ideas are a bit ridiculous,' he said.

As this had been exactly what Philly had been thinking she smiled. 'Only sometimes. I mean, I thought it was ridiculous of you to refry the chip-shop chips but they were delicious.'

He smiled back. 'I know! But in general, do I annoy you?'

She was taken aback. 'I don't know what to say!'

'Well, 'no' would do. But the reason I'm asking is . . . ' He paused, cleared his throat and carried on. 'I was having a look around earlier and there's an outbuilding that would make a perfect base for me. If I could rent it, it would be amazing.'

'Er — '

'Of course it's something I'd talk to Seamus

about and you and he would have to think about it very hard but . . . ' He paused again. 'Can I tell you my life story? Well, edited highlights, anyway?'

Philly shrugged. 'If you want to.'

'I think I told you I ran away from home — like you two did — and since then I've learnt a few things. One is, I don't really want to work as a chef in a restaurant.'

'Isn't that what chefs do?'

He shook his head. 'Not necessarily. Working in a restaurant is hell, honestly it is. Such hard work, no proper sleep, split shifts which mean you have two hours off in the afternoon but you can't really go home and sleep in that time — '

'But if it was your restaurant?'

'If I ever got enough capital to have a restaurant of my own I'd lose it all in the first six months. These are the hard business facts.'

All Philly's — admittedly very vague — impressions about the life of a chef faded. 'So?'

'I want to cook for people, either in their homes or businesses. And I want to make bread.'

'Right.' Philly sipped her drink.

'So I need a premises. Somewhere I can pre-prepare meals and, of course, bake — which is why I'm asking whether you and your grandfather would rent me that outbuilding.'

'It would take a lot of work to make it suitable — '

'I know! But I don't mind doing that work. It's got water and electricity already but I would need to have it converted to three-phase for a

109

commercial oven.' He hesitated. 'You don't need it for plants?'

Philly wondered what three-phase was but decided not to ask. She probably didn't need to know. 'No. One of the many reasons — but possibly the main one — we wanted this property so much was because of the outbuildings. But we don't need them all. Renting one out would probably be fine.' She frowned. 'But you're going to need equipment — all sorts of things. How are you going to afford that?'

Lucien had obviously thought a lot about all this. 'I'm going to save up. It'll take a while but when I've got a decent lump I'll see if I can get my godfather to put up the rest.'

'But would he?'

Lucien shrugged. 'He might. He's not as conventional as my parents. They all have enough money to lend me the entire amount but they won't because they assume I'd waste it.'

'So you need to prove — '

'That I can work hard and get some capital of my own; that I won't waste it. So, my interim plan is — with your permission — to bake what I can in your domestic oven, prove I can do the work, the getting up early, preparing everything.' He paused. 'Domestic ovens are not ideal but I've got to start somewhere.'

Philly had been thinking. 'Do professional ovens take up a lot of space?'

'Depends how big they are, obviously.'

Philly flushed. 'I know that. What I was trying to say is: Do they have to be massive?'

'Not really. What are you suggesting?'

110

'Well, there's the utility room. It's full of junk at the moment because we've never got round to clearing it out and we're fine having the washing machine in the kitchen. Maybe you could use that for the time being?'

He sucked his teeth. 'There's the phase-three thing — '

Philly realised she did need to know. 'What's that, exactly?'

'Commercial ovens need a hell of a lot more power than domestic ovens do. It would need rewiring. That would be an expense as well as the oven.'

This wasn't sounding positive. 'And I expect professional bread ovens are really expensive?'

'You can get all types and sizes second-hand. Still expensive though!' He seemed excited by all these difficulties. 'Let's have a look on eBay. It would be good to know what we're aiming for, money-wise.'

A little while later, Philly said, 'You're going to need a thousand pounds really, just for the cooker.'

Lucien nodded. 'I've got a bit stashed away but not that much. But it's OK. I've got work booked for the Newbury Races. I did a phone interview and someone I know gave me a reference.' He paused. 'I was presuming a bit. That it's OK for me to stay on for a little while? I'm not getting on your nerves?'

Her answer seemed important to him, as if he was asking for more than just somewhere to stay.

'You're not getting on my nerves and I'm sure it's OK to stay.'

His expression was suddenly too intense for

her to be able to meet his gaze. She looked away.

He cleared his throat. 'Philly?'

She blushed and glanced up and then looked away again. 'What?' Her voice was suddenly croaky.

He gazed at her for a bit longer and then said, 'Nothing! If you're sure it's all right to stay I'll see if I can get a sourdough mother started.'

Relieved he had reverted to talking about dough she relaxed. 'And if it doesn't work?'

'I've got a mate who'll give me a bit. I prefer to make my own really.'

'You're very energetic!'

He nodded. 'Used to drive my mother mad. Which is why I decided to leave — to give her some peace.' He frowned. 'It wasn't the only reason. Just one of them.'

Seeing his expression Philly felt he probably minded more being at odds with his parents than he appeared. She understood. Leaving home with her grandfather had been an adventure but hurting her family by doing it had been tough. She was glad now her parents had more or less accepted the situation. She smiled. 'So if you fall out with your birth mother you make a new one out of flour and water?'

He grinned. 'Maybe a few other things, but that's about it.'

'Talk to Grand in the morning. He might have some ideas about how to raise money. He loves impossible challenges.'

'That's good, because this is one — if you accept some things aren't do-able, which I don't, mostly.' He grinned, wickedly, Philly thought. 'I have a bit of a plan.'

'Oh?'

She didn't really want to know but curiosity got the better of her.

'Don't look like that — you'll like it.'

'Will I?'

'Yes! I'm planning a bit of a flutter while I'm at the races.'

She was horrified and obviously looked it.

'Don't look so worried.' He moved a curl away from her eyes and tucked it behind her ear. 'Although you do look pretty when you're worried.'

She took a breath. She wasn't sure if she was ready for him to say she was pretty. She was happier when they were talking about phase-three and sourdough mothers, even if she didn't remotely understand them.

'You're Irish,' Lucien went on, gently teasing. 'You're supposed to like horses.'

She felt more confident now. 'I do like horses — to ride or cuddle — but not to bet on. Not all Irish people are gamblers, you know.'

'Oh, sorry. I didn't mean to insult you. Well, anyway, I'm going to go to the races, so I'll take the van to Newbury and find somewhere to park it. Otherwise I'll have to find accommodation which is never that great.'

'The van is better?'

He nodded. 'It's very comfortable, you know. I'll take you for a ride in it sometime.'

Worried that he might pick up on the double meaning his words might have to a good Irish girl, she tossed him a smile over her shoulder and left the room.

12

The following morning, Philly and Lorna were in the garden, which, in the chilly dawn, did not look much like somewhere you'd open to the public.

'I'd just like the paths all properly edged in this bit,' said Lorna with a grand gesture of her hand. It was a part of the garden that had at one time been described as Italian but was a long way off its restoration. 'At the moment it's just full of things people have stuck in over the years. There's no proper scheme to it.'

Philly inspected it more critically, mentally running through plant lists. It was a big project and a wonderful opportunity. She felt daunted and excited at the same time. 'What sort of scheme would you have?'

'Ideally? I'd go for something quite dramatic and stylish. There's a lovely black and white garden at Highgrove.'

Philly knew the one Lorna was referring to. 'Tricky.'

'Yes, and they take the buds off dahlias — Bishop of Llandaff — to get the black foliage and I don't think I could do that.'

'Those lovely scarlet flowers? I couldn't do it either! But you could have black, white and scarlet,' she went on. 'I could do you some of those nasturtiums that don't climb but are a really good red with black leaves.'

'And they'd bulk up quickly so we could get the effect quite soon. Should we include white? Or just the two colours?'

Usually Lorna had clear ideas about what she wanted. Philly found it flattering to be consulted so closely. 'Let's see,' she suggested. 'If we run out of black and scarlet you could add in some white. There are masses of poppies, scarlet with black centres. I could grow them with some heat to make sure we have plenty in flower, like they do for Chelsea.'

'Isn't that a bit wasteful?'

'No. I can always sell the later bloomers on the stall. I think it's a great idea. What else? There are lots of black grasses.'

'It's a shame we didn't know about this last autumn. We could have done the whole thing with tulips,' said Lorna.

'I have got quite a lot of tulips in containers I could let you have. People like those really dark Queen of the Night so I planted plenty.'

'Won't that mean you won't have them for the stall?'

'It will. But I'll still be selling them.'

'Well, charge me the full retail price for them. Peter can afford it. And thinking of things Peter can afford, he said I can have help. Do you know anyone who might like a bit of gardening work?'

Philly shook her heard. 'I can't think of anyone. Why don't you put some cards up in the local garden centres? I can ring around my nursery friends and see if they know anyone who needs a bit of work. Do they need to be qualified?'

'Well, as long as they know the difference between a weed and a flower they should be OK.'

'To be honest, Lorna, I have got those two confused myself on occasion.'

Lorna laughed. 'So have I! Now let's get these beds cleared. I know I haven't got you for all that long. And while we're working, think up some more plants. And you can tell me what it's like having Lucien lodging with you.'

Philly pulled her gardening gloves out of her back pocket. 'It's fine actually. Grand loves him being there. Lucien has this mad plan to raise enough money to convert one of the outbuildings into a professional kitchen.'

'Goodness! That does make him a special kind of lodger,' said Lorna. 'That needs to cost money, does it? I mean, can't you just paint it and put in a freezer?'

Philly watched as Lorna knocked the earth off a huge clump of Michaelmas daisies before sticking her own fork into the flower bed. 'No. You need to redo the electricity to three-phase, so you can get really hot ovens and things. Expensive.'

'Oh. And Seamus is happy about that?'

'Yes! He adores Lucien. They're both a bit mad and Lucien has loads of energy and bounces around all the time like he's on springs.' She frowned suddenly.

Lorna happened to be looking at her. 'Something not right?'

'Well, it's not really my business but he has this mad plan to raise the money to do it. I don't

116

know the details but he's got work as a chef at Newbury Races.'

Lorna looked worried. 'I do hope he's not going to bet all his wages on a horse.'

Philly bit her lip. 'He mentioned having a flutter. Of course, it's his money. If he wants to throw it away on a horse it's nothing to do with me.'

Lorna nodded. 'And I suppose if you were going out with Lucien you'd have to learn to live dangerously.'

Philly flushed. 'I'm not going out with Lucien.'

Lorna shrugged. 'Of course you're not. But maybe you will? He is very attractive.'

Philly sighed. 'It's not that I don't find him attractive — of course I do. And we're fine when we're talking about practical things. But when he says anything — you know — a bit flirtatious, or looks at me in a certain way, I go all shy and can't help blushing. He must think I've never had a boyfriend and don't know how to behave around them.'

'You'll get used to it. It's early days.'

Philly nodded. 'So what about you and Jack? Are you seeing each other?'

'No! Not like that. He's far too young for me.'

'So how old is he?'

'I don't know exactly — '

'You mean you haven't googled him?'

'Have you googled Lucien?'

'Yes. He doesn't really do much on Facebook and most of his pictures are of food.' She'd been looking for pictures of him with haughty debutantes and was very relieved not to find any.

'And you think I should google Jack?'

'Yes! I mean . . . ' Philly coughed. 'I mean, you're not on Facebook, are you, Lorna?'

'I know I should be — '

'Google him,' said Philly firmly. 'If you can't find out about him on Facebook, he'll still be there on the internet. He may not be that young and anyway, why worry about it? I think he likes you!'

* * *

The following morning Philly appeared with a wrapped package for Lorna. 'Hey! This is a present from Lucien. He made bread last night to see what he could do with a domestic oven. It's not of merchantable quality, according to him, but I had some for breakfast and it's fab.'

'Oh, great! Thank you.' Lorna took the package and put it in her knapsack where there was a flask of coffee and some biscuits. 'Couldn't you have frozen it?'

'He made rather a lot, Lorna, and he wanted to find out what other people thought of it.'

'The trouble is, I'm always so hungry by lunch-time I'd think it was delicious even if it wasn't.'

'Exactly. I told him that. But he wanted you to have it and so did I.'

* * *

It was towards the end of the morning and the Italian garden was pretty much clear ready for its

118

new colour scheme when Jack appeared.

'Hello, Lorna, Philly,' he called and they both looked up.

Lorna wiped a strand of hair away from her eyes and then wished she hadn't. She knew she had replaced her hair with a streak of mud.

'Hello, Jack,' said Philly. Lorna was grateful. Since Philly had put the idea of Jack as a potential boyfriend into her head, she couldn't think about him in a normal way. The relaxed companion of the other night had somehow become something that made her wary.

'Hi,' she managed. 'What can we do for you?'

He looked at her 'I just wanted to see where I might put my sculpture.'

'Oh? I thought there was a day when all the artists were going to come round? Didn't Kirstie send an email?' She knew perfectly well she had. And she'd seen Jack's name on the list.

'I wanted to get ahead of the game. I thought being friends with the head gardener and the main supplier of plants gave me an advantage.'

Lorna smiled. 'I'm sure it does. Where do you think you might like to put it? And have you just the one piece? Or several? What sort of size is it?'

'It's quite large. I'll need to be able to get a tractor or something to wherever I put it.'

'Then quite near here then,' said Philly. 'It's not too far from a good path.'

'Sounds perfect. And if I can stake my claim I will. Other people will have problems moving things about too,' he said.

'You'd better see Kirstie then,' said Lorna. 'Once you've decided.'

'I'll have a walk round,' he said. 'I'll catch you later.' He set off towards the house.

'I hope he doesn't only do huge pieces,' said Lorna, hoping too that Philly hadn't caught her watching Jack move away with long, purposeful strides. 'Shifting it around could be tricky and churn up the ground quite a bit.'

'I don't suppose Kirstie thought about things like that when she had the idea of a sculpture trail.'

'Nor did I, at the time,' said Lorna. 'Well, let's get this lot to the compost. Shall I push and you pull? To get the barrow up the slope?'

★   ★   ★

Philly had gone home and Lorna was sweeping the paths of the Italian garden so it looked tidy, even if the beds were empty. She looked around her, content with how it looked. As yet there were no plants, but it was full of promise. As a red, black and possibly white garden it would be sophisticated and interesting. She'd probably never love it as much as the far more haphazard cottage garden, over on the other side of the house, which was full of rambling roses, poppies, lupins, stocks and phlox, but it would be immensely stylish.

She was about to go home herself, as she'd been thinking about the soup that had been simmering in the slow cooker since early that morning, when Jack came back.

'I've found the perfect spot,' he said. 'Can I take you out for lunch?'

'No,' she said. 'I've got lunch at home. But you can share it with me if you like.'

'But I've been asking you out for meals for ages and you never come! I only got you as far as the pub once! You always end up feeding me.'

Lorna laughed. 'If I went out to lunch I'd have to change. As it is I'll just get the worst of the mud off and then eat soup and bread. Lucien provided the bread so it should be delicious.'

'Sounds perfect!' said Jack.

⋆ ⋆ ⋆

Jack was outside her house, waiting for her. Because she'd known he'd have to hang around while she put away her gardening tools she'd given him her keys. But she was obscurely pleased that he hadn't used them.

'You should have gone in and made yourself at home,' she said.

'That would have felt wrong. And it's a lovely spot.' He indicated the parkland that the house looked over. 'No hardship to wait for you.'

Something about the way he said it made her wonder about what Philly had said. Did he like her in that way? Or was he just friendly and polite? As she took the keys from him and put them in the lock she allowed herself to think about him liking her in the way Philly had meant.

'Come in. Go and warm up in the kitchen. I'll just do some basic scraping and scrubbing then we can have soup. You could stir it,' she added.

'That would be helpful.' She put the bread on

121

the counter. 'The bread knife is up there if you want to cut some.'

She came back into the kitchen smelling strongly of gardeners' hand cream. She had deliberately not given her face more than a cursory check for mud as she didn't want to risk obsessing over what she looked like at the moment, practically make-up-free. Usually she was fairly content with her appearance. But now, having allowed the thought of going out with a younger man to enter her mind, she knew she had to hold her nerve.

Jack was whistling softly, having found plates and bowls and cut some bread. The bowls he had put on the Rayburn, next to the soup, possibly to warm them up.

'Sorry to keep you waiting,' she said.

'You haven't.' He smiled at her. 'Why don't you sit down? You've been working all morning.'

'Haven't you?'

'Yes,' he acknowledged. 'But not physically. Let yourself be waited on.'

'Oh, OK,' she said, and seated herself at the table. She felt strangely relaxed. She should feel hostessy and anxious but somehow it felt fine him putting a bowl of soup down in front of her and then the butter, hidden in a handmade dish with a cover.

He sat down opposite her. 'Did you get up at the crack of dawn to make this soup?' he said, having taken a sip.

'No. I did get up early, but to go to work, not to make soup. I threw the things together while I made tea this morning.'

'It's delicious. I love those beany, pulsy things but I never leave enough time to cook them.'

She took the lid off the butter dish and pushed it towards Jack. When they'd both had some she spread her bread. 'It's just a bit of forethought. What's the bread like?'

'Delicious!'

'Well, we'll get an opportunity to buy it if Lucien is ever sufficiently satisfied with it to put it on Philly and Seamus's stall.'

'He obviously has very high standards if this isn't good enough for him,' said Jack.

'I think he's a bit obsessive,' said Lorna.

'All good artists or craftsmen are,' said Jack.

'Are you?'

He laughed. 'That's a loaded question!'

'You did rather set yourself up for it.'

'I did.' He paused, holding her gaze. 'I am obsessive. There is nothing I won't do to get the end result I'm after. I don't care how many setbacks I come across.'

She looked down, finding her soup unexpectedly fascinating. 'I suppose I'm like that too. I never think 'that'll do'. It has to be as good as I can make it.' She ate the soup and looked up. 'So, tell me about being a stonemason. I know a bit about being a sculptor — I went to art school and did sculpture myself for a little while until I wanted something more secure and discovered gardening. But the stonemason bit is unknown to me. What does it entail?'

He didn't answer immediately and she began to wonder if she'd said something she shouldn't. Then he caught her gaze again and said, I think

123

I should show you. 'I think I should take you round the abbey and show you what a mason does, and has done for thousands of years.'

'Well,' she said a few seconds later, 'that would be lovely. After all, we're having this sculpture trail in aid of the abbey. It would be good to see what we're raising the money for.'

'I'd love to show you. When would be a good time?'

'I expect you're very busy . . . '

'I can make time for this. It's important. You're busy too.'

Lorna thought this conversation could go on quite a long time if she didn't do something to stop it. 'What about this afternoon? I was going to research plants but I can do that this evening.'

'I was hoping to take you out this evening. For dinner.'

'I think taking me to see your abbey this afternoon will do for today?'

He laughed ruefully. 'I keep being thwarted. I wanted to take you out the other day and we had fish and chips. I would have taken you for lunch now, and you invited me here. Please don't tell me you have to work this evening!'

'I definitely should! But why don't we play it by ear? I may start to fall asleep by this evening. I was up very early.'

He laughed. 'OK. As long as you promise that sometime you'll let me take you out for dinner!'

She laughed too but made no promises. It was fun to be courted and she didn't want him to get bored with her.

13

Jack parked the car in the staff car park, tucked away among the backstreets of the town. As always when she saw it, Lorna thought how beautiful the abbey was. It had once been very important and some past abbot had managed to do a deal with Henry VIII and so it had missed the worst of the Dissolution of the Monasteries. It was Perpendicular Gothic and had famous fan-vaulted ceilings. Being responsible for such an ancient building was a big job. Seeing it for the first time properly since she'd known Jack made Lorna see the carved golden stone with new respect.

'We'll take a quick look in at the workshop,' said Jack, 'and then I'll give you a tour of the abbey.'

He locked his car and then led her away from the abbey to a separate building. 'Here we are.'

He opened the door to a workshop filled with sound. There were three people there, all working hard. They all stopped when they saw them.

'Hey, Boss. I didn't think you were in today,' said one, a serious-looking young man wearing several jumpers and a woolly hat. She realised it was cold. Considering it was now properly spring, this was a bit of a surprise. Then she realised that the stone walls probably meant the temperature was always on the cool side.

'I'm just showing Lorna round. Lorna, this is the team.'

As he introduced her to them she realised it was clear how much they liked and respected him. He exchanged a few words with one of them while she looked around her. It was like many workshops: the walls were hung with tools, saws, chisels, hammers, mallets, all in many shapes and sizes. They were dressed for the cold and all had masks hung round their necks. The local radio station played in the background.

Jack went across to one man, hardly more than a boy, and talked to him quietly about the stone he was chipping away at.

Then he came back to Lorna. 'Ready for your tour?'

★　★　★

'Of course I have been in here before,' said Lorna as they stood in the abbey porch. 'But not since I first came to the area.'

'When was that?'

'About three years ago.'

'I don't expect it's changed much, except the bit that really needs repair. There's a major tomb awaiting restoration and part of the roof that needs doing. But it all needs attention really.'

'You mean, it's deteriorated more?'

He laughed softly. 'No! Some of it's been restored already.'

He opened the inner door to the abbey and the sound of singing drifted towards them. Lorna instantly halted. Jack whispered, 'It's all

126

right. We won't disturb them. It's a visiting choir rehearsing.'

Lorna listened as the cadences moved back and forth between the two sides of the choir. Rising and falling, loud and then soft. 'Is that Byrd?' she breathed.

'It may well be. We can find out later, if you like. They're good.'

Neither of them moved until the piece came to an end and the conductor said something to the choir and the spell was broken.

'That was lovely!' she said to Jack, still very quietly.

'Wasn't it? Now, let me show you round.'

'I really don't want to disturb the rehearsal,' she said, indicating the singers in the choir stalls.

'It's all right. Where we're going we won't do that.'

When Lorna had first visited the abbey on moving to the area, it had been fairly full of a party of Japanese tourists. She'd gone round quickly, enjoying the general magnificence of it, but not really feeling much. The fact it was nearly empty, the music, and a chance shaft of sunlight that made the ancient stone flags golden made it quite different now. She felt she'd gone back in time. The thought of all the people who'd come here over the years, with their sorrows and their celebrations, brought a lump to her throat.

Jack took her hand, as if to hurry her along. 'This way.'

He led her out through a side door and along the outside of the building.

'It's so huge!' said Lorna, partly so he would let go of her hand. She liked the feel of her hand in his large, roughened one, but it was embarrassing.

'It was built on wool, really.'

'You mean, it was a wool church?'

'That's right. They had them here and in East Anglia. It's a pity wool doesn't raise as much money now as it did then!' he said.

She nodded. 'Didn't they make people have woollen shrouds in those days? A never-ending market.' She smiled.

He returned her smile warmly. 'Come and see why we need so much money.' He opened a door that went back into the abbey. 'It's a chapel that's a memorial to the scions of a very wealthy family. It was their tomb.'

It was hugely elaborate. It was as if the couple were lying in a huge, stone four-poster bed. But although they appeared to be sharing a bed they seemed very separate from each other. Their hands were steepled as if in prayer. Elaborately carved pillars supported an equally elaborate canopy. The only thing that for Lorna showed a bit of humanity was a small dog crouched at the feet of his master.

'This is the one that needs restoring.'

'Mm, I like the little dog,' Lorna said. She did like the dog but she found the tomb a bit over the top. It was a vehicle for showing off. 'The rest is a bit . . . '

'Vulgar? Ostentatious?' suggested Jack.

She smiled, not wanting to confess she didn't like it even though he was inviting her to do so.

'The dog is definitely the best bit,' she said instead. 'He looks like a real dog. I wonder if he was one they had in real life?'

'I hope so. I copied it very carefully from an engraving of the tomb.'

'You did the dog?' She turned to him in astonishment. 'You mean it's not ancient?'

'No. It had been very badly restored in Victorian times. We were lucky that there were earlier records. They'd used entirely the wrong sort of stone.'

'Oh, well, he's adorable! So lifelike. You feel you know exactly what a cheerful little dog he'd have been.'

'Thank you. But this is what we need the money for.' He took her arm and her away from the chapel to an area under a window.

Lorna looked at what he indicated and sighed. Here was a much simpler tomb.

'This is much earlier, as you can see,' said Jack. 'Fourteenth century.'

There was no elaborate carving. The figures were in long robes, their heads on stone pillows, and they were holding hands.

For the second time since she'd been in the abbey Lorna felt her throat close with emotion. 'It's like that Philip Larkin poem. These two look as if they really loved each other.'

'"An Arundel Tomb',' said Jack, nodding. 'It always makes me think of that, too. 'They would not think to lie so long . . .''

'That's not the last line though?'

'"What will survive of us is love',' he said promptly. 'But I don't think Larkin was as sentimental about his tomb as I am about this one here.'

Lorna stood there, looking at the stone couple. The woman's face was hardly there and the man's legs were badly damaged.

'These were restored before, too,' said Jack.

'Wrong stone?'

He nodded. 'This abbey was made from Minchinhampton stone but that's all gone now. We need to go to France to get stone that's the same. There's a huge seam of it that goes under the Channel to the Cotswolds.'

They stood in silence for a few moments. Lorna was lost in her imagination, and also thinking how nice it was to find someone who understood her points of reference.

'Come on. I've got some other things to show you.'

She followed him to a spot that had what looked like a shelf attached to a section of wall.

'This is a mason's bracket,' Jack explained. 'It's thought to be a copy of the one on Gloucester Cathedral. Look up.'

She looked and saw what seemed to be a youth with outstretched arms, falling through the air. There was a man reaching out, as if trying to catch him.

'I'm not sure I quite understand what I'm looking at,' she said.

'There are two interpretations of this bracket,' Jack said. 'It could just be that the apprentice mason has fallen to his death, but imagine if the master mason was also his father?'

'I can't imagine how dreadful,' she said. 'I

130

have a son myself. How awful if I'd somehow sent him to his death. Like Kipling, making his son go to war, when the boy was desperately short-sighted and could have got out of it.'

'Hundreds of men must have died in the building of this abbey — all the great cathedrals.' She felt suddenly chilled.

He took her elbow again and they walked together. He was taller than her and, being tall herself, this was pleasant and a bit unusual. She paused in front of a quirky little statue she had almost not noticed. 'What's this?'

He laughed. 'That's an example of hubris. It's a caricature, of me and by me. It's a tradition of masons, to leave an image of themselves behind.'

'It's charming but not flattering,' Lorna said.

Jack had stopped in front of a tiny door set in the foot of a tower. Lorna hesitated. She was fine going up but had always struggled with going down spiral staircases, especially if they were confined. Should she tell him? Or maybe she'd grown out of it? After all, phobias don't necessarily last forever. She found she didn't want to disappoint him. He'd invited her into his world. She wanted to be able to share it.

As she had thought, she was fine going up the narrow, twisting steps. It was dark but Jack lit the way with a torch on his key ring. She had no trouble finding the steps and putting her feet on them, even if they were narrow and the space restricted. She even felt proud that she managed to keep up with him without audibly panting. At least her job as a gardener kept her fit. When they got to the top he opened a little door that opened out on to a lead-lined roof. You could see the roof of the abbey, the many towers and parapets and, beyond them, the town.

'Oh, this is lovely!' she said.

'It's one of my favourite bits that the rest of the world doesn't see,' said Jack. 'They don't usually bring people here on the tours. The staircase is too narrow for some of them. It's a bit private.'

Now was the moment to confess, Lorna told herself, to say that sometimes she had a problem going down spiral staircases. They didn't have to be spiral, either. She'd had a terrible time getting down the Rock of Gibraltar when she'd gone there as a student. It was the repetitive nature of it, one foot after another, time after time. It made her dizzy.

He opened the door and stood back for her to go past.

'No, actually, would you go first?' she said.

'Oh, OK. Would you like the torch? I pretty much know my way without it.'

'Thank you,' she said, praying that this time she would be fine.

She'd gone about three steps, her shoulder pressed against the wall, the torch lighting the next step, when it slipped out of her hand and skittered all the way down to the bottom of the staircase.

Lorna's mouth went dry.

'Are you OK?' came Jack's voice quite a lot further down the steps than she was.

'Not really. I've dropped the torch.'

'I know.' He hesitated. 'Can you manage without it?'

'No.' It was a squeak. 'I'm a bit claustrophobic.'

There was a pause in which he didn't comment that it was a bit late to say that and she silently thanked him. She was terrified and desperately embarrassed. Although it was dark she closed her eyes and clung to the rail, certain she would have to stay there for the rest of her life. They'd never get the fire brigade up here.

'OK.' It was Jack, right by her. 'Can you move?'

She shook her head and then whimpered.

He went on. 'As I see it, you can either bump down on your bottom, step by step, or I can carry you down.'

'You couldn't carry me down. I'm far too heavy.'

He laughed. 'I mean in a fireman's lift, over my shoulder. It'll be a squash but you won't be too heavy.'

'I'll try bumping down.' Clinging to the wall she bent her knees until she was squatting but then found she couldn't let herself move her feet so she could sit on the step.

He took hold of her arm. 'Just shuffle forward so you're sitting.'

She managed this and realised the step wasn't wide enough and this increased her panic. Somehow she worked enough saliva into her mouth. 'Can't.'

'OK, shut your eyes and don't struggle.'

She realised she had never been so dependent

on another human being for her safety. She wouldn't have known how to help herself even if she hadn't been paralysed with fear. She had to surrender herself into someone else's care completely. There was no choice.

She felt him feel for her limbs and then heave her body over his shoulder.

'Right,' he said. 'Keep your head down and your eyes closed. We're off.'

It probably only took a few minutes but it seemed to Lorna to go on forever. The blood rushing to her head, her face pressed into Jack's back smelling his washing powder and possibly his shower gel, her eyes clenched shut, she somehow got through it without crying, or vomiting, or embarrassing herself further.

They landed in a tangle at the bottom of the staircase and somehow Lorna found her feet. Her knees gave way and she had to cling on to Jack.

'Oh God, I am so sorry' she said, teeth chattering, shaking with shock and relief.

'I'm sorry for putting you through the fear,' he said. 'I should have checked.'

'It was my fault, I should have said.'

'Well, let's not argue about it. Let's get you a cup of tea.'

★ ★ ★

Lorna appreciated the tea but couldn't eat the chocolate cake Jack bought her to go with it. She pushed the plate towards him. 'You have it. Think how many calories you must have used up, carrying me down those stairs.'

'Not that many. You're not heavy, Lorna. You forget, I'm a banker mason. I'm used to heaving great blocks of stone around.'

'I'm sure you have equipment to help you with that,' she said, but she appreciated his efforts to make her feel OK about what happened.

'We do have equipment but we still have to be strong.'

'I don't suppose giving people fireman's lifts is part of the training for a mason. Even a banker mason, whatever that is.'

He laughed. 'The fireman's lift thing I learnt when I was a retained fireman at college.'

'Well, I'm very grateful that you learnt that.'

'I'm very grateful too. I always knew it would come in useful even though I never used it when I was fighting fires.'

'Did you fight many?'

He shook his head. 'Disappointingly few.' He smiled at her.

Lorna smiled back, finally acknowledging that she was more than a little in love with this big, strong man who so recently had got her out of the nastiest situation she had ever been in.

'I'm going to take you home. You must be tired after your ordeal. But although I know I shouldn't take advantage of your weakened state, I'm going to.'

He paused while she hoped he didn't ask for anything too outrageous because she knew there was no way she would refuse him.

'Will you let me take you out for dinner?'

She laughed weakly. 'I think it's the least I can do!'

★ ★ ★

This time Lorna did take pains with her appearance. She wanted Jack to stop thinking of her as the complete wimp he had to carry down the stairs. Her pride required him to fancy her, even if he had just been nice to her out of friendship up until now. And would he really be so keen to invite her to dinner if he just wanted to be friends? Surely not when they'd spent the entire day together.

Part of her would have preferred to just have a bath, eat some toast and then go to bed. But as she'd agreed to go, she would have to make an impact.

It was odd to be dressing up for a man. She had never really bothered to dress up for Peter because he never noticed her. And she couldn't dress up to garden — that would be insane.

She went for a simple look. Mid-calf black wrap dress, her best soft, long boots, amber necklace and wide silver bangle. Never in fashion, never out of it, was her trade mark look. She added a large, fine woollen shawl as although it was now nearly May, it was still quite chilly. Then she went to check her emails. You could spend too long evening up your eyebrows and seeing what you'd look like with a facelift. Her eyebrows were fine and she couldn't afford to have 'work' done.

There was an email from her son, Leo. She

smiled as she opened it. She hadn't seen him for ages and he wasn't brilliant at keeping in touch.

Hi Mum, how are you? Fancy a visit? I was thinking of coming up for a few days.

She emailed back quickly. *Lovely, darling! It will be brilliant to see you.*

She very nearly added, *I've got so much to tell you,* but decided she didn't really have anything particular to tell him. Just because she thought she might be falling in love, that wasn't anything she needed to confide in her son.

★ ★ ★

By the time they had had coffee and left the restaurant — only after the staff had done some rather overt clearing up around them — Lorna felt that she and Jack had talked about everything. She had never felt so connected to anyone.

'Well, that was really lovely,' she said, standing outside his car. 'Are you going to think I'm churlish if I don't invite you in for more coffee?'

'You're tired. You've been up at least two hours longer than I have. No, not churlish at all.'

He brushed a stray curl behind her ear and kissed her cheek, very tenderly. 'Goodnight, Lorna. I'm going to ask you out again, very soon. Shall I walk you to your door?'

'Certainly not!' Lorna was brisk, hoping it disguised her disappointment that he hadn't kissed her on the lips, or even protested when she hadn't invited him in.

He waited until she'd unlocked the door and

opened it and then, with a raise of his hand, drove away.

Hmm, thought Lorna, back in her kitchen, so much for leaving them wanting more.

She got out some milk to heat and some brandy to put in it. She didn't want thoughts about the missing kiss to keep her from badly needed sleep.

In the morning there was a text on her phone saying goodnight. She smiled, glad that she'd missed it. It made it clear she wasn't a teenager, constantly checking her phone. But she did wonder what she'd have done if she *had* seen it. Maybe she would have replied. And ended her text with kisses.

14

The following week Philly couldn't help feeling anxious about Lucien. He'd gone off in his van to Newbury at the crack of dawn on the Monday morning and they didn't expect to see him back until after the last race on Friday. As she made herself some sandwiches to take with her to Burthen House, slicing Lucien's bread, her grandfather said, 'So, child? Are you missing the young scamp already?'

She laughed. 'Not really, but I am concerned. He was talking about 'having a flutter' and I'm worried he'll get into the hands of a terrible tipster, who'll tell him there's a horse who's the secret love child of Shergar and he'll lose all his wages.'

Seamus shrugged. 'He wouldn't be the first to do that, for sure. But he's a clever lad. He won't do anything rash.'

'I think he might well do something rash, but there's nothing I can do to stop him. He's his own person.'

Philly looked up from her bread-cutting to see her grandfather gazing at her speculatively.

'He's so intent on raising enough money for his kitchen,' Philly went on. 'I just don't want him to blow it. That's all.'

'Well, no, nor do I. I think it's good having him as a lodger. He cooks better than we do and it's young company for you. I'm just not sure how long it will be before your mother comes over here to take a look at him.'

Philly laughed. What would her mother make of Lucien? Would she think he was flighty, bound to break her heart, or a good catch? 'He's got a very expensive-sounding accent. That should please her.' She paused. 'The trouble is, she's had her heart set on me marrying my childhood sweetheart since I left off being a child.' She put the lid on her sandwich box, picked it up and kissed her grandfather on the cheek. 'I'll be on my way, then.'

'Oh!' he called as she reached the back door. 'Don't worry if I'm not here when you get back in. Just carry on without me. I may be out.'

'Really? Where?'

'Just out. Now away with you, you'll be late.'

Philly was halfway to her car when she realised she didn't have to be at the garden for a few minutes yet. She'd let herself be chased out of the house, confused by her grandfather saying he'd be out and not saying where he'd be. It was very unlike him. She halted for a second, wondering why.

★ ★ ★

The days passed. On Friday, Philly and Lorna were working hard in the garden when Kirstie and Peter came to chat.

'My goodness, you are beavering away' said Peter.

'I always beavered away, Peter,' said Lorna

140

crisply, 'but now I've got help you can see the results.'

'And you've got more help coming?' said Kirstie. 'I know Peter said you could take on more people.'

Lorna nodded, glancing at Philly. 'I've put some cards up in various places — '

'I've asked around my plant friends — ' put in Philly.

'But so far, no joy,' said Lorna. 'I'm not sure there are enough people who want to do hard physical labour for the living wage.'

'I don't know why not,' said Kirstie. 'I love gardening.'

'Why don't you join us?' said Philly. 'We've got plenty of kit and we'd love to have you with us. It's fun.'

Kirstie frowned slightly. 'As much as I would really love to, I've got a whole lot of artists to sort out. They need to do a garden visit and it's like herding cats.' She paused, regarding the flat space above the red and black garden. 'That's a lovely spot.'

'That's Jack's,' said Lorna and then blushed slightly. 'He came ages ago and bagged it. His is a big piece and needs to be fairly near the path or he couldn't install it.'

'Oh, OK,' said Kirstie. 'Jack is quite famous. He should have a good spot.'

But Lorna thought she looked doubtful, as if she'd give the spot away in a heartbeat if someone more prestigious came along.

After Kirstie and Peter had gone, Philly said, 'Did you know he was famous, Lorna?'

141

Lorna shook her head.

'You didn't google him, did you?'

'No. It felt like stalking. And I don't really want to know how old he is.'

'Well, it obviously doesn't matter. You're — seeing each other?'

Lorna nodded. 'Nothing serious, of course.'

'Why of course? Don't you like him?'

'I do but — well, you know, it doesn't seem right . . . ' She decided to change the subject before it got too complicated. 'Hey? Did I tell you my son is coming to stay for a few days? I'll invite you all to dinner. If I dare have Lucien to dinner, that is!'

'That would be great. Though I'm not sure he'd be able to come. He's working at the races at the moment, and when he's not doing that he's trying to raise money to set up a bakery by devious means.' She made a face. At that moment her phone pinged. She pulled off her gardening glove and retrieved it from her pocket. 'Oh. Speak of angels. A text from Lucien.'

'Open it, then,' said Lorna.

Philly scanned the text. *Hi! Van broken down. Any chance you or Seamus could bring the tow truck and collect me? Wouldn't ask but I'm desperate.*

'Oh my goodness,' said Philly. 'He took his van to the races but needs a tow. I'd better ring Grand.'

She did, asking him if he could pick up Lucien in the tow truck.

'Actually, Philly darling, why don't you do it? I'm a bit busy here,' said Seamus.

142

'Are you? But I thought you'd have loved to go!' Philly knew her grandfather loved rescuing people more than anything. It made him feel needed and useful.

'The crowds will be terrible. I'd rather not. You go.'

'I'm working!' said Philly, looking at Lorna who, she noted, seemed amused.

'You're your own boss, Philly. Go and get Lucien from the den of iniquity you sent him off to on Monday.'

'It's Newbury Races, Grand — '

'Go on,' Seamus persisted. 'You drive that truck as well as I do.'

Philly disconnected her phone. 'Grand won't pick him up. Would you mind if I went?'

' 'Course not. You're your own boss, after all. And I need a break too. I must put more effort into finding more help, or this garden opening could be an embarrassment.'

Philly was gathering her things, putting her thermos into her bag. 'I'll put effort into it too. Are you sure you don't mind me leaving now?'

'Get on with you. Go and get your boyfriend.'

'He's not my boyfriend!' But as Philly denied it, she wondered how long it would be true. Her heart gave a little skip.

★ ★ ★

Later, when Philly had arrived in Newbury, she allowed herself to feel excited. She'd missed Lucien. He was exhilarating to be around as well as being very cute.

143

'OK!' she said to Lucien on the phone. 'I'm here. The car park is full. Where's your van? The traffic was awful.'

'Just pull in and I'll come. Where are you?'

When she'd given Lucien as many clues as she could as to her whereabouts, and got out of the way, Philly resigned herself to a long wait. There were thousands of cars here. Lucien would never find her. At least he didn't expect her to find him.

But waiting for him wasn't boring. All the world seemed to file past her. Some were wearing proper racing clothes: tweeds, elegant long coats in shades of lovat green, straight out of gentlemen's outfitters who'd been in business for years. Others were wearing their ancient Barbour jackets over corduroys, and yet others were looking, Philly felt, what her mother would describe as chavvy. She didn't see many women in outrageous hats; they'd all be in the boxes, waiting for the last race. There was a really great atmosphere and she identified plenty of her countrymen, recognisably Irish, ruddy-cheeked, good-natured and laughing.

At last she spotted Lucien running towards her, still in chef's whites, looking unfairly handsome, considering his hurry and dishevelment.

He got into the truck and kissed her cheek. 'OK, this way. Follow that car. He's my mate. He'll show you where you can park.'

'What about the van? Shouldn't we pick that up?'

'Not until after the last race. I've got money on it!'

'Oh God, you didn't bet your day's wages on a horse?'

'Um, not exactly.'

Philly didn't dare take her eyes off the car leading her through the crowds so she couldn't look at him. 'Which means?'

'I have an accumulator. That's when you put money on one race and if it wins you put that on the — '

'I know what an accumulator is. You are mad, you know that?'

'Not mad, desperate. I need money to get my career going, you know that. If this comes off I'll have enough to be able to go to my godfather and ask him to lend me the rest.'

'You could save up to do that,' said Philly. 'Why not just do what you're doing, working hard and saving up?' As she spoke, she had a horrible feeling she sounded like her mother.

'I'm impatient. I could win over three thousand pounds. That would be enough.'

'Would you have to tell your godfather how you got it? Wouldn't he disapprove?'

Lucien laughed loudly. 'Good God, no! He's always been a terrific gambler. Which is why I hope he'll take a gamble on me. Now, can you see where Spike is going?'

★ ★ ★

As Lucien pulled her along behind him, through the crowds, most of whom seemed to be going in the opposite direction, Philly picked up the excitement. Here she was, with a boy she really

145

liked, on a sort of adventure. He had a lot at stake — literally — and because she cared about him, she had a lot too.

He dragged her forward, towards the rail. 'We've got a good spot here.'

'Shouldn't you be working?'

He shook his head. 'It's all over except the clearing up. My boss knows what I'm doing with the money — and my share of the tips — so said I could find you and watch the last race.' He paused. 'Although strictly speaking we're not allowed to bet if we're working.'

'Grand couldn't come. He should have done really, he loves racing.'

'Don't you like it?'

'Not like he does.'

'I'm glad it was you who came. You've been so supportive, you should be here when my horse comes in!'

Philly shook her head, laughing ruefully. 'Horses quite often don't come in, you know. I have a gambling uncle too. It didn't work out for him, mostly.'

'It's going to be different for me, you'll see.' Lucien was oozing confidence.

They happened to be standing within easy earshot of the commentary, which gave Philly a speedy lesson on the riders and runners. Everyone seemed to think the favourite would win. She relaxed a little. It seemed Lucien hadn't been so crazy after all. She moved a little nearer and squeezed his hand with the one of hers he still had hold of. He looked down at her and grinned. 'This is going to be the start of my own business, Philly. You'll see!'

It seemed to take ages for the horses to get ready. Philly and Lucien were near the finishing line and could only see what was going on at the start if they could see the television, and although she tried, Philly found screwing her head round at such an awkward angle too painful. At last came the cry, 'They're off!'

The commentator was set on the favourite. He seemed to be passing everything. Philly found she was clutching Lucien's hand in excitement. She glanced up at him, keen to share the moment with him. He wasn't smiling.

'Lucien?' she shouted. 'Are you OK?'

'Not really. I didn't bet on the favourite. The odds were much better on an outsider.'

Philly felt cold suddenly. She moistened her lips. He was going to lose everything. Now was not the time to tell him you didn't bet on a horse with the best odds, you bet on the horse most likely to win.

Then there was an 'Oh no!' from the commentator. 'The favourite's fallen. It's all right, he's got up again but he's lost his lead. Doubt if he'll catch up now. It's anyone's race — '

'Which horse? Which is your horse?' Philly had to bellow to make herself heard over the crowd that was now roaring so loud she could feel the vibration in her feet.

Lucien shouted something into her ear but she couldn't hear.

She squeezed round so she could see the television. There was a big pack of horses at the front and a lone galloper coming up the outside. Some sixth sense told her this was the horse with the great odds that Lucien had bet on.

She managed to catch the name from the commentator: Baker's Dozen. She turned back to stand by Lucien and briefly closed her eyes. She didn't want to see it limp home five minutes after everyone else, and Lucien would need her support.

'It's Baker's Dozen, isn't it? You bet on it because you liked the name and it had great odds?' He probably couldn't hear her, she realised, and that was a good thing. He knew what a hideous mistake he had made. He didn't need her to point it out. She braced herself for his desperate disappointment, glad she was there to drive him home.

Then his hand became a vice, crunching her fingers together. The crowd was so impossibly loud she could hardly hear the commentary, but the name Baker's Dozen seemed to emerge. The thunder of the horses sounded like a rockfall getting nearer and nearer. As they shot by, Philly had no clue about who was in the lead.

And then the roar was co-ordinated into one great shout. 'Baker's Dozen!'

The commentator called, 'Baker's Dozen has won — he's gone past every other horse — '

Lucien picked Philly up and hugged her so tight she couldn't breathe or move. 'We've won!' he shouted. 'We've won!'

They jumped up and down together like two pogo sticks welded together. Then he kissed her, first her cheek and then on the mouth.

148

'Come on, let's claim our winnings. The bookie should be just down here — '

He was so excited, Philly couldn't bring herself to suggest the bookie might have done a runner. She berated herself for being so negative but in her mind money was always worked for. You didn't get it by putting hard-earned wages on the right horse.

She ran after him, pulled along by his hand, struggling to keep up as he ducked and dived between the groups of people, her heart sinking with every step. She did not have a good feeling about this.

She fell against Lucien as he drew to a halt suddenly. 'He was here! The bookie was here.'

'How much was he due to pay you?' Philly asked.

'Over three thousand pounds.'

She bit her lip. She should be brave and explain that over three thousand pounds was a huge amount and a small bookie might not be able to find that even if he wanted to.

'Oh!' said Lucien. 'There he is. The one in the emerald-green suit.'

Philly followed more slowly. She was there to pick up the pieces; she hoped she wouldn't have to stop Lucien getting into a fight.

However, everyone was being very good-natured though she could see Lucien was patting his pockets in a rather dramatic way.

'You haven't lost your betting slip?' Philly asked, wishing her stomach would stop behaving like a washing machine churning over as each crisis was faced and then averted. This last one could be the worst of the lot, the only one that couldn't be blamed on someone else — the tipster, the horse or the bookie. This was down to Lucien.

Then he put his hand in his top pocket and pulled out a very scruffy bit of paper that had bright green horseshoes all round the edge. He glanced at Philly, who had a trickle of sweat running down her spine. 'Had you going there, didn't I?'

'Time to be smug when you've got the money in your hand, Lucien.'

'Whoa there, me darlin',' said the bookie. 'You wouldn't be suggestin' I might not pay up, now would you?'

'It's a lot of money,' said Philly firmly, emphasising her Irish accent in the hope it would give her a bit of authority. For all he knew, her favourite uncle could be Paddy Power, or one of the other huge bookmakers.

''Tis, so,' said the bookie, winking at her, 'but I've laid it all off, and as the favourite didn't win, the bookies are all happy.'

She summoned a smile, wishing she knew what he was talking about. But when she saw the wodge of notes he was withdrawing from his inside pocket and beginning to count into Lucien's hand, her smile became genuine.

'Now,' said the bookie, winking again, 'go and blow the lot on getting back on the right side of your girlfriend.'

Lucien grinned and put his arm round Philly, hugging her to him. 'I'll do that,' he said.

'What that chap doesn't know is that getting

on the right side of you involves doing something very sensible with the money,' he went on when they were out of earshot.

'What he also doesn't know is that I'm not your girlfriend,' said Philly.

'Really? I think we should work on that. I think you'd be a great girlfriend!' He paused and put his arms round her and pulled her close. 'Now I'm no longer an itinerant chef but a man of means, will you consider taking me on as a boyfriend?'

'I might,' she said happily.

15

A couple of weeks later, Lorna opened the door and opened her arms. Her son, impossibly tall and good-looking, stood on the doorstep.

They kissed, embraced, and then she said, 'How lovely to see you! Come in.'

Leo lowered his rucksack on to the floor. 'I've got more stuff in the car but it can stay there for a bit.'

'Of course,' said Lorna, wondering why he needed more than just a rucksackful of clothes. 'It's nearly suppertime. Do you want tea or wine?'

'Both!' Leo grinned fondly down at her. 'Tea first though.'

They went into the kitchen. 'It is a very nice place you've got here,' he said, looking around. 'I'd forgotten it was so roomy.'

'That's because you've only visited me here once when you helped me move, and it's not really that roomy, it only has one bedroom.' She smiled to show there were no hard feelings.

'You've made it nice.' He pulled out a chair and sat down. 'And you've made chocolate cake! You are a mum in a million.'

'Well, I am,' Lorna agreed, putting the kettle on, 'but not because I made you a cake.'

When she'd made tea and they were both eating cake, she said, 'So, what's your news?'

'Good and bad. Which do you want first?'

Lorna's heart sank a bit. Although she and Leo got on really well, he didn't visit often and she usually had to invite him specially so an unrequested visit was a bit ominous. 'Well, let's have the bad while we're still eating cake.'

'My job came to an end. It wasn't my fault, the company folded.' He sighed and smiled ruefully. 'And I finished with my girlfriend at the same time. The two were not related.'

'Oh, darling, that's two bad things. What's the good news?'

'I've come to live with you for a bit! You're always on at me to visit more so now you'll have me every day.'

Lorna took a sip of tea. Of course it was lovely to see him but having a grown-up son living with her wasn't something she'd planned for. He wasn't the easiest to share with. He needed space. 'But, darling, this house has only one bedroom,' she reminded him.

He looked a bit deflated. 'Oh. Bummer. Still, we'll manage. I can sleep on the sofa.'

'Of course you can stay as long as you need to, but it can't be a permanent arrangement. The house just isn't big enough.'

He frowned. 'Oh. I've got a job interview in Grantminster. It's not great money but I thought it would be nice to be near you.' He grinned the grin that had got her to write letters explaining why he hadn't done his homework on many an occasion. 'With you, actually.'

Lorna reached across the table to pat his arm. 'More cake?'

'Yes please. Why don't you want me? Have you

153

got a man-friend you don't want me to know about?' He laughed to indicate he thought this idea ridiculous.

'Of course not!' She laughed too. 'But there is only one bedroom,' she repeated. 'There is a tiny box room but it would take a lot of clearing out.'

'I always wondered if that Peter didn't have a soft spot for you.'

Leo didn't seem to want to consider lack of bedroom space. Lorna mentally resigned herself to sorting out the box room. 'Well, he hasn't. He has a new girlfriend, much younger and prettier than I am.'

'Can't say I'm sorry. I thought he was a bit of a . . . ' He hesitated.

'What?' Lorna prompted.

'A bit of a letch?' He sounded apologetic.

Lorna frowned. 'As you haven't seen him often since you've been grown up, I don't know how you could have got that impression.'

Leo raised his hands in surrender. 'I don't know! Maybe it's just because I don't like the thought of a man getting it on with my mum.'

Guilt trickled over Lorna as if she were having a full-blown affair with a man the same age as her Leo, which she most decidedly was not. 'It's not that horrifying a thought, is it?'

He shrugged. 'Well, yes, it is. But don't worry, Mum, being single is the new . . . '

'Being single?' she provided kindly.

'Well, yeah. But you don't mind, do you? You've got lots of friends.'

She did have friends but not that many of them in this area. Lorna realised that he was

154

probably thinking about when they lived in the small town where he'd grown up: she'd had a wide circle of friends and acquaintances there. But it was much harder to meet people when you didn't have small children and, although she was perfectly content here in her cottage on the Burthen estate, he was wrong to assume that she hadn't sometimes been lonely. 'It's not quite like it was when we lived in Surrey' she said mildly, 'but I do all right.'

'So where's the bathroom? Then I'll get my stuff in.' Leo got to his feet and stretched, instantly making the kitchen seem smaller than it was.

'Fine,' she said. 'But it has to be a temporary arrangement. Until you find somewhere more suitable.'

★ ★ ★

As Lorna finished getting supper ready while Leo watched television in the sitting room, which had suddenly shrunk because of his possessions, she realised her joy at seeing her son was marred. She should be thrilled to have him — she *was* thrilled — but the thought of her nice little house being full of his speakers and computers and stuff that she felt no need for was daunting. And supposing she did want a boyfriend? Was having your son living with you like having a Victorian parent? Would her darling boy turn into Mr Barrett of Wimpole Street if Jack came over? Would they have to have secret assignations? While that did sound quite fun in a way, it was a bit bloody ridiculous. She was in her fifties: surely it was up to her if she had a love-life or not?

But as she opened another bottle of wine, the first having been shared equally between her, Leo and the casserole, she realised she was jumping to conclusions. He had expressed misgivings about a man getting it on with his mum (she shivered slightly as she remembered how he'd phrased it) but that was in the abstract, surely. If he met Jack and saw what a nice, honourable man he was, he'd think differently. Wouldn't he?

★ ★ ★

A few days later, Lorna got up extra early. It was the day before the great garden and sculpture show and she wanted to be there as early as possible. She had a box of black pansies she wanted to get in before the artwork started arriving, possibly taking her away from her main concern.

But although it was only 7 a.m. when she arrived, Kirstie was already there with a clipboard, looking agitated.

'It is going to be finished, isn't it, Lorna?'

'Of course,' said Lorna, hoping her irritation wasn't too obvious. 'I have two women coming at eight to help us with the planting up. My son will be here soon to do sweeping and tidying, and Philly and I are doing everything else. It's up to the sculptors to get their work into position now.'

'Well, they are doing that. Jack texted to say he's going to be late.'

Lorna brushed her hair out of her eyes. 'Yes.' He'd texted her, too. She hadn't seen him since Leo had moved in just under a week ago and was anxious about their meeting. The two men would probably get on fine, she realised, but she was still worried.

'So,' Kirstie went on, unaware of what was going through Lorna's mind while she appeared to be listening attentively. 'I don't know if I told you but we've got Ben Hennessy at the last minute!'

Lorna frowned. She knew she ought to recognise this name but was currently struggling to place him. Kirstie had said his name as if he was really famous.

'You know?' Kirstie was impatient. 'He only won the Turner Prize!'

Lorna relaxed. Not a well-known celebrity then. 'Oh! Well, that's brilliant!'

'Yes. He's coming over later. We're giving him and his team lunch, then they'll decide where his piece should go.' She paused. 'Actually it would be great up there, overlooking this garden.'

Her hand indicated the very spot Jack had chosen. Kirstie knew that; it had been discussed. It should be written on her clipboard. Lorna swallowed, trying to second-guess Kirstie. If she reminded her that Jack wanted that spot, would it make it more desirable for Ben Hennessy?

'Well,' she said casually, 'I don't know the piece but if it's fairly small it might look OK there.' She paused. 'But if it's substantial the

157

absolute prime spot is by the lake.'

'It is quite big, actually,' said Kirstie. 'It's a modern take on *The Burghers of Calais*. You know? Rodin? Large figures?'

'I know the piece you mean. I did go to art school.'

'Well, Ben's isn't quite like that. Instead of being actual figures, his has shards of bronze, clustered together, reaching for the light.'

'Oh.' Lorna struggled to match this up with *The Burghers of Calais* she knew of.

'You don't think it would be difficult to install by the lake?' said Kirstie. 'I mean, it's quite a steep slope down to it.'

'He'll be having it professionally installed,' said Lorna, feigning confidence in this being true. 'And it would look stunning there.' Jack's piece would probably look stunning there too but as she was virtually certain Jack didn't have a team of installers at his command she wanted him to have the site he could access.

Luckily, Kirstie smiled. 'I see where you're coming from. It could look great there. Reflecting in the water and all that.' She paused. 'Peter and I are thinking of buying it. It's several hundred thousand pounds, of course, but it will increase in value and I do think the garden would be improved by some artwork.'

For some reason Lorna had always disliked the expression 'artwork'. To her it sounded like something you'd order from the internet which would arrive in your porch ten days later. 'Why don't you buy Jack's piece? It wouldn't be nearly so expensive.'

Kirstie gave her a look. 'Because Jack hasn't won the Turner Prize.'

Lorna shrugged. 'Nor did Rodin.'

★ ★ ★

Although she'd worked in the garden until the light failed, which was very late, and fallen into bed exhausted, Lorna woke early the next day. This was it; this was the day they'd all been working towards. It seemed they had been doing it forever. Although as Lorna stepped into the shower she knew it hadn't been that long at all.

She knew that Kirstie had been checking the weather app on her phone obsessively as she paced round the garden, announcing the results of her weather-checks, giving instructions, banging in sign-posts and supervising installations. But as it changed fairly regularly and nothing could be done about it, Lorna didn't pay much attention.

She dressed hurriedly, put on a little bit of make-up and, after a quick cup of tea and a bit of bread and butter, set off for the garden. She wanted to be there before Kirstie and her clipboard arrived.

She was aware she'd left the house in a certain amount of chaos but maybe Leo would tidy up before he joined her. She had decided she did enjoy having him, even though he took up a lot of space by sleeping in the sitting room. But she missed coming back to peace in her little haven when she was tired.

It was going to be a perfect day, she thought as

she walked through the morning mist towards the gate and up the drive. Now, there were huge tubs of flowers in front of the columns of the house and below, evidence of the recently acquired ride-on mower was everywhere. Burthen House and its surroundings seemed to glow.

Only allowing herself a couple of seconds to appreciate the house's recent upgrade, she went straight to the Italian garden that was now satisfyingly red and black. Philly had managed to get hold of masses of Queen of the Night tulips a fellow nursery had grown in shallow containers for a garden show. Bishop of Llandaff dahlias with their scarlet blooms and dark foliage, Black Barlow aquilegias, auriculas and dark-leaved bergenias were all filled in with the scarlet nasturtiums and their dark foliage. Both Lorna and Philly were delighted with it.

Jack's sculpture, a male figure carrying a lamb, now installed and overlooking the garden, was perfect, she thought.

She was just trying to decide if she so admired it because it really was a magnificent example of figurative sculpture, where every muscle and sinew of the man was clearly defined, or if it was just because Jack had done it, when he appeared.

'I hoped I'd find you here,' he said. 'If I hadn't, I'd have knocked on your door.'

Only briefly did she allow herself to think what sort of welcome he'd have got from Leo if he'd woken up to find his mother having breakfast with a strange man.

'Well, here I am. It looks good, doesn't it?' She indicated his sculpture, staring, stern and brave, over her black and red Italian garden.

'Yes,' he said, not looking at the garden but at her. She blushed.

'I'm just going to walk around and check on the rest of it. I've concentrated most of my efforts — and my team's efforts — on this.'

'That seems sensible. If you can't restore the entire garden in the time you had, even if you'd had hundreds of assistants — you might as well do one bit perfectly.'

'That's what I thought.' On impulse, because she wanted to stop him moving away to do whatever it was he'd come to do — apart from talk to her — she said, 'Have you heard we've got a Turner Prize winner exhibiting?'

'Ben Hennessy? Yes. My old mate. Known him for years. I'm looking forward to seeing his piece. Do you know where it is?'

'By the lake,' said Lorna. 'I suggested it. I thought it sounded — well, you know, a good spot.'

'Not as good as my spot though,' said Jack.

'Kirstie wasn't to know that,' said Lorna.

'You saved this' — he indicated his sculpture with a casual flick of his hand — 'for me?'

Lorna nodded. 'You were here first. I didn't see why you shouldn't keep your chosen position.'

He gave a slightly crooked smile. 'That's good to hear,' he said. But Lorna wondered if he didn't mean something different.

'Do you want to come on my garden tour with

me?' she suggested. 'You can check out the competition.'

'I'd like to have a look at Ben's piece. That must have been fun to install.'

'I don't think it was fun for the installers.'

He laughed. 'Oh, don't worry about them. They get paid handsomely to do it.'

'I think he brought his own heavy-lifting gear.'

Jack nodded. 'Sounds like Ben. Great guy though. Very talented artist.'

'Kirstie's very impressed by him. She said she and Peter are considering buying his piece for hundreds of thousands of pounds.' Lorna knew she should end it there but couldn't stop herself adding, 'I suggested they buy your piece. Much better value.'

Jack shrugged. 'I didn't win the Turner.'

'That's what Kirstie said. I said that Rodin didn't either.'

He laughed. 'Maybe you should be my agent.'

She shook her head. 'I'd be hopeless. Now come, I ought to be checking on the garden.'

She lost him when he came across his old friend Ben, who was inspecting his bronze shards, which, Lorna was forced to admit, did look very good. She walked on, leaving them chatting and laughing together, to continue her tour.

She was in front of the house trying to spot anything that needed her attention when Peter came up and stood beside her.

'It's all very splendid, isn't it?' she said.

'Mm. But you know what? I sort of miss the times when we used to sit on the step together and put the world to rights.'

'We could still do that,' she said. 'But maybe not now. Kirstie would feel — quite rightly — that we should be doing something more useful.'

Peter grunted. 'In many ways Kirstie is the best thing that's ever happened to me, but life was more peaceful before.'

'Well, she's certainly been the best thing that's happened to this garden,' said Lorna. 'You would never have spent all this money on it if it hadn't been for her.'

'I'm glad you like her,' he said.

As Lorna hadn't actually said she liked Kirstie she didn't comment; instead she considered how she did feel about her. She certainly didn't dislike her, but she didn't think she'd ever be a real friend. 'Well, why wouldn't I?' she said, as Peter seemed to be waiting for some sort of response.

'I think she worries that she's so much younger than people round here. You and my mother, for example.'

While Lorna was certainly older than Kirstie, she wasn't quite sure how she felt about being put into his mother's age group. 'Well, there's Philly. She's young.'

'Too young, apparently' said Peter.

'I don't think age is an issue when it comes to friendships,' she said firmly and then instantly thought about Jack. It might be a bit of an issue when it came to the sort of friendship she contemplated having with him.

'No,' said Peter, 'but there is something about

being with someone who gets your references.'

'But Kirstie does that! You told me when you first met her?'

'No — yes — she does. It's great having Kirstie, it really is.'

'You sound doubtful.'

'I'm not really doubtful,' he said slowly. 'But it is very expensive having a younger partner.'

She laughed. 'You've always been such an old skinflint. It's good for you to actually spend some of the money you've worked so hard to accumulate.'

'Maybe,' he said glumly. 'But I might have to go and accumulate some more, if Kirstie's plans go the way she wants them too.'

'You'd like that. You're too young to retire.'

'I am, aren't I?'

Kirstie joined them. 'So what are you two talking so earnestly about? Haven't you got things to do?' She looked at Lorna when she said this.

'Lorna was just telling me I'm too young to retire,' said Peter.

'And I have got things I ought to be doing,' said Lorna, setting off in the direction of the lake, feeling dismissed and disgruntled.

She found Leo by the lake. 'Hi, Mum. Sorry I slept in. Have you met Ben?' Ben, tall and athletic, smiled at Lorna.

'Not properly. Hi, Ben. I'm Lorna.'

'I know. You're Jack's friend, aren't you?'

'Who's Jack?' said Leo.

'One of the artists,' said Lorna. 'But he's local. Here he is.' She looked at her son as Jack

164

approached and saw him stiffen. 'Jack, come and meet Leo, my son.'

'Oh, hi,' said Jack, putting out his hand.

Leo took it but he didn't smile. He nodded and said, 'Jack.'

Lorna sighed and was glad to see Kirstie bustling towards them, clipboard in hand.

'Come on, everyone! The paying public are arriving at any minute.'

'Before we all rush off,' said Lorna, 'Kirstie, I'd like to introduce you to Leo, my son. He's been helping with the tidying up in the garden.'

'Leo!' said Kirstie, smiling broadly. 'Lovely to meet you.'

It occurred to Lorna, as she caught the expression in Kirstie's eyes, that Kirstie didn't share her doubts about younger men.

'Leo?' said Lorna. 'Will you come with me and see if Philly needs any help?'

'Actually Lorna, if you wouldn't mind, could I borrow Leo?' said Kirstie. 'I've got some stuff that needs a bit of manly brawn.'

Lorna smiled graciously, forbearing to say that Kirstie could borrow Leo as long as she promised to give him back.

Walking back to where she thought she'd last seen Philly, Lorna wondered if she could ask if Leo might have a room in Burthen House. There was plenty of space, after all. After today, if it went well, she thought she might do just that.

16

Kirstie had done a brilliant job with the publicity, Lorna thought. She was by the Italian garden and as the gates were officially opened, people came streaming in. The weather helped, of course, and so probably did the presence of a Turner Prize winner (who, as Jack had said, seemed extremely nice).

She was there to answer questions about the garden and had a plant list, kindly provided by Philly, who had a stall by the old stables. The artists were all being interviewed by various members of the press because the event had attracted quite a lot of media attention. She hoped to catch up with Jack later.

'So, what can you tell me about the people who live here?' asked one man.

'Unless *you* live here?' added his wife.

'No, I don't live here,' said Lorna calmly, suddenly wishing she'd predicted interest in Peter and Kirstie and had a strategy to deal with it. 'The couple who do have very kindly opened their garden to raise money to help with the abbey-restoration fund.'

'So you don't know them then?' The woman was eager for gossip.

'Not really,' said Lorna, smiling sadly.

They wandered off.

Fortunately most of the rest of the people who came were really interested in the garden and the history of the house. Several wanted to know if rooms in it could be hired. Lorna thought she should tell Kirstie about this, in case she and Peter ever wanted to raise money for the house itself. Peter would hate the idea, of course, but they could do it while they were away, if someone else were in charge. It could be a wedding venue, she thought: Kirstie, who organised events as her day job, would thrive on hosting occasions like that. Maybe she wouldn't mention it, she decided. Kirstie could think of it for herself. She no longer had romantic feelings for Peter but she was still very fond of him. She didn't want him to be pushed too far out of his comfort zone.

When Lorna had answered enough questions about how she had created a red and black garden, whether she had borrowed any ideas from the garden at Highgrove (yes) and were the plants available for sale at the plant stall (some of them), she decided to go and see how Philly was getting on.

Jack intercepted her. 'Wait!' he called. He caught up with her a few seconds later. 'Come,' he said, 'let's go somewhere where we can not talk.'

Lorna laughed, ridiculously pleased to see him. 'Aren't you supposed to take me somewhere where we *can* talk?'

He shook his head. 'I've been talking to people all day. I just want to be quiet somewhere, with you.'

'Well, I know a little corner. It's behind a tree that's on the path that leads to the summer house. I don't expect anyone will see us there.'

They walked in silence and soon were settled in the sunshine. Lorna closed her eyes. Suddenly she realised how tired she was. It was bliss sitting there on the grass, her back supported by a tree, feeling the sun on her face with Jack at her side.

'There you are, Mum!' said Leo, sounding out of breath and cross. 'Kirstie needs you.' He glared at Jack.

'Oh, OK,' said Lorna, not moving, wondering if she had actually dropped off. 'Where is she?'

'By the stables. A journalist wants to talk to you.'

'Really?' Lorna felt exhausted all over again at the prospect. 'Why?'

'They're interested in the garden.' He set off and reluctantly Lorna and Jack got to their feet.

'I am sorry. I can't think why he's so rude,' she said.

'It's natural. The young stag trying to head off the older one and not managing it.' Jack smiled at her and Lorna's heart suddenly beat faster.

'We'd better find the journalists,' she said.

'Before we do, or while we're going, there's something I want to say.'

'I thought you wanted to be silent?'

'I did, but I might not get you on your own again.' He paused. 'I've been plucking up the courage, debating whether it's too early in our relationship but I have to go away for a week.' He paused, looking down at her in a way that made her stomach melt. 'I was wondering if you could come with me.'

It took her a few seconds to think of

something to say. It was such a huge thing — from being two people who were getting to know each other at a reasonable speed to being a couple who went away together. 'Where are you going?'

'To France. I need to source some stone. I don't want to be away from you for so long.'

Lorna didn't know how to respond.

He went on urgently. 'I know it's too soon really, but otherwise — well — I won't see you. It's tomorrow. Please say you'll come?'

Every word of wisdom Lorna had ever heard, in poetry, prose, song or real life, about love and how to handle it, rushed through her head and out again, unheeded. 'I'd love to.'

★ ★ ★

She could think of nothing else all day. After they'd discussed the practicalities of how and when they were going, she talked to the journalists, to other people, to Philly about how well her plants had sold and how delicious the tea and cakes were, and how many people had come and how much money had been raised. But inside she vacillated between euphoria that she and Jack were going to sleep together and horror at her rashness in agreeing to it.

She only really came to when everyone had gone home and Kirstie had organised a team of teenagers to litter pick. All the other helpers were in the courtyard. There were Peter and Kirstie, obviously very thrilled by how it had all gone, Anthea and, for some reason Lorna couldn't fathom, Seamus. While she was very fond of Philly's grandfather, she didn't know how he'd been dragged into it all. Maybe it was to support Philly, who had produced a stunning plant stall — mostly, she had confided to Lorna, provided by colleagues in the business. Nearly all Philly had produced had gone into the Burthen House garden. Leo was there, and in spite of his slight surliness around Jack, Lorna had been proud of how hard he'd worked. And she wasn't the only one who'd noticed. She'd seen Kirstie kissing his cheek after she'd thanked him for something.

Kirstie cleared her throat and got everyone's attention. 'Well, I think that was bloody brilliant!' she declared to murmurs of agreement. 'And I think we should have a wash-up meeting here. Would ten o'clock tomorrow morning suit?'

'And what, if I may ask, is a 'wash-up' meeting?' asked Anthea haughtily.

'Oh come on, Mother,' said Peter, sounding tired and therefore irritable. 'You know perfectly well what it is.'

'Sorry,' said Kirstie, far more respectful than Peter had been. 'We'll discuss how it all went and what we'll do differently next year.'

'Are we doing it next year?' said Peter, shocked by the idea.

'I think we should, sweetie. Build on our success?'

Lorna thought she heard him groan.

'I'm afraid Lorna and I won't be there,' said Jack. 'We're going to France.'

'Mum?' said Leo. 'Really?' He looked stunned

and not at all happy.

Lorna would have preferred to tell her son in private, along with a lot of reassurance that his mother had not lost her senses, but Jack had taken the matter out of her hands. 'Yes,' she said.

Leo didn't speak but Kirstie came in quickly. 'Does it have to be tomorrow? And since when have you been an item?'

'You're not an item, are you, Mum?' said Leo. Lorna looked at Jack, unable to speak.

'Yes,' he said. 'Lorna and I are definitely an item. Now if you lot don't mind I think we should go home. Lorna's got packing to do.'

★ ★ ★

'Honestly Leo, it's fine. It won't affect you in any way. I'm still your mum!' Lorna put another drapey cardigan into her bag. She no longer knew what she'd packed already. As long as she remembered her credit card she could buy anything vital.

'How can you be my mum when you've got a — boyfriend?' Leo was obviously really distressed.

'In the same way you're still my son when you've got a girlfriend. It doesn't change anything.'

'But it's natural for me to have a girlfriend. It's not right that you should have — God, I can hardly say it!'

'Why isn't it natural for me to have a boyfriend? Peter's roughly the same age as me, and he's got Kirstie.'

171

'Yes, but he's the man, he's the older one. You and Jack, it's — '

She saw him stop before he could say what he was thinking: that it was 'disgusting' for his mother to have a boyfriend who was younger than she was.

Lorna was torn. She'd been a single mother for so long and sacrificing herself for her son was her default setting. But this was a chance of happiness she'd never dreamt of. And if Jack wasn't bothered by her being older, why should she be?

But what about other people? How would she feel if people she loved and respected — Anthea, Philly, even Peter, for example — despised her?

She decided she couldn't allow herself to care. She had to grab this chance of happiness.

'I'm really sorry you can't be happy for me,' she said decisively, 'but I'm still going. If you want to move into my bedroom while I'm away that's fine. But I suggest you ask Kirstie if she could put you up in the house. I'm sure she'd find a corner. And I don't think Peter would mind.'

'Are you throwing me out?' Leo was outraged. 'Are you throwing me out because you've got a toy boy?'

Lorna almost laughed. 'Of course not! I just feel this house is rather small for two people.'

'So you won't be moving Jack in here then?'

'No! But if I do, then you'll definitely have to move out. And it doesn't mean I love you any less, so don't get all hurt and touchy about it.'

When they eventually went to bed, Lorna was

nearly crying with tiredness and frustration. But the more Leo argued that what she was doing was wrong, the more she was determined to do it, and as she finally got into bed and closed her eyes she couldn't help smiling. All this fuss about a couple who hadn't even really kissed properly yet.

★ ★ ★

In spite of her resolution the night before, in the morning, as she put her stuff into her car and got ready to drive to Jack's house, she felt herself wavering. Leo, who had been so difficult, had been remorseful over breakfast.

'I'm so sorry, Mum. I really didn't mean to be so vile. It was just the shock. Of course you're entitled to a life. I'll get over it, I really will, it's just . . . '

'What?' Lorna's slice of toast hovered between her mouth and the plate.

'It's just he's a bit younger . . . '

She put the toast down, her appetite having departed. 'I know. It's a shock for me too. But we get on so well . . . '

Leo didn't answer for a while. 'I think I don't want things to change between us. If you hook up with someone — Jack — they will.'

Lorna realised this was true. 'But not necessarily in a bad way. You don't want your old mother dependent on you when you've got a family of your own. You'd prefer to have her being happily looked after by her toy boy.'

Leo became very serious. 'Do you think he'll

173

do that? Do you think he's your forever one?'

Lorna sighed, suddenly despondent. 'I really don't know.'

'I just don't want you to get hurt,' said Leo. 'That's all it is. Honestly.'

All the euphoria of the previous day had melted. By the time she'd parked outside Jack's house, ready to pick him up to drive them both to the airport, Lorna felt she was on the path to destruction. Why on earth did she think a man like him would like a woman like her in the long term? She was mad! She doubted the relationship would last the week they'd agreed to be away for. But because she really wanted it to work, and she really wanted a romantic break with Jack in France, looking at stone, drinking café crème in little bars, eating at lovely restaurants, generally being on holiday, she took a deep breath, locked the car, picked up her handbag and knocked at the door.

The sight and smell of Jack, fresh from the shower, was extremely reassuring. He swept her into his arms, into a bear hug that reminded her he worked with heavy objects. He was strong and he hugged her tightly. And then he planted his lips on hers in a kiss that gave a lot and promised more. She felt weak with relief.

'Come and have a cup of coffee. I've just got to send a couple of emails before we go.'

'Actually, I'd love to visit the loo first,' she said.

'No problem.' He ushered her into his bedroom. 'The en-suite is the only one I've got, I'm afraid. But I hope I left it reasonably respectable.'

174

She realised his flat was even smaller than her house and that if living together became a possibility, they would have to live in hers. Then she stopped her thoughts in their tracks. Why on earth was she thinking about that?

She washed her hands and came out into the bedroom, looking for a towel. There was one on the bed, damp from the shower. As she dried her hands her attention was caught by a drawing, framed and hung on the wall. It was of a nude woman and it was good. So she put down the towel and went nearer to inspect it.

Then she gave a little stifled scream. Her knees gave way and she staggered back to sit on the bed. Jack, presumably hearing her scream, came rushing in. 'What's the matter? Are you all right? Oh. You've seen the drawing.'

Lorna nodded. Her head was swimming and she felt sick. The naked woman in the drawing was her, when she was about eighteen years old. When she had a body she could be proud of. 'Where did you get it?' she whispered.

'I bought it. The artist is very well respected. Didn't you know that?'

She shook her head. 'I was an art student. I did life modelling for the money. I didn't know who was in the class drawing me.'

'You look terribly shocked. I don't understand?'

Lorna wasn't quite sure herself why she felt so terrible but for some reason she felt like a teenager who'd sent her boyfriend a naked selfie. He had a picture of her, naked, on his wall. 'Why didn't you tell me?' Her voice was shaking.

'I didn't mean not to tell you. But when I worked out how I knew you from somewhere, it felt a bit awkward.'

Lorna was feeling more than a bit awkward. He had this picture of her, in his bedroom. If it had just been her body, that wouldn't have mattered so much, but it was identifiably her. How could she ever take off her clothes in front of him now, when he was used to looking at her teenaged body? She was well over fifty, and older than he was. She couldn't do it. Not now.

'Look, let's go and have a cup of coffee.' He glanced at his watch. 'We've plenty of time.'

'I can't come with you,' said Lorna.

'Don't be silly A cup of something will sort you out.'

She looked at him. 'I'm not being the slightest bit silly. And how could you think a cup of coffee would 'sort me out'?'

'You're overreacting. It's just a drawing.'

'Of me. On your wall.'

'I don't know why you're making such a big thing of it. It's because of the drawing I was so attracted to you.'

Lorna caught her breath and managed to choke back a rising sob. 'Well, you're attracted to the wrong version of me! You were probably still in junior school when that was drawn.'

'Maybe — I don't know. But why does it matter?'

She realised he would never understand that for her, the fact that he had her at eighteen imprinted on his mind, and would see her body, nearly forty years older, meant she couldn't go

176

through with this trip.

She had thought she was in love with him, she fancied him as much as she ever had anyone, but she could not sleep with him. And she certainly couldn't go on holiday with him.

'I'm sorry, Jack, I really am. But this has all been a horrible mistake. I'm going home.'

'Oh, for God's sake, Lorna, it's a piece of art, not a porno movie! You're not ashamed of being a life model, are you? Why on God's earth should you be?'

But she was, and the fact that he didn't understand why it mattered so much somehow made it even worse.

'I'm going, Jack,' she said. 'Goodbye.

Without waiting for him to react, she walked out of the house and got into her car, picking up her handbag on the way.

★   ★   ★

Setting off for home didn't seem possible, not if Leo might be there. She needed somewhere she could cry, undisturbed, and then have time to disguise the fact that she'd been crying. She drove until she found a lay-by and then parked.

She realised she felt too numb to cry. She felt so stupid. What had she been thinking of? She had been about to go off to France with a man several years younger than herself. She had even been thinking about moving in with him. If it wasn't so heartbreaking it would have been almost funny.

She switched on the radio. Maybe Radio 4

177

would help her see sense. She closed her eyes and tried very hard not to think about Jack.

She opened them again shortly afterwards, disturbed by someone banging on her car window. It was Anthea.

'What on earth are you doing here? I thought you were off to France with your toy boy?'

Lorna wound down the window. 'Oh, Anthea, I've been such a fool.'

'There's no fool like an old fool!' said Anthea gaily. 'Come to my house and I'll feed you gin until you feel better. Good excuse not to go to this wretched washing-up meeting that Kirstie has called.'

As Lorna didn't have a better plan, she followed Anthea's car to her house.

'Now,' said Anthea, sitting her down at the kitchen table with a gin and tonic strong enough to anaesthetise an elephant. 'Get that down you. You can tell me all about it later.'

Lorna allowed herself to take a couple of sips of gin before she spoke. 'It's a bit early for gin, isn't it?' she said shakily.

'The sun is over the yardarm somewhere.'

'I suppose it is.'

'Now I'm going to make you a sandwich. Did you have breakfast?'

Lorna remembered the toast she'd tried to eat when talking to Leo. 'Not really.'

'You're lucky. I've got some smoked salmon.'

A few minutes later, one sandwich down and half the gin, Lorna said, 'I'm not going to be able to drive home.' The thought of walking back to her house, bag in hand, having to explain to Leo that, actually, she wasn't going to France made her have another sip of her drink.

'Seamus would run you back if I asked him, or you could stay the night. Now, tell me what happened.'

When Lorna had finished, Anthea said, 'So, you're turning down the chance of a fling with a rather gorgeous man because he's got a picture of you naked?'

'Put like that it does seem silly but I felt betrayed. He'd had that picture all the time we've known each other and he never told me. And I was eighteen when that drawing was done; I'm not eighteen now. He'd have got the saggy, wrinkly, dyed-hair version. He'd have been revolted. I couldn't bear it.'

Anthea's raised eyebrows indicated just how neurotic and silly she thought Lorna had been. Lorna persisted. 'Honestly, Leo was disgusted at the thought of me and Jack being together.'

'Not at all the same, dear. But you feel like you feel.' She narrowed her eyes at Lorna. 'So what do you want to do now? Go home and pick up the pieces? Or, may I suggest, as you've got a bag packed, that you go away somewhere else? Tell Leo, obviously, although why one's children feel they have to know all about one's private life I do not understand.' She said this so vehemently it made Lorna wonder for a moment if she was speaking personally.

'Well, I'm not looking forward to going back to do a walk of shame when I've done nothing to be ashamed of. Apart from being a bloody idiot.'

'Find somewhere nice to go, either a good B

179

and B or an Airbnb. You can mope about where no one knows you and come back refreshed. Then get in touch with Jack and tell him it was all a huge mistake.'

'I don't know about that. Agreeing to go away with him was a huge mistake but breaking up with him wasn't. But I do like the idea of a holiday.'

'Splendid. Let's find you something.'

To Lorna's surprise, Anthea produced a laptop from under a pile of newspapers and opened it up. 'Now, where do you fancy? What about the seaside? Nothing like the sound of breakers on shingle for bringing on a good self-pitying howl. Devon suit you?'

By the time Lorna had finished her drink and refused a second one she was booked in to a very charming-looking B and B near Salcombe. Anthea had telephoned Kirstie and made some excuse for not being at the meeting and then turned to Lorna. 'What now? I'm busy this afternoon but what would you like to do? A boxed set of something on the telly? I've got quite a good selection. Or there's Netflix.'

Lorna had a sudden vision of Anthea curling up of an evening in front of *Breaking Bad* and almost smiled. 'You're very up on the latest technology. I'm impressed.'

'I've taken to it in my old age. So, what do you fancy? I've got *Brief Encounter* if you really want to cut your throat.'

Lorna shook her head. 'What I'd really like to do is some weeding. Have you got a bed that needs clearing? Preferably full of convolvulus? I find digging up bindweed very therapeutic.'

Anthea looked thoughtful. 'Can't promise bindweed but I've got frightfully behind on the weeding lately. If you want to get stuck in, I'll find you my gardening gloves. The tools are all in the shed.'

★ ★ ★

That evening, when Lorna had had a relaxing bath after a hard afternoon's digging and they were eating omelettes at the kitchen table, she said to Anthea, 'I've been wondering, what goes on behind all those self-sown ash trees? At the end?'

Anthea shrugged. 'To be honest, Lorna, I don't know. I've always just ignored it. I've got enough garden to look after without investigating new bits.' She picked up the bottle. 'More wine?'

17

Philly perched on the edge of a chair at the kitchen table, drumming one heel and picking up cake crumbs with her finger. Her grandfather sat opposite, looking at her with a mixture of amusement and bafflement.

'Can you not just calm down, child?' he said. 'You're jumpy as a cat in a room full of rocking chairs. Is it the young fella coming back that's eating you?'

'Yes. No. I don't know. It seems such a long time since he won all that money at Newbury.'

'Credit to him that he went straight off on another cheffing job. He could have just come back and made bread,' said Seamus.

Philly agreed with her grandfather but she'd missed him horribly. 'I know. He's so determined to get as much money as he can, he works all the hours.'

'So, he doesn't even know how well the garden opening went? What a triumph it was for you all?'

'I wouldn't say it was a triumph, exactly.'

'Why not? The garden looked great, you sold all your plants and it made the papers. What's not a triumph about that?'

'Well, if I could have produced all the plants myself and if I hadn't been left with nothing to sell so I'm now having to work my socks off, filling the new polytunnel with seed trays so I'll have plants to sell again — '

'You text him, don't you?'

Philly nodded. 'Little bit.'

'And are you walking out together?'

Philly smiled, knowing he was using this outdated expression to amuse her. 'Well, he was quite friendly after Newbury, but he's been away since then. And . . . ' She paused for dramatic effect but also because she was worried. ' . . . will he have gambled away all his wages?'

Her grandfather, who was shaving off another slice of cake to give to Philly, didn't answer immediately. 'I understand why you're worried. It only needs a couple of lucky wins on the horses and people think they can work the system and end up losing everything. But I think he's more sensible than that. He's a hard worker. He wouldn't want to go throwing it away.'

Philly accepted the cake. She and her grandfather had agreed long since that several very thin slices of cake weren't nearly as fattening as one ordinary slice. 'I do hope you're right.'

'So what are you going to feed him on? The feast for the conquering hero? I'd offer but I know you want to do it. Besides I won't be back till six.'

'Oh, God, Grand, I can't cook for him!' Just the thought of it made her shake with nerves. 'I'll get a ready meal. He'll complain but he'll understand.'

'Not at all. I'll ask Anthea if she's got an easy recipe. Simple home cooking is always acceptable.'

'Yes, but you know how busy I am.'

'You need a break from the polytunnels. You've spent so much time in them recently I've been checking you for powdery mildew. Out of the plastic, into the kitchen. It'll be good for you. Besides, cooking's not that hard.'

'Says you, who only makes cakes.'

'Many people say baking is harder than cooking,' said her grandfather. 'Your young man is coming home and you need to make him a meal. He'll be hungry.'

Philly sighed. It was true what he'd said was a bit old-fashioned, but it was also true. It was just she was panicked at the thought of cooking for such a demanding diner.

'OK,' she said reluctantly. 'You get me the recipe and I'll give it a go.'

Some hours later, she was just shutting the oven door, having made sure all was well, when she heard Lucien's van. She had a moment or two to feel excited and nervous, fluff up her hair and smooth it down again, and wish she hadn't put on a dress — he'd think she'd made a special effort and know she cared. She stepped away from the cooker.

He came in carrying a bottle of champagne and wearing a big smile. He put the bottle on the table and came over to Philly and hugged her, tucking her into his arms so her head was under his chin. She couldn't breathe but she didn't mind.

He let go of her and stepped back to look at her. 'God, I've missed you! And you look so pretty! You've put on a dress. Wow! Actual legs!'

Philly couldn't stop smiling. She was so happy to see him, so happy that he was so happy 'Hi, Lucien,' she said and hoped she didn't sound squeaky. 'How are you?'

'Super good now I'm back home with you. I have missed you so much! Have you missed me?'

She shrugged, hoping just how much she'd missed him wasn't written all over her face. 'I've hardly had time to miss you . . . '

He waited, looking just a bit worried.

' . . . but I have,' she finished, still smiling.

He relaxed. 'Let's put this bottle in the freezer and then I'll get my things in. You won't believe how much I'm looking forward to sleeping in a bed — even if it's on my own.'

When he came back, his hair was damp and his shirt sticking to him in places. 'I had to have a quick shower. I must have been stinking when I arrived.'

She hadn't noticed him stinking, precisely, but now he smelled of something lemony and a little bitter: it reminded her of lemon balm and artemisia and maybe some vervain. It was fresh, clean and sophisticated. While he was fetching the champagne from the freezer she decided to grow more of the unusual herbs, just for their smell. She found her brain was frantically distracting itself from the matter in hand. She was so happy but also nervous.

Lucien found two wine glasses and opened the bottle. 'No champagne flutes?'

She shook her head. 'Paris goblets or tumblers, you know that.'

He nodded and handed her a glass. 'I'd drink

185

it from your shoe if it came to it but I don't think you'd fancy drinking it from mine.'

She smiled. 'Not your trainer, no.'

'Here's to being home,' he said, and they clinked.

'Here's to you being home,' said Philly, delighted that he referred to her home as his home.

'What's for dinner? Something smells good.'

Philly put down her glass, some of her euphoria dispelled by anxiety. 'Stew. Anthea's recipe. I hope it's all right.' She frowned. 'I don't suppose I'll ever dare call Anthea that to her face.'

'Why not?'

She shrugged. 'She scares me.'

'Why?'

'She's so — well — posh.'

'Don't say that. I mean, I'm going to need you to be brave.'

'Why? Please don't tell me you really have lost all your money on the horses.'

'No! Of course not. Why would I do that? I'm not an idiot.'

Philly sighed with relief. 'Then why — '

'I'll tell you later. Is Seamus going to be with us for dinner?'

'Yes. He said he would be.'

'Good.' He watched as she got the casserole dish out of the oven and took the lid off. Then he could bear staying on the sidelines no longer and joined her at the stove.

'What's it got in it?'

'Meat, vegetables — can't remember.' She

sighed. 'Actually I am brave. I cooked for you.'

He laughed. 'That is quite brave.'

She looked at him. 'If I go and set the table can I trust you not to taste the stew?'

He considered and then shook his head. 'I'll set the table.'

Inside, Philly smiled. He made her heart sing, he really did.

★　★　★

Seamus had got out one of his good bottles of wine, having rejected champagne. By a 'good' bottle, he meant one that hadn't been part of any kind of deal. It could have cost as much as five pounds. Philly realised that to many people — Lucien included — this would not be considered enough to ensure quality, but she and her grandfather were frugal. And to be fair to Lucien, while he'd been staying with them, if wine had been produced, he always just drank it.

'Well now, Lucien,' said Seamus, having filled the glasses. 'I can tell you've got something to tell us. You'd better get it off your chest before you pop.'

'Oh, Grand! Let him taste the stew first,' said Philly, who'd taken a large gulp of wine without waiting for any kind of toast. 'I'm in agony here!'

Lucien gave her a look that filled her with a mixture of desire and terror. What would he think about it? Its only advantage, she thought, was that it had been cooked very slowly for a very long time.

'Actually,' Lucien said, having eaten quite a lot

187

of it, 'it's very good. The mashed potato has a few lumps in it, but I don't suppose you've got a drum sieve to pass it through.' He grinned.

Philly was sorely tempted to flick a bit of the mash at him but refrained. 'Grand doesn't like mashed potato without a few lumps,' she said.

'I don't,' said Seamus. 'I don't trust it to really be potato if it hasn't got a few wee lumps.'

'Actually, it's fine,' said Lucien. 'I was teasing you. Not about the lumps, they are there, but it's still delicious. Frozen peas are a very safe choice of veg though.'

This time she did flick a pea at him.

Lucien ducked. 'When you've stopped throwing vegetables, I have something to say. To both of you.'

'Go on then, lad. But don't forget to eat.' Seamus topped up the glasses.

'Well,' said Lucien. 'You know we've talked about me turning that outhouse into a professional kitchen? One where I can bake retail quantities of bread? Changing the electricity system, making some big alterations?'

'Yup,' said Seamus.

Philly just nodded, scared he might be going to say it couldn't be done. Then he'd move away and she might never see him again, however pleased he'd been to see her.

'I just want to make sure that you're still OK with that? I mean, I think I've got enough money now to go and ask my godfather to back me. But if you don't want a pro kitchen on your land, I need to find another premises.'

Philly took another sip to stop herself saying

'That's fine!' when really it was her grandfather's decision.

'We agreed,' said Seamus. 'We're happy, aren't we, Philly?'

She nodded.

'Great,' said Lucien. 'Well, the other thing I wanted to say — ask — was: Will you come with me to ask him, Philly?'

'Sorry?' She tried to work out what he meant.

'I want you to come to Uncle Roderick — I call him that — and ask him to back me financially.'

'Why? Do you think Philly being there would help?' asked Seamus.

'I do. The thing is, I've always been a bit — well . . . My girlfriends haven't always been . . . '

'What are you trying to say?' Philly put down her wine glass. 'What have your girlfriends always been?'

'Flighty,' said Lucien. 'That's what Anthea would call them.'

Seamus leant back in his chair and laughed. 'She probably would.'

'But no one would call you flighty, Philly,' said Lucien firmly. 'And before you ask, that is definitely a good thing.'

'You think young Philly here would add gravitas to your request for money?'

'I do.' Lucien took a breath. 'But mostly, I don't want to go away again and leave her when I've only just got back.'

'Should I be after asking your intentions with regard to my granddaughter?'

'No you should not! Grand! Really!' Philly was indignant. 'You can't ask things like that nowadays. Queen Victoria has been dead a long time.'

'I think he has a right to look after your safety, Philly,' said Lucien seriously. 'After all, he's your family here in England. He'll get it in the neck if you elope with a bounder.'

It took her a couple of seconds to work out Lucien was joking about the last bit.

'He's right there, you know, child. I am responsible for your safety. Your mother would have me guts for garters if anything bad happened to you.'

'So will you come with me?' asked Lucien, serious again. 'Uncle Roderick is great — much more laid-back than the rest of my family — but I know he thinks I'm a bit of a waster. No one liked it when I left home to be a chef. I have to prove to him that I'm responsible enough to set up my business, to be a baker. With you there it'll make me seem more . . . I dunno . . . as if I've got my life sorted out. With a proper girlfriend who'll support me and not just dress up and want me to take her clubbing all the time.'

Philly frowned. 'Does this mean, if I go with you, that you won't take me clubbing?'

Lucien rolled his eyes. 'I'll take you clubbing the moment we secure the deal, but when I'm getting up a four a.m. to bake, probably not so often.'

'That's all right then,' said Philly, beaming at him. 'But you know? Until you mentioned it just then, I've never particularly wanted to do those sorts of things. That's why I'm a bit of a social misfit. But I would like to do it once, with you.'

'And I'll take you, to all the best ones. I'm on the guest list of a lot of them,' said Lucien. 'So is it a yes?'

Philly thought about all the work she should be doing, and then about all the work she had done.

'Have you taken a holiday since we came to England?' Her grandfather interrupted her thoughts. 'Apart from going home to see your parents, I mean?'

She shook her head. 'No.' Then she looked across at Lucien. 'I'll come!'

* * *

They set off two days later, in Lucien's van. Philly had packed her smartest clothes, usually reserved for visiting relations back in Ireland. Her mother was anxious that her cousins and aunts didn't think Philly had 'let herself go' so Philly actually put a dress and jacket, bought for a wedding, in the bag, just in case.

'OK?' Lucien glanced at her as they sped off down the road.

'Think so,' said Philly.

She felt more than OK. She felt excited. She knew she'd feel crippled with shyness as they approached Lucien's godfather's house, but now she was on a road trip, with the boy she was fairly sure she loved at her side.

She was a bit worried about how many bedrooms they'd be given. Lucien had said there were plenty but she couldn't decide if she wanted her first time (she did know she wanted to sleep with him) to be accompanied by tiptoeing along creaking corridors. But she didn't fancy going down to breakfast in a strange house having been put in the same bedroom as her boyfriend. Growing up in an isolated part of Ireland with strict parents hadn't really prepared her for the modern world. But she was an independent woman (if you overlooked her grandfather, which was actually quite hard) who had her own business. She would cope.

They stopped for lunch in a pub with low beams, horse brasses and an empty fireplace. Of course not many places would light the fire in early June, Philly reasoned, but she was a bit chilly. While the day was bright with sunshine it wasn't actually very warm. She was in her summer clothes, a dress with a cardigan. She missed her jeans and fleece.

'It's like we're having all the dates we've never had in one day,' said Lucien, frowning at the menu. 'Only I'd have taken you to lunch somewhere a bit more . . . '

'Pretentious?' suggested Philly.

He smiled. 'Probably. I was going to say food-focused. But there's something to be said for lasagne and chips.'

'With garlic bread,' said Philly. 'To make sure we're not low on carbs.'

'Nothing wrong with carbs,' said Lucien. 'I want to be a baker, remember, but they've got to

192

be good-quality carbs.'

'I'd like a half of cider with mine, please,' she said, beginning to enjoy herself.

They both had a fork into a portion of sticky toffee pudding when Philly became aware of Lucien losing some of his *joie de vivre*. He kept rearranging the salt and pepper and staring into space. As he was always so positive and enthusiastic this seemed odd.

'You're not having second thoughts about this, are you? We don't have to go. You could take me home and then go on your own.'

He shook his head. 'No. I really want you with me, for all sorts of reasons. It's just there's something I should tell you.'

Philly bit her lip. 'What?'

'It's nothing really.'

'It's something! You've gone all twitchy.'

'OK. My godfather has a housekeeper.'

'And?'

He bit his lip. 'It's just she used to be my nanny. She is a devoted family retainer. Not that she's horrid or anything but — well, she's a bit devoted.'

'Go on.'

'She might be a bit funny with you. I think she thinks I should wait for Princess Charlotte to grow up so I can marry her. Princess Anne is married already and is a bit old for me.'

'She's a royalist?'

'She's a snob. No woman will be good enough for me.' Lucien obviously felt better now he'd shared his secret. 'But that really won't affect you. She just might be a bit — well — sniffy.'

193

'She's your godfather's housekeeper? That's not a euphemism?'

Lucien paled at the thought. 'Oh, Philly, I wish you hadn't suggested that. The thought of them in bed together — ergh!' He regarded her in a way that made her heart skip. 'Maybe you should have another drink?'

★ ★ ★

Philly had tried to make light of it for Lucien's sake, but she'd been quite nervous before he'd mentioned the housekeeper. Now she was no longer enjoying herself and instead felt sick and had visions of throwing up on an antique Persian rug that had turned dozens of children blind in its creation. She could tell that Lucien was fretting now, too. After his confession about his old nanny he'd been his usual self while she'd drunk her second half of cider. Now they were only a few miles away he'd gone quiet.

After the housekeeper revelation Philly didn't dare ask where Lucien's godfather lived. If he had a housekeeper a quiet suburban semi seemed out of the question. It would be like Burthen House, she decided, only with more antiques. Especially the rugs that she might well throw up on. And after that she'd break a priceless Ming vase. This was going to be terrific fun.

He turned into a drive. In front of them was one of the grandest houses she'd ever seen that wasn't owned by the National Trust. It made Burthen House seem a bit on the small side.

194

'It's big,' she said.

'Yup.'

'And have you got your business plan?'

'Yup.' He pulled up in front of the house. 'Well, here goes.'

'Scary nanny, here we come.'

'I wish I'd never put that idea in your head. She was fine. Like Mary Poppins.'

'Mary Poppins had a dark side. You mustn't get her muddled up with Julie Andrews.'

'I wasn't,' said Lucien.

18

They weren't left on the doorstep of the house for long, but long enough for Philly to look wistfully at the van and work out how quickly she could get to it. Then, just as she remembered that Lucien had the keys, the door was opened.

Philly recognised Evil Mary Poppins as soon as she saw her and if she'd been in any doubt about her evilness, her narrow smile confirmed it. The chill Philly felt as she entered the house, wearing her spring-like cardigan and summer dress, added to her sense of doom.

'Lucien, dear, how very nice to see you. We don't see you nearly often enough. I know your godfather would appreciate far more frequent visits.' Then she glanced at Philly. 'Hello.'

Lucien took his old nanny in his arms and gave her hug but even as he did so Philly wondered if she could really have been 'fine' as a nanny. She was so formal and thin.

'I'm not going to say you've grown, dear,' said Evil Mary Poppins, looking at Lucien with a critical gaze, 'but you've lost your lovely golden curls. And you have filled out a bit.'

As Lucien was far from being fat, Philly decided that his nanny had underfed him, and this added to her evilness. She cleared her throat, having realised that she had forgotten to ask Lucien what the woman imprinted on her mind as Evil Mary Poppins was really called. This

196

could be a serious problem, one that she had to tackle now. She couldn't spend their entire stay calling her 'you' and her personal soubriquet might slip out. 'Lucien? You haven't introduced us.'

'Oh, sorry!' He seemed flustered. 'This is Miss — Sarah Hopkins.' He too obviously had to struggle for her real name, Philly noticed. He probably just called her 'Nanny'. Maybe he'd had a series of them. She shuddered at the thought. 'Nanny — um — Sarah, this is Philly.'

'How do you do, Miss Hopkins,' said Philly, holding out her hand, hoping her recent efforts with various hand products designed for gardeners had done their job.

'How do you do,' said Miss Hopkins, not inviting her to use her given name, which was obviously what Lucien had expected. 'Mr Roderick is in the library, if you'd like to follow me. Then I'll bring tea.'

'Oh, no need to show us,' said Lucien. 'I know my way.'

'In which case, Lucien, I'll organise tea.' She bowed formally.

'Oh my God, she's so much worse than I expected,' muttered Philly in a rapid whisper as she followed Lucien down a stone-flagged corridor. 'And is your godfather's name really Roderick? Roderick Roderick?' She knew posh people were often called the most ridiculous things.

'No, he's Sir Roderick Mythson. She just calls him Mr Roderick because she's always worked in the family He's a distant relation of ours.'

'Was she his nanny too?'

'Don't think so. She's not old enough. Now, here we are.'

Lucien's godfather got up as they entered. He was in his fifties, wearing red corduroy trousers, a check shirt and a cravat. His socks were red too, worn with very shiny brogues. He still had quite a lot of hair and had ruddy cheeks. He was, Philly decided, what her mother would describe as raffish, but as he was smiling fairly warmly, she didn't mind.

'Lucien! Dear boy!' They didn't hug but shook hands. 'And who's this pretty little thing?'

'This is Philly,' said Lucien, possibly embarrassed by his godfather's description of her.

'Hello,' said Philly, 'it's lovely to meet you.'

'And you, m'dear. Now, come and sit down. I might light the fire. It's gone quite chilly.'

Philly, who was very chilly now, made appreciative noises which she hoped would encourage him. Alas, he made no move to the fireplace but went to a table of drinks instead. 'Drink? Glass of sherry? Help to warm you up?'

Philly felt a glass of sherry would have both warmed her up and calmed her nerves. 'That would be lovely but Miss Hopkins is bringing tea.'

'Miss Hopkins? Oh, you mean Sarah. Well, we'd better not have a drink then, not if she's bringing tea.'

Philly noted a slightly anxious look about him: he wanted a drink but didn't dare risk putting his housekeeper out.

Lucien spoke. 'Shall I light the fire, Rod?' He

198

addressed his godfather (in a very informal way, Philly thought) but looked at her. She nodded.

'Yes, do. Then I can tell Sarah that you did it and she won't tell me off.' Roderick laughed in a way that told Philly he was completely serious — he was accustomed to being told off by his housekeeper.

Philly quite wanted to light the fire herself, being better at it that Lucien was, but she knew this would be a step too far for Evil Mary Poppins.

'And what do you get up to?' Roderick asked her while Lucien got on with the fire.

'I have a plant nursery,' said Philly. 'I have a couple of polytunnels and raise plants — mostly for a friend who gardens for a big house. A bit like this one.' She smiled, feeling she'd done quite well with her description.

'Plants eh?' Roderick gave Philly the impression of not really knowing what a plant was but maybe she was being unfair. 'Money in it?'

'Not as much as there should be, given what hard work it is, but I do all right.'

'Hard work?' He frowned as if this was a foreign concept for him.

'I don't mind getting my hands dirty,' said Philly, just as Miss Hopkins came in with a trolley.

'Would you like to wash your hands before tea, miss?' said Miss Hopkins, who'd obviously overheard this.

Wishing she could drop breadcrumbs so she could guarantee being able to find her way back, Philly allowed herself to be led along the corridors to a large, freezing downstairs loo.

The soap was old and had cracks in it and the towel was rough and not clean. Philly felt willing to bet on there being a much nicer bathroom she could have been shown to, but Evil Mary Poppins had obviously decided she was not worth the good bathroom, with the nice hand towel and new soap. Philly, who considered herself to be a bit of a wimp a lot of the time, felt her courage rise along with her hackles.

She was glad to see that Lucien had got the fire going in the library and went to stand beside it. Miss Hopkins was serving tea.

'There you are,' she said, as if Philly had taken hours. 'I've put your tea down over there.' She indicated a chair far too far from the fire.

'Thank you,' said Philly meekly and crossed the room. Then she picked up the tea and took it back to the fire. As she sipped it she wondered why, when Lady Anthea scared her so, she could be so defiant with Lucien's ex-nanny. It was because Miss Hopkins was almost openly hostile while Lady Anthea was just posh. She resolved to be braver when she got home.

Eventually Miss Hopkins left the room and Philly sensed she wasn't the only one who relaxed after she'd gone. She felt bold enough to pick up a pouffe and take it to the fireside. Lucien put down the bourbon biscuit he had taken only one bite of and Roderick went to the drinks table again.

'Not a baker, Sarah, is she?' said Lucien.

'Cakes are empty calories,' said Roderick. 'Shall we have sherry? Or go straight to the hard stuff?'

'Hard stuff,' said Lucien. 'Not keen on sherry.'

'Sherry for me please,' said Philly draining the cup of tea that was cold, too weak and had too much milk.

'Will she be cross?' said Lucien, taking the glass his godfather offered.

'I'll blame you,' he said. 'You always were her blue-eyed boy.'

'God knows why,' said Lucien. 'I played her up terribly.'

'Was she your nanny for long?' asked Philly.

'Couple of years. But I went to prep school when I was seven. She only came when I was six so it was only in the holidays for one of those years. She left when I was eight. Went to look after an ancient aunt.'

'Then when the aunt died,' said Roderick, 'I inherited her. She's very efficient but a bit, well . . . puritanical. She still talks about looking after Lucien as the height of her career.'

'So, Rod,' said Lucien after a couple of sips of whisky. 'You might have guessed we haven't only come for the pleasure of your company.'

'You've come because you want money, I understand that perfectly. What's the story?'

Philly perched on her pouffe by the fire, sipping sherry and eating the bits of bread and butter that the others had ignored.

'Well — ' Lucien began but was interrupted.

'Why did you run away from home, boy? You had everything! A great education, loving parents, very comfortably off. You had anything your heart desired! Cricket coaching at Lord's, skiing every winter, tennis coaching, sailing lessons, everything. And you just ran away from it all?'

Philly was a little startled. She knew Lucien came from a privileged background but she hadn't realised quite how privileged.

'Broke your parents' hearts,' Roderick finished.

'Obviously I was sorry they were upset,' said Lucien, a little stiffly, 'but I just didn't want the life they'd marked me out for. I wanted to be a chef. They wouldn't even discuss it.'

'And respect to you that you knew that,' said Roderick, 'but now you want to be a baker? What happened to the cheffing? You need a bit of sticking power in this world, m'boy. It's no good just picking things up and then giving up when the going gets tough.'

Lucien exhaled, took another sip of his drink and another breath. 'I'm not going to set myself up as a baker because the going got tough as a chef. Being a baker is far harder in many ways. As a chef I can have quite an easy life, especially now I'm known on the racecourse and sporting events circuit. It's fairly well paid and I can do as many days as I like.'

'So why give that up? Although I'm sure your mother would rather see you as a head chef with your own restaurant.'

'I'm afraid what my mother wants for me and what I want for myself are two different things. It's why I left.'

Roderick nodded and drained his glass. When he'd refilled it he said, 'That's fair enough. And she's a very strong woman, your

202

mother. Likes her own way.'

Philly seeing how much whisky he poured into his glass, felt a tiny glimmer of sympathy for Roderick's housekeeper, who obviously tried to moderate his drinking. But she quailed at the thought of Lucien's mother. If it was tough facing his nanny, God knows how terrifying his mother would be.

'Which is why I've come to you for backing,' went on Lucien. 'I explained a bit in my email — '

Just as he was about to expand the door opened and Miss Hopkins came in, presumably to clear away the tea. 'Oh,' she said. 'You've moved on to drinks.'

Entirely unfairly, Philly thought, Miss Hopkins fixed her with a gimlet eye, managing to make Philly feel responsible for the debauchery. 'Perhaps the young lady would like to see her room? It's nearly time to change for dinner.'

There was nothing for it but to leave the fireside and follow Miss Hopkins. At least, Philly thought, she'd have an opportunity to find some warmer clothes in her bag. Although she doubted that changing for dinner meant putting her jeans and fleece back on.

Lucien had left her bag in the hall and Philly picked it up and followed Miss Hopkins up the stairs and along a lengthy and very draughty corridor that Philly was convinced led to the haunted east wing. She knew she would be miles away from Lucien and so any worries about tiptoeing along corridors were banished. There may well be a mad family retainer locked up in the same wing, of course, thoughts of *Jane Eyre* coming into her mind. She also knew, before she'd even been shown her bedroom, that she'd need to sleep in all her clothes.

She decided to put on her jeans and a strappy top under her dress, and layer her cardigan back on over the top. She doubted Evil Mary Poppins would comment on her slightly outlandish costume and if she did, Philly resolved, she'd make out it was a 'look'.

As she set off back down the corridors, searching for the library and some warmth, she realised that most of her life people had looked kindly on her and she'd just been happy to be liked. Now she was faced with almost open hostility she found herself becoming stronger. It was heartening, she decided. So much better than it would have been the other way round.

But before she could reach the comfort of the fire, she was intercepted. 'The gentlemen are in the drawing room,' said Miss Hopkins, giving Philly a glance that told her that jeans with a dress would never be a 'look' in her eyes.

The fireplace in the drawing room was filled with a huge vase of dried flowers that stated firmly that it was summer and under no circumstances would the fire be lit.

Roderick and Lucien were both wearing cashmere V-necked jumpers, Roderick's slightly attacked by moth. He was also wearing a cravat that Philly could have done with borrowing.

'Philly,' said Lucien. 'Come and sit down.' He handed her a glass of sherry. 'Nanny — Sarah — says dinner won't be long. Did you find everything you needed?'

She nodded, feeling it was too rude to say that she had failed to find a wardrobe full of fur coats. For a start it wasn't Roderick's fault she had packed inadequately for June in a big old country house, and secondly he and Lucien might not have got her reference to *The Lion, the Witch and the Wardrobe*. There was something about this place that reminded her of adventure stories she had read as a child. It was more like a fictional setting than an actual house where somebody lived.

'Drink that quickly,' said Lucien, standing over her with the decanter, 'then you can get another one in before Nanny comes back with cheesy biscuits.'

Roderick was clutching a cut-glass tumbler and standing near a different decanter. Was it Nanny who had driven him to drink? Or was she keeping an eye on his drinking because she cared? Possibly both.

By the time Miss Hopkins came in with a plate of biscuits spread with something pale pink everyone was seated with a suitably modest amount of alcohol in their glasses.

'Dinner won't be long,' she said, handing round the plate. 'So don't spoil your appetites.'

'What are we having?' asked Lucien, who, as the favourite, had the required temerity.

'Wait and find out, dear. Then it'll be a lovely surprise.'

'It may not be that lovely,' said Roderick gloomily when she had left. 'She's good at nursery food — macaroni cheese, shepherd's pie, etc. — but if people come she feels obliged to do a recipe.'

Lucien groaned softly 'I could have cooked for you,' he said.

'I'm sure, but that would have hurt her feelings horribly,' said Roderick.

Philly wasn't convinced Evil Mary Poppins had feelings, but didn't comment.

'I've got out some nice wine,' said Roderick. 'Managed to get two bottles into the dining room. We'll have to get the first bottle drunk quite quickly if we're to be allowed to open the second.'

'I'll do my best,' said Philly. She was already looking forward to telling her grandfather about the goings on. And Lorna. Thinking about Lorna she hoped she'd had a lovely time in France with Jack. She felt rather envious: at least it must have been warm in France.

As predicted, they weren't given too much time to sit over their sherry and fish-paste crackers. Before long they were ushered into a dining room that was even colder than the other rooms.

'Sorry,' muttered Roderick, seeing Philly unable to suppress a shiver. 'Coldest bloody house in the county.'

She smiled politely, not wanting to contradict him.

As Roderick predicted, the food was disgusting. The first course was a pale pink pâté, which turned out to be the same as the one served on the biscuits. Then there were chicken breasts in what may well have been tinned soup of indeterminate flavour with undercooked rice.

Miss Hopkins served, which meant no one wanted to say much, and while she was out of the room, Lucien topped up the glasses. Philly was by now tempted to follow her host's example and down hers, in order to get a refill before Miss Hopkins returned with the next course.

The pudding caused Lucien to exclaim in excitement. Whether this was happy excitement or dismay, Philly couldn't tell. It was pale brown and served in little dishes.

'Oh, Nanny,' said Lucien. 'you've done my favourite. Angel Delight!'

'Mr Lucien!' Nanny protested, adding a title to give her reproach emphasis. 'May you be forgiven. All my food is made from scratch, just like the government says we have to.'

'It's lovely,' said Philly gulping down her wine, which made it taste disgusting. 'I love — er — chocolate — chocolate things.'

'There's cheese' said Roderick. 'Sarah, could we have the cheese? I've got some rather nice port. I'd like us to have that. Don't worry though; I'll get it.'

'I wasn't planning on serving cheese, Mr Roderick,' said Miss Hopkins reprovingly.

'I do think Lucien should try the port,' said Roderick. 'As his godfather it's my job to educate his palate.'

Lucien coughed into his hand.

'I'll fetch the cheese then,' said Miss Hopkins with a sniff. 'But I doubt the young lady will want to eat or drink any more. You go along to the drawing room, miss, and leave the gentle-men.'

'I think Philly would like a glass of port,' said Lucien.

'And we have a damn fine Stilton. Lucien put it in the post for me,' said Roderick.

Miss Hopkins stood with the door open. 'You gentlemen might want to discuss business.'

'I assure you we're not going to be discussing anything Philly can't hear. She knows all my business plans,' said Lucien.

'I've had too much to drink to talk business anyway,' said Roderick.

'So we'll sit down and have some port and cheese!' said Lucien.

'I think the young lady would prefer to leave you gentlemen,' said Miss Hopkins persistently.

Philly was finding this quite amusing. 'I'm happy to leave you two to get drunk,' she said, 'if I could have a cup of tea in the drawing room?'

Philly realised Miss Hopkins hadn't intended to offer her anything but now, having made such a big fuss about her leaving the gentlemen, she was obliged to make tea.

Philly nipped along to the library and raided the fireplace for kindling, firelighters, logs and matches. She was slightly tempted to steal some of the actual fire and carry it on a shovel to the fireplace in the drawing room but realised that would be extremely dangerous and, almost more importantly, she'd get very told off if she dropped any on an antique Persian rug. She removed the flower arrangement to under the window.

Annoyingly, she was on her knees in front of the fire, blowing it, when Miss Hopkins came in with tea. Philly took the initiative.

'So silly of me,' she said, 'I should have just asked if I could have had tea in the library, but I'll soon have a good blaze here.'

'It's June. Fires shouldn't be necessary. And I would not have liked you to be in Mr Roderick's library unattended.'

Quite right, said Philly to herself. I would have defaced all the precious first editions. How clever of you to spot I was like that. Out loud she said, 'I'll be quite happy here. Thank you so much for the tea. I expect you must be dying to get to bed. Guests are so tiring, aren't they?'

Miss Hopkins pursed her lips in agreement. 'Breakfast is at eight o'clock. In the dining room. I wish you a very good night, miss.'

19

Philly was soon bored waiting for the others and for some reason didn't feel like going back to the dining room. Perhaps Lucien and Roderick *were* talking about the loan. Instead of waiting any longer for them, she found her way to her bedroom and got ready for bed.

She didn't even attempt to have a shower or a bath. The guest bathroom was ill equipped and had a spidery feel about it. Ball-and-claw baths were all very well in newly updated rooms full of shiny porcelain and stainless steel. In this bathroom full of 'original features' they just made the place seem even more draughty and unpromising than it did already. Maybe if they'd visited in spring, not early summer, the pipes to the towel rail would have been hot.

Back in her spooky, chilly room, Philly got into bed with all her clothes on. She planned to warm up the bed a bit and then get undressed and into bed properly.

She could just about read her novel by the bulb in her bedside lamp that was so dim a jam jar full of fireflies would have been more efficient. She felt cold and very far from sleep, but she must have drifted off, fully clothed and hunched over her book, because when she heard the door open she jumped.

It was Lucien. 'Shhh,' he said before she'd had a chance to make a sound. 'If Nanny finds out

I'm here, all hell will break loose!'

'OK,' breathed Philly. 'But what could she do about it?'

'Tell my parents. Believe me, it's not worth it. I just came to give you these.'

He handed her a mug and then, from under his arm, a hot-water bottle. 'Nanny made the hot chocolate and the hot bottle for me.' Then he took off his jumper. 'It's old but warm. Now I must go. Nanny isn't young but she has the hearing of a bat.'

'An old bat, obviously,' said Philly, unable to resist.

'You!' He kissed her cheek and then fled.

Philly smiled. The chocolate wasn't terribly hot and far too sweet but it was comforting, and the hot-water bottle even more welcome. What was most precious of all was that Lucien had brought them to her, risking the wrath of Evil Mary Poppins, and had gone without cocoa and a hot-water bottle for her.

★ ★ ★

She was in the dining room at eight o'clock sharp the next morning. It was still cold, and although she knew it might invite comment, she had Lucien's cashmere jumper on. As a gesture to it being morning, she hadn't put her dress on over the jeans.

Lucien arrived not many minutes later. His hair was damp but he looked on top of things. He had obviously slept better than she had.

Miss Hopkins came into the dining room at

211

almost the same moment, possibly having been listening out for Lucien. 'Good morning. I trust you slept well,' she said, staring at Philly's jumper.

What she trusted, thought Philly, was the certainty that she wouldn't say if she hadn't slept well. Annoyingly, Evil Mary Poppins was right: she didn't say the bed had been unbelievably uncomfortable and a bit damp. 'Fine, thank you,' she muttered.

'I did too, thank you,' said Lucien.

'You always were a good sleeper, Lucien, even when you were little.'

'The hot-water bottle and drinking chocolate helped,' he said, winking at Philly in a way she was sure must be visible.

Miss Hopkins turned to Philly. 'Would you like cereal or toast?'

'I suppose a full English is out of the question?' said Lucien.

'Indeed it is. Heart attack on a plate. Mr Roderick wouldn't be able to tolerate it.'

'Will Roderick be up for breakfast?' asked Lucien.

'No. He didn't sleep very well so I've taken him up his breakfast.'

'Well, we've got to push off quite soon,' said Lucien, helping himself to a slice of toast. 'Is toast enough for you, Philly?'

Philly nodded. Her stomach was growling, and was part of the reason she hadn't slept all that well. 'Plenty,' she said.

'I must say, miss, you don't have the look of one who eats like a bird.'

She's saying I'm fat, Philly realised. She gave her the sort of smile she'd given the nuns at school when she didn't like them. 'Appearances can be so deceptive.'

Actually she hadn't meant to imply anything but she saw Evil Mary Poppins wince.

★ ★ ★

Lucien ran up to his godfather's bedroom to say goodbye and then they were off.

'Put 'greasy spoon' into the satnav and take us there!' said Lucien.

Philly laughed. 'I must say, my stomach thinks my throat is cut.'

'You sound like Seamus.'

'I feel very hungry.'

'I am so sorry to have put you through that. If I had any idea how ghastly it was going to be I'd have booked us in at a bed and breakfast.'

'Where 'a heart attack on a plate' is part of the deal,' said Philly. 'We would have been warm!'

He glanced at her. 'We would have been together.'

'Yes.' She felt suddenly shy. 'I think we'll find somewhere for breakfast if we head into the centre of town.'

They found a little café and ordered everything: beans, fried bread, hash browns, pints of too-strong tea, toast and marmalade.

'You know what? As a chef, I find it hard to get up a better plate of food than a full English.' Lucien wiped up the last of the bacon fat with a bit of toast.

'Which is why you want to be a baker?'

Lucien shrugged. 'It's not that really. It's just the yeast, wild yeast especially — all that stuff, is magic. And not everyone can afford gourmet meals, but most people could buy decent bread.'

'I don't think your old nanny would agree with you.'

'Oh, she'd agree with me!' said Lucien. 'She just wouldn't buy the bread herself.'

'I've been thinking about whether your godfather has enough money to back your business,' said Philly. 'They don't exactly live on the pig's back, do they? I mean, there's no great wealth apparent in that house, if you overlook the house itself.'

'I don't blame you for thinking that but the thing is, Roderick doesn't greatly care about food and comfort, as long as he has enough to drink, and mostly he has — '

'Some would say too much!' said Philly and then wished she hadn't sounded critical.

'I know Nanny would say that, but my parents have always said that Roderick is rolling in it. And people do say the reason rich people are mean is because that was how they got rich in the first place.'

'What did Roderick do to earn money?'

'He didn't earn it, honey, he inherited it.'

Philly shrugged. Having money without having had to work for it was a concept she knew of but didn't relate to. 'Will he give it to you, though? If he's mean?'

'He was a generous godfather. I don't think he's mean really, I just think he doesn't like change. Having proper central heating in that house would mean massive upheaval. He wouldn't like that. I think we'll be all right.'

'So you talked through it all after dinner? He understood your vision?'

'Ha! Sorry to laugh, but if I used words like 'vision' to Roderick, he'd throw me out of the house. I said things like 'business plan', 'projected profit' and 'growing market'.'

'And he got that?'

'I really think he did. Didn't want to commit himself on the spot but I'm sure he'll see the light.'

'Won't it mean upheaval? Which he doesn't like?'

'Not really. He'd just get his accountant to sort it all out for him.' He paused. 'More tea? Or shall we get on?'

Philly took the wheel and, while she was driving, Lucien plotted the route to a little pub for lunch that he knew had been taken over by a promising young chef. The sun came out and they sat in the garden.

'Just as well we had such a big breakfast,' she said teasingly. 'If it's nouvelle cuisine there won't be enough to fill the holes in our teeth.'

'It'll be plenty!' said Lucien. 'Just you wait and see. If you didn't have the appetite of a horse you wouldn't even say things like that.'

'I'm a working woman. I have a healthy appetite and I'm not ashamed of it.'

'That is one of the many things I love about you.' He started the sentence light-heartedly but became more sombre by the end. 'Please, Philly.

215

Look at me. I'm being serious for once in my life.'

She made herself look at him. He was indeed looking serious. 'Yes?' she said softly.

'I think I love you, Philly.'

'But you're not sure?'

'Don't tease! I've never told anyone I love them before. They're not words that come easily to me, that I am sure about. But you're so lovely. It's not just about sex — '

Philly blushed.

'It's because I really admire and respect you. You make me laugh, you're supportive — and as for the sex part, it's not going to be long before I show you exactly how I feel.'

'I never have before, you know, Lucien.' Philly knew she was a deep rose pink by now. 'You would be my first. I know that must seem weird but I'm Irish, and was brought up very strictly.'

'It doesn't seem weird. It seems perfect. And was the strict upbringing the only reason?'

She shook her head. It was best to tell the truth. 'Not really. I never fancied anyone enough.'

He brought his hand up to cup her face. 'I'm glad.'

Philly let Lucien drive for the last bit but she wouldn't have noticed if the wheel had been taken over by an orang-utan. She was on a cloud of happiness. She was in love with someone who was in love with her. It was the most wonderful feeling in the world.

20

When Lorna had unlocked her front door and gone into her little house after her holiday she had felt as if she'd been away for years, not a week. She had felt years older, too, although when she'd glanced in the hall mirror she'd noticed she'd caught a bit of sun, which had made her feel a bit better.

Moving through to the kitchen she had been aware of a certain amount of mess. Leo had moved out, and had only taken what he needed, which sadly didn't include the washing up.

As she put the kettle on and gathered the dirty dishes she wondered if her holiday by the seaside had actually done her any good at all emotionally. She'd walked a lot, eaten delicious food and slept, yet she'd come back not cured of Jack but missing him more than ever.

Later, when she'd sorted herself out a bit, she lit the wood-burner, more for comfort than warmth, and wondered for the millionth time if she'd over-reacted to finding a picture of her naked on his wall. But unlike all the previous times she decided that she had, and this time she would do something about it.

She wasn't of the generation of women who invited men out on dates and her own personal rules meant she should wait for him to get in touch with her. But he hadn't, and old-fashioned or not she knew she had to take the initiative and get in touch with him. She composed a text.

Sorry for being so hysterical. Can we meet and talk? Hope France was good and you found your stone. Love, L x.

She agonised only briefly about the correct text etiquette regarding crosses. She didn't know it, and although younger than her, she was fairly sure that Jack didn't know it either.

Having sent the text she was now in agony about whether or not he was going to reply. She went into the kitchen and began making comfort food: spaghetti with cheese, no vegetables, nothing healthy to go with it except wine. Fortunately Leo didn't like white wine and there was a bottle in the fridge.

When an hour had passed with no reassuring ting from her phone indicating Jack had replied she called Leo.

'Hi, love. I'm back. How are you?'

'Oh, hi, Mum! All good here. Good holiday?'

Lorna realised Leo didn't really know what was behind her sudden change of destination although he had been pleased, unmistakably, when she'd told him that she hadn't gone away with Jack. 'Really nice. I caught a bit of sun and the B and B was lovely.'

It had been an excellent B and B — just what she'd needed as a single person who needed to be alone but not isolated. She had someone to chat to if she needed, even if they never really got beyond the weather.

'You see I've moved out?' said Leo.

Lorna didn't comment on the detritus he'd left behind. 'Yes. So Kirstie and Peter found room for you in the house? You're not getting in their way?'

'Oh no. Anyway, Peter has gone away. Work as a consultant. The money too good to turn down apparently.' He paused. 'I've been helping Kirstie clear out. The house is absolutely full of stuff.'

'I know. Peter bought it like that. The previous owners just upped and left. It was one of the reasons it was such a bargain.'

'Of course. I'd forgotten you knew the house before Kirstie came.'

'Not everything is left over from the previous owners though,' said Lorna, suddenly worried. 'Quite a lot of it is Anthea's. When she downsized from the family home, she stored a lot of things in Burthen House. Don't let Kirstie throw anything away without checking with her first. In fact, you should invite Anthea to look through what you're clearing out, before anything actually leaves the house.'

'Oh.'

There was something a bit worrying about how he said this. 'Please don't tell me you've been chucking roomfuls of stuff into a skip?'

'Well, not whole roomfuls, but there have been some bonfires. Although everything has been real rubbish. I'll tell Kirstie. And actually, I'll have to go now. Kirstie is cooking me dinner.'

Later, as she ate her spaghetti, Lorna wondered if Leo and Kirstie were developing a relationship. She was quite a bit older than he was, but who was she to talk? Jack was quite a bit younger than her. And where did this leave Peter? Then she decided it wasn't her job to protect Peter's romantic interests while he was away. Not that long ago she'd have been delighted to think that Peter's younger-woman-off-the-internet was losing interest in her millionaire. But she discovered that although she had lost Jack (still no reply to her text) she didn't want Peter instead, even if he'd been offered to her.

Funny old thing, love, Lorna thought, pouring a second glass of wine. It was like a disease. You caught it, and then it went away, or it didn't. But there was no logic to it. You couldn't turn it on and off according to the suitability or otherwise of the love object.

Actually, it wasn't funny, it was really annoying.

★　★　★

The following morning, having taken a herbal sleeping pill and slept quite well, she had decided to be proactive. She would go and visit Jack at work. He hadn't replied to her text, and nor to the email she sent later.

She had to remind herself about a hundred times that she was an adult visiting another adult. It was a perfectly reasonable thing to do. In fact, to rely on technology and assume it always worked was foolish. Everyone knew that phones broke, or lacked signal or battery. But she still felt terribly anxious as she parked and walked to the abbey.

It was so different from the last time she'd visited with Jack. Although this time the ancient building was bathed in sunshine, in her heart all was darkness and dread. She didn't pause to admire her surroundings as she walked through and found the workshop.

Jack wasn't there. It took her a little time to get the attention of the young men who were chiselling and carving, using noisy tools. When finally she was able to ask where Jack was, they shook their heads. He was on a sabbatical, they said. And no, they didn't know when he was coming back. She hadn't wanted to ask if he was coming back. It would make her look even more foolish and needy than she already felt. And had the answer been no, she would have despaired.

It was only fifteen minutes later, but when she walked out of the church and through the town to where she'd parked her car she felt her whole life had changed. For the worse.

Before she met Jack she had been contented, if suffering with unrequited love for Peter. But her feelings for Peter now seemed so girlish, so amateur, compared to the deep yearning she had for Jack. It wasn't going to be easy to get herself back on track. But she would do it.

There was the garden in Burthen House — although the garden was now infected with memories of when Jack had been in it, what he'd said to her, how she'd felt.

There was her home, which she loved, even more now she was back in it and her beloved son was not. She was very lucky, she knew that. She had work she was good at and really enjoyed and which kept her fit; she had friends — not many but they were true friends. She lived in a lovely

221

part of the world. She was solvent, if not rich.

Sadly, the positive thoughts she had forced into her brain with such determination fizzled away when she saw Kirstie's car outside her house. When she discovered that Kirstie was actually inside, they were replaced by outrage and fear.

'Er — Kirstie?' Lorna said, holding on to her temper. 'Should I have been expecting you?'

Kirstie seemed put out but not as embarrassed as she should have been. 'No. Actually, I thought you were still away. Sorry to intrude.'

Hadn't Leo mentioned to her that his mother was home? Apparently not. 'So, can I help you?' Lorna's hard-wired rules of hospitality rebelled. She was not going to offer this woman coffee as if she'd been invited, or even just knocked on the door.

'I just want to look round,' said Kirstie, as if she had the right. 'I do think this place would make the ideal holiday cottage, don't you?'

'No, I don't,' said Lorna bluntly. 'I live here. And I'm not on holiday.'

'But you don't actually own it?'

'No. It's a tied cottage. It's part of my wages.' Anthea had been very insistent that Lorna was given somewhere nice to live. Lorna had been very grateful. Not having to buy a house meant she had some savings, so she could buy one when she retired.

'Oh, I see!' Then Kirstie became thoughtful. 'So I gather you didn't go to France with Jack?'

'No. I went to Salcombe. It was lovely,' she snapped. 'Does Peter know you're here?'

'He's away. He got a consultancy gig — money too good to refuse. I'm keeping an eye on things for him, looking after his assets. As you probably know, he's a bit idle about things like that.' She paused. 'I'm also doing a bit of clearing out, something he's also quite idle about. The house is full of junk, all left by the previous people.'

'I know. Peter and I saw the house together when he first considered buying the estate. I encouraged him,' she added. 'It's a lovely property.'

Something in her wanted to lay claim to Peter, not because she wanted him any more, but to make it clear to Kirstie that she and Peter had known each other all their lives. Peter would not throw her out of her cottage as long as she needed it.

She went on. 'And not all the 'junk' as you call it was there; a lot of the things are Anthea's. I was telling Leo. I do hope you haven't thrown away anything precious of hers.'

A flash of concern crossed Kirstie's features. 'Oh. I didn't realise that. But so far we've only got rid of real rubbish.'

'That's what Leo said, but you can't always tell what's rubbish and what's precious.' She gave Kirstie a warning look. 'Really, ask Anthea to come up and tell you what's hers. Peter would never forgive you if you upset his mother.'

Kirstie's anxiety appeared to increase. 'I really don't think we have chucked anything precious, but I will check.' She paused, obviously terrified of ringing up her potential mother-in-law and

223

revealing the possible destruction of precious possessions or her old school reports. She swallowed. 'I don't suppose you'd like to ask her?'

Lorna sighed. Kirstie was a bit crass but she had taken Leo in. 'OK,' she said. 'I'll need to ring her to tell her I'm back anyway. And thank you so much for finding space for Leo.'

Kirstie seemed relieved. 'Oh, that's no bother. He's been really helpful. He's been giving me all his spare time after he gets back from work.'

'Well, if you're giving him a roof over his head I'm sure it's the least he can do,' said Lorna, who really wanted to know if it was just Leo's handiness Kirstie was interested in. As a mother it was hard to tell, but she thought Leo was gorgeous. It was possible Kirstie did too.

'He's going to clear out the coach house. We're going to convert it to a holiday let, but Leo can have it for as long as he needs it.' She smiled. 'Just like you can have this place.'

'How kind,' said Lorna coolly. Really it wasn't up to Kirstie to say who could live where and for how long — at least until she was married to Peter.

Kirstie smiled apologetically. 'I'm sorry to have been here when you got home. I was really hoping you and Jack were going to get it together.' She shrugged. 'But I suppose there is a bit of an age gap. Anyway, I'll be off. You will give Anthea a call, won't you?'

* * *

Lorna had just been wondering if it would be a waste of time to sit down and have a good cry

224

when there was a knock on the door. It was Anthea. She was brandishing a bottle of champagne.

'Hello,' said Lorna. 'I was going to ring you to say I was back and to give you a message from Kirstie.'

'Seamus saw you arrive so no need. Can I come in? You get glasses.'

Lorna couldn't help smiling just a little at her friend's abrupt entry and abrupt instructions. 'What are we celebrating?'

'Nothing,' declared Anthea. 'Life is a pile of horse droppings for you just at the moment. What better reason to drink champagne?'

In spite of herself Lorna laughed. 'Well, before we get too drunk, I'd better tell you that Kirstie has called round. She wants me to ask you to go up to the house and identify your belongings. She and Leo are clearing things out. I warned her that some of them might be yours and she shouldn't until you've checked.'

'Thank you. I think I have all the things I really value at the Dower House, but I'd better check.' She paused. 'Oh, you've got lovely old-fashioned champagne saucers. Flutes are such a nuisance in the dishwasher, aren't they?'

Anthea extracted Lorna's tale of woe: how she'd come back and made herself go and see Jack at his stonemason's yard. Then, having heard that Jack was on indefinite leave, and wondering if it was because of her, she found Kirstie in her house, sizing it up as a holiday let.

'So I wonder if I should move away from all my humiliation and just start again,' said Lorna,

225

topping up their glasses.

'Definitely not. It's outrageous what Kirstie has been up to. Honestly! Seeing your home as a holiday let? I shall have words with that young woman!'

'Oh, no need. I think I made the situation perfectly clear. Now, we've finished the champagne, shall we move on to white wine?'

'Oh, why not!' said Anthea. 'I'll get Seamus to give me a lift home.'

★   ★   ★

The following morning, slightly fuzzy, Lorna had walked through the garden towards the steps where she and Anthea had agreed to meet and unexpectedly her heart had lifted a little.

Dew sparkled on the grass and the sun cast long shadows across it. It was looking glorious. The hasty plantings done before the garden being opened had settled in and were beginning to flower. Bright phlox, scarlet crocosmia and white tree poppies filled the borders. She loved the garden and wouldn't leave it just because of a man.

And it would be fine. She could go back to how she had been before Jack. It was only a couple of months of her life, after all. Easy enough to forget all about. All she had to do was put Jack out of her mind. But the trouble was, making that resolution just put Jack right back into the forefront.

Kirstie was there when Lorna arrived. 'I'm sure you won't find anything of value,' she was saying to Anthea, obviously still not sure how to address her, 'but if you'd like to check — '

'I'll volunteer for skip-diving,' said Lorna, forcing herself to sound upbeat.

'Great! So do you mind if I leave you to it?' said Kirstie, desperate to get away. 'Leo and I are going to source some statues to go on top of the plinths by the gate. There's a reclamation yard in Somerset that has some on their website.'

When permission to depart had been given, Anthea said, 'In my day one bought things, now apparently the word is 'source'.'

Lorna clambered towards the rim of the skip. 'Here, take this,' she said to Anthea. 'I don't know what's in here, maybe rubbish, but I like the folder.'

'What else is in there?' asked Anthea. 'I must say, I'm very tempted to get in too. People throw away such wonderful things.'

'Well, there's lots of what could be old pictures but they're unframed and grubby,' said Lorna.

'Oh, goodness,' said Anthea. 'Kirstie could have been throwing away works of art. Do I have to get in there?'

'Well, if you're up for it!'

Anthea was up the stepladder and over the top before Lorna could stop her.

Half an hour later, Lorna and Anthea were still flinging sheaves of old papers out of the skip, Anthea exclaiming with enthusiasm every time. At last the skip was empty and there was a huge pile of paper next to it.

'So, is there anything precious of yours we've rescued?' asked Lorna.

'Oh, none of this is mine,' said Anthea, reading something intently. 'But it is fascinating.'

'It's starting to rain,' said Lorna. 'What shall we do? Abandon it or try and get it into the dry?'

'Dry,' said Anthea. 'We can't afford to miss any of this.'

Lorna found she was enjoying heaving papers about — it was different from anything she usually did. They'd found some cardboard boxes and were filling them with papers, taking them into Burthen House, emptying the boxes and going back outside to rescue more papers from the increasingly heavy rain.

At last all was safe and, they hoped, not too damp. 'Tell you what,' suggested Anthea, brushing rain off her face with a casual arm. 'Let's look at them all, and the ones of no interest we can leave here to burn later.'

'Good idea, but didn't Kirstie say there was a whole bedroom full of stuff upstairs?' said Lorna. 'We should check none of it is yours before we start burning things.'

'True,' said Anthea, her gaze not lifting from the paper she was reading. 'This is an old plan of the house. We have to keep this.'

'Well, let's check upstairs,' said Lorna. 'Then we can stop for lunch. I'm quite hungry.' She was glad about this. Although she hadn't stopped eating, agonising about Jack had severely reduced her appetite.

'Seamus is making soup at my house,' said Anthea. 'Couldn't you go up and see what's in the bedroom? I'm too gripped by this to want to bother.'

'Well, what did you store here?' said Lorna. 'I don't know what's precious and what's not.'

'Furniture mostly. You go up. Leave me here. Then we'll have lunch.'

* * *

As Seamus thought 'a little glass of rosé' was the perfect accompaniment to soup, bread and cheese, they went back to the house feeling a bit more cheerful even if Lorna was yawning. But Anthea's blood was up. Her plans for sorting through the stuff in the skip were not to be put off by people being heartbroken or in need of naps.

Before they'd stopped for lunch they'd got everything upstairs to a bedroom which was large and would possibly have been the master had it not been for a huge damp patch in the ceiling with corresponding buckets on the floor. The water must have had to go through the attics and the upper storeys for it to have reached this level. If the roof needed doing, in a house this size, thought Lorna, it would be very, very expensive.

All around the bucket were boxes and crates of stuff. Some of it was newer, possibly from Anthea's old house, and some of it had obviously been in the house before. It was mostly papers, but some blanket boxes and chests too. Anthea was fixated on the papers, but Lorna preferred the boxes.

She'd just come across a large box of shells, all heaped together, all sorts and sizes, when Anthea

229

exclaimed, making Lorna turn quickly.

'Look! I've found it! I thought I might.'

'What? What have you found?' asked Lorna.

'A plan of the house and garden.' She gestured with her hand. 'Look out of the window. It's all there.'

Lorna hurried over. Anthea was holding the plan up and Lorna, having looked out of the window, burrowed in her pocket for her reading glasses. She scrutinised the plan for a couple of moments. 'Oh. I see what you mean. The plan must have been done from this level — possibly this room.' She paused. 'We can see everything,' she quietly thrilled. 'The whole garden and the Dower House.'

'Except the Dower House garden is much bigger than it is now,' said Anthea, frowning.

Something stirred in Lorna's memory. 'I've an idea I've seen something — when we were carrying papers upstairs. Something nearly slipped and I caught it.' She went to the corner where she'd dumped that particular load. 'Now I've seen the plan . . . ' Rapidly she riffled through the pile, flat now and easier to see. 'Here it is. It's a painting. Same view!'

She brought it to the window so Anthea could see it.

'Well,' said Lorna after a few seconds, 'the artist has either been in this room and painted the view or copied the plan and added detail.'

'Look at that little row of saplings,' said Lorna. 'Those must be the limes when they were planted. And now they're huge. And look at the Italian garden,' she went on. 'That's how it should be again, really. Although I was very pleased with the red, black and white garden.

'I do wonder what goes on behind all those self-sown ash and sycamore trees. On the plan there's a garden but I wonder if it was ever made? Is this a record of what was there then, or a plan for the future? You remember you asked me the other day and I didn't really care? Now I need to find out!'

Lorna laughed. 'So do I. I'll need some tools though, in case we need to hack our way through all that undergrowth.'

'You keep the tools in the stables, don't you?' said Anthea. 'Why don't I ring Seamus to pick us up?' Before she could do anything her phone started to ring.

'Seamus? I was just about to ring you!'

Then she didn't speak for a little while. Finally she said, 'I'm so sorry, Lorna, can we do this tomorrow? Seamus needs me. It's urgent!'

As she walked home Lorna reflected that she'd been aware that Anthea rang Seamus whenever she needed him. It was interesting, and pleasing, to know that it was reciprocal. If Seamus needed Anthea, he rang too. It was really sweet.

21

'Holy shit!' said Lucien, stepping on the brakes of the van.

Philly's eyes snapped open. Panic ripped through her. They were on their way home from Uncle Roderick's and she'd dozed off. Now she expected to see an oncoming lorry, tree or something that had made Lucien brake so hard and swear.

'What's the matter?' She realised they were very nearly in the lane that led only to their house.

'You see that car ahead? It's my parents.'

'Oh no.' Philly didn't feel like swearing, she felt like melting into the car seat and disappearing. She was going to meet Lucien's parents. This would have been an ordeal even if she'd had weeks to prepare, and not when she was travel-stained and grubby and wearing their son's ancient sweater. It couldn't be worse. She must look like a tramp he'd picked up on the side of the road.

Lucien didn't speak as he followed the Range Rover down the track. He veered off when it had been parked in front of the house and took the van round the back, where it usually lived.

'Roderick — or, more likely, Nanny — must have called them,' he said. 'Given them my address.' He glanced at Philly and grasped her hand. 'But it's going to be fine. We'll walk round to the front. Get to them before Seamus.'

As they walked round Philly realised that Seamus would be fine. He was good with people. Although she realised Lucien's parents probably weren't quite the same as normal people.

All too soon they were in front of the house and closing in on their uninvited guests. Lucien's mother was wearing cream-coloured slacks and had a navy jacket slung over her arm. To avoid making eye contact until she had to, Philly noticed she was wearing driving shoes with gold buckles. She was looking towards the front door so Philly could take note of her expertly highlighted caramel-coloured hair. She decided her look could be defined as casual, and very, very expensive.

Lucien's father was wearing pretty much the same as Roderick had worn — obviously the uniform of the upper middle classes: bright red cords and a V-necked cashmere sweater. Although, unlike Roderick, there were no signs of moth. He had very shiny brogues that were probably handmade.

All this meant that if her hand hadn't been tightly held, Philly would have run away and hidden in her polytunnel, where she felt safe.

'Hi!' said Lucien, at the same time as Seamus opened the door.

'Lucien!' said his mother. 'Darling!' She rushed forward and snatched Lucien to her, ignoring Philly. 'Thank God we've found you! I can't tell you how worried we've been!'

Lucien patted his mother. 'Come on, Ma. You've told me exactly how worried you've been every time I've called. Which has been quite often.'

'But we didn't know where you were!' his mother wailed. 'You could have been anywhere!'

'You knew I was in England, living perfectly happily, and not in a cult or anything.'

'We didn't know where in England.' She let go of Lucien and turned her attention to Philly. 'Is this the Irish girl?'

'I am Irish, yes,' said Philly, finding from somewhere the strength to speak. She didn't want Lucien to feel obliged to speak for her. 'My name is Philly, short for Philomena.' She held out her hand, unable to do anything about it being slightly sticky from the journey.

Lucien's mother took the very tip of her fingers. 'I'm Camilla Camberley.'

Lucien's father strode across. 'I'm Lucien's father,' he said.

Philly realised it was possible this was the only name he was willing to own up to.

'Now what's all this going on?' Seamus had opened the front door and was looking at the embraces and introduction questioningly.

Lucien got to the door. 'Seamus, these are my parents. Jasper and Camilla Camberley. Ma, Dad, this is Seamus, who's very kindly taken me in.'

His mother gave him a stricken look. 'Mr — I don't know your name — we've come to get our son back!'

Philly could tell her grandfather was amused and some of her tension went. He was brilliant in tricky social situations and this was definitely one of those.

'Sure, I didn't realise we were keeping him

under lock and key,' said Seamus, unabashed. 'Won't you come in now? We can't be having this sort of conversation on the doorstep.'

Philly mentally scanned the house. How tidy had she left it? Would it now be better or worse? The ghastly swirly wallpaper they'd never done anything about, the woodchip, the orange woodwork: Lucien's parents would see that and think it was their taste. She felt judged already.

Seamus ushered everyone into the sitting room. Seeing it through Lucien's parents' eyes, Philly thought it looked like something out of a sordid soap opera. There was another swirly carpet with not-quite-matching wallpaper, a huge, comfortable but very worn fake-leather sofa and armchairs, a dark oak sideboard covered with plant pots and motoring magazines. A very marked coffee table in front of the sofa bore witness to meals eaten in front of the television. It was just about as bad as it could be. She wanted to tell them they'd bought most of the furniture with the house, which was true.

'I'll make tea!' said Philly in the manner someone might say, 'I'll send for help!'

'No,' said her grandfather firmly. 'I'll make tea. You get to know the boy's parents.'

Philly didn't protest; she just hoped Grand had a cake ready to go. There weren't many situations not helped by cake.

'Do sit down,' said Philly, and was forced to watch as Camilla lowered herself to the sofa as if it were a dirty lavatory. At least Jasper, Lucien's father, just sat in the armchair.

'Lucien,' said his mother. 'We were so shocked

when Nanny called us.'

'Why?' said Lucien. 'What could she have possibly said to make you so shocked?'

'Well, for a start — ' His mother shot Philly a look. 'Is she pregnant?'

Philly gasped at this. Would she have said that if her grandfather had been in the room?

'No,' said Lucien, 'and she has a name. It's Philly, in case you've forgotten already. And I'm in love with her.'

Philly gasped again and turned a deep pink. She felt ridiculously pleased that he should be sticking up for her so firmly.

'Calm down,' said Jasper. He reached into his back pocket and withdrew his wallet. 'These things can be simple to fix, if you change your mind.'

Philly, who'd been hovering, felt her knees give way and then found herself sitting next to Camilla on the sofa.

'There's no need to be insulting,' said Lucien, white with anger. 'Maybe we should talk outside?'

'No!'

To Philly's relief, Camilla held up her hand. 'We need to speak to . . . '

'Philly,' supplied Lucien curtly.

His mother shook her head. 'We need to speak to Philly's grandfather. I'm sure this can be sorted out.' In spite of her calm words, Lucien's mother looked ashen.

'There's no need to sort anything out,' said Philly. 'Lucien is a free agent. We're not keeping him here. If he wants to go back to you, he will.'

'I don't want to,' said Lucien firmly.

'You have him under your spell,' hissed Camilla to Philly.

Fortunately for Philly, who would normally have laughed hysterically at the thought of having anyone under her spell, her grandfather came in with a tea tray.

Philly couldn't decide if his decision to use the best china was right. She didn't want Lucien's parents to think he'd made a special effort — they were so horrendously rude. On the other hand, various chipped mugs sporting a selection of advertising and bad jokes weren't really an option either. Thank goodness there was a very splendid coffee and walnut cake on the tray.

'I'll go and get the plates,' said Philly, without bothering to see if they were already on the tray, and fled.

By the time she came back into the room everyone had a cup of tea and Seamus had a knife in his hand.

'Now, Mrs Camberley, you'll have a piece of cake? I made it myself and I'd be offended if you didn't.'

Philly realised Lucien's mother probably never ate cake and wouldn't care about offending Seamus, and yet somehow she was saying, 'Well, only a very small slice. It looks delicious.' Seamus's Irish charm had worked its magic — as far as the cake went, anyway.

Jasper took a large slice without comment. When Seamus offered Philly a bit she shook her head. She felt as if she could never eat again.

To Philly it took forever and a day to get

237

everyone served with tea and cake. Eventually Seamus, who had taken charge, said, 'Now, what can we do for you good people?'

Camilla and Jasper exchanged glances. 'Basically, we want our son to come back home with us,' said Camilla.

'I'm not a possession,' said Lucien, icily calm. 'I make my own mind up about where to live.'

Jasper cleared his throat. 'I think we need to discuss this in private.' He glared at Philly and Seamus, possibly forgetting he was in their house and they weren't in his board meeting.

Seamus took charge of the situation. 'Come on now, Philly, we'll leave these people to their private conversation.'

★ ★ ★

'Oh, Grand!' said Philly when they were both in the kitchen sitting at the table. 'I can't bear it. They're going to take him away from me, I know they are.'

'Come now, darling. No need to panic. They can't do anything he doesn't want them to do.' He took her hand. 'Is it true what Lucien says? That you love each other?'

Philly nodded. 'Yes. He told me he loved me when we were on our way home.'

'And you feel the same?'

She nodded. 'I really do.'

'Then we must do what we can to keep you together.'

Philly sighed deeply. 'I don't suppose we can do anything. Those sort of people — they think they own the world and can arrange things just as they like.'

'Lucien's a very strong-minded boy. They won't bully him into doing anything he doesn't want to do. You mark my words.'

Philly heard a car. 'Oh God! Guests! That's the last thing we need.'

'That's not guests, that's the cavalry and the timing is perfect. I phoned Anthea when I went out to make the tea. She'll know how to handle these ghastly people.'

Still in her gardening clothes, Anthea swept into the house like an aristocratic hurricane. 'Hello, Philly' She kissed Philly's cheek in a casual way that Philly appreciated. It stated they were on the same side, even though they hadn't really been on kissing terms before.

Just as Philly realised they couldn't all go back into the sitting room with Anthea and say, 'This is our posh friend,' Lucien came out. He seemed crushed but determined, as if he'd been tortured but hadn't succumbed.

His parents followed, looking as if they'd achieved a pyrrhic victory: they'd won the battle but it was giving them no joy.

'Oh,' said Anthea, 'you have visitors. I should have telephoned before I came. I'm so sorry, Seamus!' She saw Lucien. 'Lucien! How are you? I haven't seen you for ages. I must say, I've seen you look perkier.'

'Anthea,' said Seamus. 'Let me introduce you to Lucien's parents. This is Mr and Mrs Camberley, Lady Anthea Leonard-Stanley.'

Anthea regarded the Camberleys through

239

slightly narrowed eyes. Then she held out her hand. Philly noticed that her scrutiny had put Lucien's parents on their mettle and that their social confidence had faded a bit.

Having shaken hands Anthea said, 'Have we met? You seem familiar to me, but maybe that's just your likeness to Lucien.' This time her narrowed gaze seemed more benign.

'It's possible,' said Camilla, obviously honoured by Anthea's suggestion that they knew each other. 'Do you go to the Standforths' garden party? Everyone I know always seems to be there.'

Anthea shook her head. 'Not for years, too far and too tiring. Don't worry, I'll think of it eventually. Seamus, darling, is it too much to ask for a cup of tea?'

'We were having tea in the sitting room,' said Philly, who felt she should show some hostessing skills however much she wanted to run away and hide in her polytunnel.

'Oh, not in that dreary room. The kitchen!' declared Anthea. 'Until you get rid of that furniture I just can't go in there. If only it wasn't so bloody cold we could sit in the garden. What has got into this weather?'

While Anthea behaved as if she was very much at home, Philly slipped into the sitting room to rescue the best china and the cake.

Lucien joined her in there and took her into his arms and hugged her hard. 'Oh God, Philly, what a nightmare!'

'Whatever happens between you and your parents, we'll make it OK,' she said, finding strength from his well-muscled arms being around her.

'We must stick together, Philly. They'll separate us if they can,' he whispered into her hair before kissing her hard.

22

By the time they'd gathered the tea things everyone was standing around and Seamus was pouring sherry but as they didn't have any sherry glasses, he was using Paris goblets instead.

'Grand!' Philly said as she came up beside him with the cake. 'You'll have them all under the table.'

'Best place for them,' he murmured and then handed a full glass to Camilla.

'I know it's not fashionable,' said Anthea loudly, obviously very happy with her knockout quantity of alcohol, 'but I like a glass of sherry about this time of day. Goes excellently with cake.'

'Actually sherry is quite fashionable,' said Lucien. 'Although gin is more so.'

'Well, if I'd known that,' said Anthea, laughing, 'I'd have gone for a G and T.' She took a large sip, and addressed Lucien's parents. 'Have you come to see how your boy is getting on? You must be very proud of him.'

'I don't know about that,' said Jasper. 'We haven't seen hide nor hair of him for nearly a year. The first couple of years after he left home he at least visited regularly.'

'He decided not to take up the very nice position we found for him in the City when he said he didn't want to go to university but go off and be a cook instead.' Camilla was obviously

242

very disappointed by her son's career choice.

'But he's so good at it!' said Anthea. 'Have you never eaten his cooking?'

'I have,' said Camilla, 'but really, cooking isn't a proper career, is it?'

Lucien's mouth compressed into stubbornness.

'I think you don't know how good he is at it,' said Seamus quickly. 'I think if you stayed for dinner — '

'What a good idea!' said Anthea. 'I do hope I'm invited.'

'Of course,' said Seamus. 'You're always more than welcome.'

Philly noticed Lucien's mother looking between Anthea and Seamus and wondering what on earth Anthea, who was a 'lady' officially as well as socially, was doing among such people. She didn't blame Camilla for being confused; she was quite surprised herself at the friendship that was blossoming between her car-mechanic grandfather from Ireland and an aristocratic woman such as Anthea. But they did seem to make each other happy.

'I don't think we can stay' said Camilla. 'We've got quite a long way to go back.'

'There's a very nice B and B in town,' said Anthea. 'I'm sure you don't want to miss this opportunity to see what your talented son can do.'

'We can see what he's done,' said Camilla. Then she stopped suddenly as if she'd realised she'd been about to say her son had got himself involved with a girl who had an accent. It

243

wouldn't have mattered what kind of accent it was. Lucien's future wife had to share the tortured vowels of the rest of the family.

'Why don't we stay for dinner, darling?' Jasper said to Camilla. 'You can drink. I'll drive home.'

As he'd recently consumed about a tumblerful of sherry, Philly thought that his ship had sailed, but it was none of her business.

'Run along then.' Camilla addressed Philly directly. 'You'd better go with Lucien and help him.'

Philly smiled. 'Actually Lucien can manage perfectly well without me but I do have to go and check on my plants. See you guys later!'

As she fled in the direction of her polytunnels she wondered at herself. Where did 'See you guys later' come from? She realised she wanted to make herself seem as dreadful as possible in front of Lucien's parents, just to spite them. Although she knew really she was only spiting herself.

★　★　★

Philly felt soothed when she came back to the house. Time spent with plants that didn't judge, or criticise, and responded to care even if they didn't really love you, made you feel a lot calmer.

Camilla and Jasper had been taken off by Anthea to see Peter's garden, which now included a couple of sculptures that hadn't been there before. Lucien had taken over the kitchen.

'Hi,' said Philly, seeing at a glance that he had used every saucepan in the place. Although he

244

was a tidy cook, there was a lot of equipment. 'Need a kitchen porter?'

He caught her round the waist and kissed her swiftly. 'I'd love one. And I love you — you do know that? And I wouldn't have put you through all this for anything.' He put his arms round her and hugged her to him. This turned into quite a long kiss.

'I'd have had to meet them sometime,' said Philly a little later.

'If we're going to be a couple, you mean? Does this mean we are going to be a couple?' He wrapped himself round her again. 'Mm?' he prompted. 'Put me out of my misery.'

Philly laughed. She felt so happy, in spite of his parents. 'Of course we're going to be a couple. We're a couple already.'

Lucien felt obliged to seal this with a kiss and it was only catching sight of the kitchen sink over his shoulder that made Philly break away. 'We'd better not do this now,' she said. 'You've got your parents to cook for. What are you making?'

A quick look told her it wasn't what his parents would no doubt describe as 'kitchen sups'. This would be 'Fine Dining' with a capital 'F' and 'D'. She started emptying the sink of dirty saucepans and running the hot tap.

Lucien pushed his hair back from his forehead. 'I thought I'd keep it simple. Start with a parfait; that's in the freezer, chilling. Then a good old beef Wellington, using what Seamus probably meant to have for Sunday lunch. Didn't have time to make make my own pastry but you had some in the freezer. Then for

245

pudding, a chocolate roulade. All pretty simple, really.'

Philly couldn't help smiling, mostly because she was so happy and loved him so. 'I thought you'd push the boat out a bit, for your parents,' she said.

It took him a few seconds to realise she was joking. 'They don't deserve to have the boat pushed out.' He frowned, looking worried. 'They'll bully us if we let them.'

Concerned by his stern look, Philly said, 'Then we won't let them.'

* * *

Anthea reappeared with Lucien's parents at eight o'clock. She also brought some very good wine that Peter had given her. Lucien rejected Philly's suggestion that they put it in the microwave to get it up to temperature and he decanted it instead. It wasn't necessarily noticeable that he poured the wine into the jug that usually contained the flowers Philly put on their stall to make it look pretty.

'Right,' said Seamus from the head of the table, 'let's get the wine going. Jasper? Would you mind seeing to that side of the table? Save me reaching across.'

'Hmm,' said Camilla, narrowing her eyes at the wine her husband was pouring. 'Unless I'm much mistaken that's a flower vase. Have you slipped up, Lucien?'

'Certainly he hasn't,' said Seamus firmly. 'It's a tradition of the house that we serve wine in a flower vase. Isn't it, Philly?'

Philly coughed assent and held out the butter to Camilla. She'd found a butter curler in the drawer full of kitchen utensils and had created a pile of golden curls that, according to her grandfather, wouldn't have shamed Shirley Temple — whoever she was.

'Oh, how retro!' said Camilla. 'I was taught to make these at finishing school.' She glanced at Philly as if she realised that Philly must have worked out how to make them herself, as she would never have been sent off to Switzerland to acquire polish.

'Have we got a drink now? Anthea, m'dear, are you only having half a glass?'

'I'm driving, Seamus,' said Anthea sternly.

'In which case, I won't drink myself and drive you back. Now, everyone?' He raised his glass, determined to lighten the atmosphere. 'To our wonderful chef, Lucien.'

'Time will be the judge as to whether he's wonderful,' said Jasper tersely.

'He is wonderful, take it from me,' said Seamus, losing his bluff Irish charm for a minute.

'He really is,' said Anthea. 'And I'm not remotely involved so wouldn't say it if it weren't true. Now, let me tell you, the big clear-out Kirstie is having up at the house could be getting out of hand.' She turned to Jasper and Camilla. 'I showed you the stacks of papers and piles of furniture? All destined for the skip!'

'De-cluttering is very fashionable at the moment,' said Camilla.

Anthea sniffed. 'It can go too far,' she stated. 'And I can't help wondering if that girl has got her feet a bit too well under the table.'

Camilla nodded. 'She did give the impression she owned the place,' she said to Anthea. 'It must be heartbreaking for you to see your son under the thumb of someone like that.' Then she glanced at Philly, frowned and picked up her wine glass.

Anthea tossed her head dismissively. 'Peter's quite capable of looking after himself,' she said. 'Lucien? This pâté is really rather good. I like the toast.'

'I made the bread myself,' Lucien said meaningfully.

'Back in the day we made Melba toast,' said Camilla. 'Rather fun!'

'Did you learn that at finishing school along with the butter curls?' asked Philly, sounding innocent but feeling she was having a dig.

'Yes. Cooking in the morning, other things in the afternoon,' Camilla explained and then turned to her son. 'So, how was Nanny, darling? She always adored you! We always knew you were safe when you were with her. And you adored her back.'

'Really? What I most remember is her truly horrible cooking and how miserable her portion sizes were. I had to go into the kitchen and beg for snacks.'

'Oh, surely not — ' Camilla interjected.

'And she cut my fingernails far too short and they hurt for days,' said Lucien. 'Anyone want more parfait?'

'Never thought I'd hear those words spoken in anger,' muttered Seamus.

Anthea reached across the table and took another piece of toast. 'Lorna's son was with Kirstie. Helping her sort things out.'

'How did she and Jack get on in France?' asked Philly.

'She didn't actually go to France,' said Anthea, 'she went to Salcombe. But I'm sure you'll find out soon enough. She wasn't with Jack.'

This was a shock, but as it wasn't a topic for general conversation Philly looked around the table to see if people had finished. 'I'll clear now, shall I?' she asked, the waitress in her surfacing.

'Oh no,' said Anthea, 'we'll all just pass our plates along.'

'I'll help Lucien, then.'

For someone who was just cooking dinner for his parents, eating in the kitchen with wine served from a flower vase, Lucien took a lot of time plating up.

Fortunately, trained by her grandfather, Philly had the plates red-hot. She watched as he carefully sliced the Wellington, cutting through the pastry, the layer of Parma ham, the finely chopped mushrooms, and finally the beef. 'Perfect,' he said as he saw the middle was exactly as he wanted it.

This much, Philly understood. It was the obsessive placing she found a bit irritating. When she saw him blobbing on the gravy and pulling out the blob into an exclamation mark, she got impatient. 'For God's sake! Just get it on the plate!'

But he wouldn't be hurried. The game chips were propped into a pyramid and the mash put into a perfect pile.

'At least you haven't got the piping bag out,' said Philly. 'Are these ready to go now?'

'We need carrots — '

'We'll just put them in a dish with the extra potatoes. Now come on! It's only family!'

'They're testing me, Philly,' he said grimly. 'I need to make sure I pass.'

She could see how hard he was concentrating on making it perfect and her heart went out to him. She had trouble with her own parents, but at least she knew they really loved her. Lucien's parents didn't make this at all clear. They wanted him to do well, but on their terms. 'Of course you'll pass,' she said briskly. 'You're amazing.'

★ ★ ★

The beef Wellington was eaten, the roulade served. Philly thought it was perfect but although when she said so others joined in, its chocolatey-lightness couldn't dispel the atmosphere of impending doom.

'We need to have a talk, Lucien,' said Jasper, possibly irritated because he wasn't drinking and people around him were.

'Why don't you go into the office?' Seamus suggested.

'And put the heater on if you need to,' added Philly.

Anthea and Camilla discussed mutual acquaintances over coffee while Philly and Seamus did their best with the clearing up. The food had been wonderful, but the quantity of saucepans and crockery was too much for the dishwasher, in spite of Philly washing up at half-time during the cooking.

While she washed and wiped and found homes for things, she worried. Would Jasper, impressed by his favourite meal being produced, produce some funding in return?

Eventually he and Lucien came out of the office. 'Come on, Camilla. We're going home,' Jasper said curtly. 'I can't get the boy to see sense.'

Lucien looked grimmer than his father did, which was saying something. Philly took his arm and drew him to one side. 'What happened?'

'It's quite simple, m'dear,' said Jasper, sounding patronising and overbearing at the same time. 'I know Lucien was depending on Roderick for backing but I'd rather do it myself.'

'Would you do that?' asked Philly.

Jasper inclined his head. 'Under certain conditions. If Lucien wants me to back him in this ridiculous bakery project, he's got to show commitment. That means coming back home, working for a real baker and really learning his craft. And ending his relationship with you.' He bared his teeth. 'No offence, but if he wants to set up a business he can't be distracted by women. Even if they are pretty' He shot Philly a look implying this was not meant as a compliment.

'And I refused,' said Lucien. 'The conditions are unacceptable. I'll get backing from somewhere else.'

'Well, you won't get it from Roderick,' said Jasper, glaring at him. 'He promised me he wouldn't give you money. He completely understood I wanted to be the one you owed money to and no one else.' He paused. 'I think you'll find that if I refuse to back you, no one will.'

Philly felt sick. 'Lucien? Come with me to the garden. We need to talk.'

'We're not waiting for you,' said Camilla. 'I want to get home.'

'I'm not dependent on you for transport,' said Lucien. 'I've got my van.'

'Come on, Lucien.' Philly took hold of his arm.

It was lovely to get out of the house, away from the dominating presence of Lucien's parents. Philly breathed in the scent of honeysuckle for a moment and then took hold of Lucien's hand.

'Listen,' she said urgently, gripping on to him and looking up at him. 'If they're prepared to back you, set you up in a bakery, you've got to accept.'

'No! Not if it means giving you up. Dad just can't understand that. To him business has always been more important than people — than love.'

Philly bit her lip, suddenly fighting tears. 'But they can't keep you prisoner for ever. When your business is up and running — or even before — I'll come and join you. You can't give up this amazing opportunity because of me.'

'You've got your business here. You can't give

that up for me just because my vile father has other ideas,'

'I could start another nursery somewhere else — '

'No, darling,' He was more gentle now. 'Your life is here. I'm not tearing you away from everything you've built up. And I want mine to be here too.' He sighed. 'I tried to explain to Dad how perfect it is — even apart from you — but he wouldn't have it. I won't go!'

Philly gulped. 'Go with him now. Do what he wants you to do. Work for a baker. Show him commitment. Then we'll try and work round the other stuff. Seriously Lucien. I want you to do this!'

'You don't understand! He won't let us keep in touch. If I go we're saying goodbye for months possibly. I can't do that.'

Philly screwed up her eyes to stop the tears and so she couldn't see him, because she knew if she could she wouldn't have the courage to say what she knew she had to. 'We're young, Lucien. We've got the rest of our lives to spend together. Take this opportunity — you may not get another one.'

Lucien sighed sharply. 'My father thinks if we don't have contact with each other I'll forget about you. But I won't! I never could!'

'Then we must prove him wrong,' said Philly desperately, through her tears. 'We must prove that our love will survive this. Do what they want, get the backing you need; we'll make it work somehow.'

'Oh God . . . ' he said hoarsely.

They clung on to each other until eventually they heard a voice. It was Seamus.

'Philly? Lucien's parents need a decision.'

'Go!' she said.

He cupped her face with his hand for a second and then turned and walked back to the house.

'Are you all right, little one?' said Seamus.

Philly nodded. 'It's not as if he's going to war or anything.' Then she threw herself into her grandfather's arms and sobbed.

23

There was nothing like a new project for raising the spirits, thought Lorna, checking the back of her car for missing tools that she might need at Anthea's. While Jack was a constant presence, a nagging ache, having the extra bit of Anthea's garden to focus on gave her conscious brain something positive to focus on.

Most of her gardening tools had gone ahead but she was adding things like twine, secateurs, loppers, a selection of pruning saws, some plastic sacks and gardening gloves in several weights, include Kevlar ones for brambles. She was already wearing thorn-proof overtrousers. She'd made a batch of chocolate brownies and some flapjacks as well as a flask of coffee.

'It's like going on safari,' she muttered as she set off. 'I just need a couple of pith helmets and a compass and I'll be all set.'

While she was laughing at herself she did feel it was a bit of a journey into the unknown and she relished it. She wanted to get so physically tired that she'd be able to sleep, and not be kept awake by 'if only' thoughts about Jack.

Anthea was waiting for her; she too was geared up for a good battle with nature, and nature would not win, Lorna decided, not this time.

'Morning, Lorna!' Anthea called. 'Philly will be over soon. I'll let her tell you all about it but

Seamus rang first thing asking if we could use her.'

Lorna got the impression that Anthea knew more about 'it' than she was letting on and was cross about whatever 'it' was. 'It's brilliant that she wants to come. We need all the help we can get. Oh — here she is.'

Philly came over, dumping her own selection of tools in the wheelbarrow that already held Anthea and Lorna's. 'Hi.' She looked as if she'd been crying all night. Her eyes were pink and puffy and matched her nose.

'Oh, darling!' said Lorna, unable to help herself. 'You look awful. What's wrong?'

Philly shrugged. 'I sent Lucien away. He went back to his parents. We won't see each other for months.'

Lorna was astounded. 'Why? He's lovely! How could you send him away?'

'He is lovely' Philly agreed. 'But his parents aren't. They won't back his business unless he demonstrates he can do it and doesn't see me until he has proved himself.' She shrugged. 'It's not that unreasonable but they were so vile about it. And, really, I don't think it's to do with him. I think they might back him right now if I wasn't in the picture. They really want to separate us.' She cleared her throat as if tears might come again. 'But they won't. Not forever. So, shall we get on?'

'Good idea,' said Lorna. 'Where shall we start? We should probably get rid of the saplings first?'

'We need a chainsaw,' said Philly. 'Grand's got

one. Will I ring him and ask him to come over with it, Anthea?'

'Or get a tree surgeon?' suggested Lorna.

Philly and Lorna looked at Anthea, waiting for an answer.

Anthea shook her head. 'No. I don't want to wait for a tree surgeon and Seamus kindly offered to help but I want us to do this ourselves. This is our adventure.'

'But what about the trees?' objected Lorna. 'It'll take us ages to saw them all down.'

'We could borrow the chainsaw,' said Philly, 'but I don't think we should, not if we're not qualified to use it.'

'It's fine,' said Anthea crisply. 'I have a chainsaw and I'm qualified to use one.'

'How come?' said Lorna. Philly was too surprised to speak.

Anthea made a dismissive gesture. 'Oh, a couple of years ago Peter gave me a voucher to do a course at this rather nice place. When I tried to book one everything was full up except crochet and chainsawing.'

'Goodness,' said Lorna, hoping this was a suitable response.

'I know it sounds a bit eccentric but I thought chainsawing would come in handy' said Anthea, as if it had been an obvious thing to do. 'And so it's proved. I'd better get kitted up.'

'Typical of Anthea to prefer a chainsaw course to crochet,' said Philly while she and Lorna were waiting. 'But what are we here for? Grand just told me to get over here and be prepared for hard work.'

'Anthea and I were at Burthen House, going through all the things that Kirstie had decided should be thrown away. We came across an old painting of the garden done from an upstairs room — probably the room we were actually in at the time, which was rather exciting.'

'And?' prompted Philly when Lorna stopped for breath.

'There are also plans. There seems to be a garden behind Anthea's current garden that no one was aware of. But a lot of self-seeded ash trees and sycamores have grown up around it over the years. Some of them are really big, in which case we'll have to leave them. But Anthea is determined to investigate it.'

Philly nodded. 'And why didn't you go to France with Jack?'

Taken by surprise Lorna said, 'Oh — well — something happened — or at least it had happened ages ago . . . I changed my mind. I didn't want to go.'

'Would you rather not talk about it?'

Lorna shrugged. 'I feel such a fool.'

'I'm sure there's no need.'

'I'll tell you about it when I don't feel so stupid. You'll probably laugh.'

Philly shrugged. 'I could do with a laugh. Life's a bit bleak just now. For at least three months, maybe even six.'

'Oh, Philly. OK, I'll make you laugh,' and she told Philly about the drawing and how embarrassed it made her feel.

'Actually that's not funny' said Philly when

Lorna had finished her tale. 'I think I'd feel weird about it too.'

Lorna sighed. 'I think Anthea thinks I'm being ridiculous.'

Before Philly could respond, Anthea appeared.

She looked, Lorna thought, rather like a Lego figure. She was carrying a chainsaw and fully kitted up in Kevlar protective clothing. This involved a helmet, gloves, overtrousers and big boots. She heard Philly snort and suddenly felt like giggling herself. It was funny! There was an awful moment when she thought she might find herself in hysterics at a woman in her seventies wearing protective clothing. She bit her lip.

Anthea removed the helmet. 'It's all right, you can laugh. I won't wear all this, I don't suppose. My generation doesn't believe in health and safety; we all think it's fine for a child to suck on a nice bit of lead-based paint, but they made you buy all the kit on the course.'

Lorna realised Anthea had put it all on to cheer them up. It had worked. But instead of stifled guffaws they now just smiled and felt better. 'It would be a shame not to use it, if you've got it. But has the saw got fuel in it?'

Anthea nodded. 'I checked all that first thing. Now, let's get going!'

★   ★   ★

Quite a few of the trees were too big for Anthea's starter-model chainsaw, so they left those after Lorna had put a dab of paint on the ones they thought should go. The smaller ones, Anthea

259

attacked with determination. They soon developed a technique that meant the saplings were despatched quickly and safely. As their confidence grew, they took on some of the larger ones. Anthea did tire though and, having watched her do it quite a lot of times, Philly donned the protective clothing and took over the chainsaw.

They finally reached an old wall, swathed in generations of ivy, traveller's joy and brambles. Lorna caught the whiff of honeysuckle and spotted a wild hop.

'I wonder how long all this has been here,' she said.

'Could be hundreds of years, could be far less,' said Anthea. 'I don't know how to tell. But it's all coming off. I wonder whether we will find a door. It looks like the type of wall that might have a door.'

'Oh, like in *The Secret Garden!*' said Philly, who, Lorna noted, was looking far more cheerful after her stint on the chainsaw. 'I loved that book as a child.'

'I still do love it,' said Lorna.

'Hmm,' said Anthea, less sentimental. 'I seem to remember there was a key involved to that particular secret garden. If we find a locked door we haven't an earthly chance of finding the key for it. We'll have to knock it down.'

'We can do that,' said Philly. 'We're hardcore!' Then she stopped. 'Sorry. It's this Kevlar clothing. It's gone to my head.'

'It'll probably be rotten but there must be a door,' said Lorna, 'and it'll probably be in the middle of the wall. I think that's where we should start looking.'

She retrieved her loppers from the wheelbarrow, went to where she judged was the middle, reached up as high as she could and snipped a line of brambles, strands of ivy and some traveller's joy. While she gathered them up to get them out of the way, Anthea and Philly took her place. Lorna had just decided they should start a bonfire when Anthea said, 'Found it!'

There was the door, roughly where Lorna had thought it would be. It was quite high and wide and was arched.

'And it's not locked,' said Philly excitedly. 'In fact it's ajar.'

'It's just a shame it's got several hundred years' worth of undergrowth behind it stopping us opening it enough to actually get through it,' said Anthea.

'I think we should have a coffee break,' said Lorna. 'And then we'll get the door open. Or down.'

Anthea found a stump to perch on as she sipped coffee from Lorna's flask and ate a flapjack. Philly and Lorna had theirs standing up. Although glad of the coffee, Lorna was itching to get on. She sensed Philly was too.

'I was thinking maybe we should have a bonfire,' said Lorna. 'It'll be fairly smoky as lots of the stuff is green but we're quite far from other houses so it shouldn't bother anyone.'

'There's a by-law, I think,' said Philly. 'It has to be after six o'clock.'

'Oh, nonsense!' said Anthea. 'We'll have a bonfire and if anyone complains we'll put it out. But you're right, Lorna. We're too far away from anyone's washing to get smuts on it. Once we're through the door, I'll get what we need to start it.'

Getting through the door took some effort, mostly because they couldn't get to the roots of the plants that were preventing it opening away from them. When there was a gap big enough, Lorna squeezed through to the other side.

'What's it like through there?' asked Anthea, obviously desperate to see it for herself.

'Hang on. I'll get rid of a bit of this jungle so I can open the door a bit more.'

Soon she had forced a gap wide enough for Anthea to get through and Philly followed.

'Oh my word,' said Anthea eventually after the three women had surveyed the scene. 'It really is a secret garden, but it's also a jungle.'

Just then the sun came out and changed everything. 'It's magical,' said Lorna softly.

And it was. It was silent apart from birdsong, and the light coming through the trees turned everything green. While most of what surrounded them was wild and thorny there was still a sense of peace.

'It's going to be wonderful,' said Philly. 'But it'll be a lot of work.'

'And we might need more help,' said Lorna.

'Then we'll get more help,' said Anthea. 'But are you two up for helping me restore it?'

'Abso-bloody-lutely!' said Philly and everyone laughed.

They didn't hang around admiring the tranquillity for long. They fetched the wheelbarrow full of equipment and soon every cutting tool was in use. Philly started a bonfire and every so often, when they couldn't move for pulled-down brambles, ivy, young trees and elders, they gathered up the detritus and piled it on the fire.

'We should compost some of this really' said Lorna.

'Not at all,' said Anthea, sounding a bit like Seamus. 'We'd have to put it through a chipper first and there's too much.'

'Well, we can heap up the softer stuff in piles as we go and decide what to do with it later.' She brushed her hair back from her face. 'Is it time for another break?'

'Hope so,' said Philly. 'Grand has sent a cake.'

'I need lunch not cake,' said Anthea. 'At least, I'd like a sandwich first. Shall I go and make sandwiches or do you want to come in, wash and have a rest and a drink while I do so?'

There was no doubt about what the right answer was and Lorna gave it. 'We'll carry on if you're happy to bring us the sandwiches here.'

Although they were carrying on in theory, Lorna and Philly did take a break.

'I wonder what this garden was for?' asked Philly. 'Why would there be a garden separate from the rest of the house?'

'Women — at least those who could afford them — have always had gardens as places of sanctuary, to pray in, or just to get away from male oppression,' said Lorna. 'I read a book about it once. It was fascinating. I must try and find it so you can read it too.'

'I can imagine if you were a great lady who always had to be doing things it would be wonderful to have somewhere you could be private.' Philly frowned. 'But would the great ladies have done the actual weeding and stuff? Or would they have had gardeners to do it?'

Lorna shrugged. 'I expect they'd have had men to do the heavy lifting.'

'There's something to be said for that,' said Philly. 'Anthea is inexhaustible! She was amazing last night, with Lucien's parents.'

'Tell me about it?' Not only was Lorna desperately curious, she sensed Philly needed to talk about it.

Philly sighed and propped her foot on a fork she'd stuck under a bramble root that possibly went down to Australia. 'One day I'll think it was quite funny. Even now, part of me does.'

Lorna nodded encouragingly.

'Lucien and I just got back from visiting his godfather and the scariest nanny ever.'

'Lucien's godfather had a nanny?' Very disturbing images involving grown men in nappies flitted into Lorna's head.

'No! She was Lucien's nanny. But now she's looking after his godfather, Roderick. He puts up with her but her cooking is dreadful and she hardly gives him anything to eat. She tries to restrict his drinking too, but he's quite cunning about that.'

264

'Sorry, I've missed a bit. Why did you and Lucien go there?'

'To see if Roderick would lend Lucien enough money for him to set up his bakery. But Evil Mary Poppins, as I called her, must have got on to Lucien's parents the moment we'd left and they were waiting for us at home when we got there.'

'Oh, love, I don't think that sounds funny at all. It sounds a nightmare.'

'It was a nightmare. The funny part was how dreadful they were and how desperately shabby our house is with the swirly carpets and enormous sofas with the stuffing coming out of them.' Philly shrugged. 'You know what it's like. Only we've got used to it and have other things on our minds than making it more civilised.'

Lorna nodded. Philly and Seamus's house wasn't remotely elegant but it was their home and she felt prickly at the thought of people being snooty about it. 'Were they appallingly snobbish?'

Philly nodded. 'Grand sent for Anthea and I must say she was a great help. Although eventually, nothing worked. They told Lucien he had to go home with them if he wanted backing. He refused. But I made him leave.'

Her voice faltered a little and she stopped.

'That was the right and brave thing to do,' Lorna said. 'If you two can prove you can survive being apart for a while, his parents will come round to the idea of you and probably adore you in the end.' This was how it was supposed to

265

work out anyway, Lorna thought, and with luck it would.

Anthea arrived with the picnic. It involved packets of smoked salmon sandwiches, flasks that turned out to have gin and tonic in them, and Seamus's cake and a knife.

'Let's find somewhere more comfy to eat this,' suggested Anthea. 'Look, there are some stones in there we could perch on.'

They were chewing happily when Lorna said, 'I think these are plinths that we're sitting on.'

'Oh yes!' said Philly. 'And you can just see what might be the statues to go on them under all that ivy' She pointed with her sandwich.

Anthea nodded. 'So what's that huge heap? It's like a creature from outer space, only covered with greenery.'

'I've been thinking about that,' said Lorna. 'I think it might be a grotto.'

'Wow!' said Philly.

'That would be terrific,' said Anthea. 'But what makes you think that?'

'If this is a secret garden, belonging to the lady of the house — or, more likely, the lady of the Dower House — it might well have had a grotto.'

Anthea swallowed. 'Well, come on, girls. Hurry up with your lunch. We need to investigate.'

Lorna stopped wondering if a strong gin and tonic at lunchtime was a mistake as, with Philly and Anthea, she tore at the greenery that covered what might be a grotto. There were brambles as thick as hawsers tangled up with ivy that brought fragments of stone with it as they tugged at the mass of vegetation. At last they were able to stop.

'It's definitely a grotto,' said Anthea. 'How absolutely splendid.'

'That explains all those shells we found in Burthen House!' said Lorna excitedly. 'They used to ship them back from the West Indies by the barrel load.'

'Really?' asked Philly. 'Why?'

'Shell-work was a suitable occupation for women. And the ships were coming back empty,' said Lorna.

'So if the grotto is damaged, we can repair it,' said Anthea.

'If you can do shell-work,' said Lorna, teasing. 'You've probably done a course on it.'

'It can't be hard, if it's a suitable occupation for women,' said Anthea.

'What about the statues?' asked Philly. 'Can we repair them? I had a closer look a bit earlier and they could be really lovely except there seems to be bits of them missing.'

'Let's go and look,' said Anthea, and stepped nimbly over the tangles of greenery to where Philly had pointed.

'Their middles aren't there. They look a bit sad without them,' said Philly after they'd pulled away the vegetation. 'But they must have been really beautiful, don't you think, Lorna?'

Lorna was aware the others were looking at her oddly. 'Yes. Really beautiful originally. But they're no good with the mid-section missing. It would take ages for anyone to make new torsos. Probably not worth doing.'

Anthea frowned at her. 'Not like you, Lorna. You're a great recycler.'

267

Lorna made a gesture, wishing she could explain how she felt about the broken statues. She went for honesty. 'The thing is,' she said bluntly, 'they remind me of Jack. It's the sort of thing he deals with as a stonemason. I loved this space being man-free.'

Anthea studied her again for a few seconds. 'Very well. We won't repair them. I'll get Seamus to take them out of here and this can be a man-free space again.'

Feeling she'd got a result she hadn't worked hard enough for, Lorna smiled faintly. 'Thank you so much for being so understanding, Anthea.'

'I can be, you know,' she said. 'Now, I'm going in to put the kettle on and get in touch with Peter. I need to tell him this garden might be quite expensive to restore.'

'He won't like that!' said Lorna, somewhat aghast.

'He will,' said Anthea confidently. 'It can be my birthday present. He never knows what to get me, hence the chainsaw course. I might even let it be my Christmas present too.'

Watching her make her way towards the house, Philly said, 'It may have to be several years' worth of birthday presents.'

'I know. But if he's happy to pay, I'd be delighted. It's a wonderful project. It will really help to take our minds off our miserable love lives.'

Anthea turned back. 'I've had a brilliant idea!' she called. 'We can have my birthday party here!'

Lorna gasped, frantically trying to remember

when Anthea's birthday was.

Fortunately, Philly, who couldn't possibly know, asked the question. 'When is your birthday, Anthea?'

'Ages away! The sixteenth of September.'

'But, Anthea!' Lorna was horrified. 'By next year, certainly, it'll be lovely, but look at what a state it's in now!'

Anthea gave the surrounding flattened greenery, fallen trees and heaps of brambles a cursory glance. 'Oh come on,' she said bracingly. 'We can do it. We'll throw money at it. Or better, we'll get Peter to throw money at it. Think how brilliantly you got the house's garden up to scratch for the sculpture show!'

Lorna swallowed and then began to laugh weakly. Anthea was not a woman to accept excuses. 'It will be a lot of money, Anthea. We'll have to buy heaps of stuff — most of it really — full-grown.'

Philly nodded. 'But I might be able to help out there.'

'Good-oh. I'm glad you've accepted the challenge. You know what? Never mind the kettle. I think we all need another very large gin.'

24

Philly was in the secret garden admiring all the work that had been done since its discovery early in the summer. She hadn't been able to sleep and had got up and gone straight to the garden. It was really early — about daybreak — and Lorna probably wouldn't be there for a couple of hours yet. She was alone, making notes of plants she still needed to source for Anthea's big day.

Now September was adding red and gold to the fields and trees and in the garden blocks of colour took the place of elder, sycamore and brambles. The birthday was less than two weeks off and the garden was very far from completed.

Although, if she hadn't felt so sad all the time, she'd have been full of satisfaction for what they had achieved, which was immense.

She thought back to that first day, when the three women, including Anthea in Kevlar, were hacking through the jungle. They'd made some discoveries apart from the grotto and the statues that Lorna had wanted to get rid of. There had been several climbing roses. Lorna had cut them right back and fed them, watered them, possibly read poetry to them and they'd responded with strong new shoots. Next year, with luck, they'd begin to flower again. There had been some specimen trees that were beginning to show autumn colour. Sumach, with long pointed leaves, which had sent up suckers all over the place, was now under control and flame red. A ginkgo with fan-shaped leaves was turning yellow. There were some Japanese maples that were also tinged with scarlet.

The three women hadn't done it all on their own. Seamus, Leo and various other young men with muscles had been brought in for some of the heavier work.

One of the walls of the grotto had collapsed and emptying the fallen soil, which included quite a lot of the ceiling, had been a big job. Whenever the weather was too bad for gardening, Lorna had taken a camping lantern into the grotto and replaced the shells.

They'd also made a proper path from Anthea's original garden through to this one. The gate had been repaired and although it was mostly left wide open, the garden still felt secret and special.

Everyone had worked so hard yet there was still so much to be done. Although, to be fair, if it hadn't been for Anthea's bonkers idea about having her birthday party in the garden, they wouldn't have achieved nearly so much.

Working together so hard, she and Lorna hadn't talked much, but once, while they were resting after having got rid of a huge tree root, Philly admitted her only regret. 'I knew I was right to send him away, but I didn't tell him I loved him, in so many words. I should have done. I know he can't get in touch with me but I'm so worried.'

'I'm sure he knows you love him,' Lorna had said, still panting a little. 'Only someone who loved him could have sent him away for his own good. It was a very tough thing for you to do. I really don't think you should worry.'

But Philly did worry — or did she just long for him? Maybe if they'd made love she'd feel more certain about things? Maybe it was 'out of sight, out of mind' for him? Men were different. He was young, healthy and gorgeous. Maybe there'd be another woman there, pretty, willing and — more importantly — within easy reach.

She had just felt her throat constrict and was wondering if another bout of self-pity was about to overcome her when she heard a ping from her phone to indicate she had an email.

She pulled it out from her back pocket.

It was from Lucien and it had come through her website. Seeing his name gave her such a shock it took a second before she could read the message.

Parents took away my phone with all my details, and my laptop, but hope you get this. Can you ring me on my new phone? Here he gave the number. *I'm allowed to have a phone, just not one with your details on it. I'm here 24/7. It's really urgent.*

With shaking and slightly sweating fingers, she pressed in the numbers. Through the long days and nights since that awful scene, when she'd watched Lucien get into his van to follow his parents, she'd longed to hear from him. But also, she had hoped not to hear from him. While he was silent she knew he was doing what he wanted to do. She hardly ever let herself imagine that he'd gone out of her life forever — only about once a day, maybe twice. And not for longer than a couple of hours at a time.

'Philly?'

She nearly fainted to hear his voice saying her name. 'Yes!'

'Oh God, I've missed you so much and they'll kill me if they find out I've contacted you but I need you!'

Philly found herself smiling and smiling. It was so good to hear him sounding just the same. 'Whatever you want, I'm there!' she said.

'Can you come to me? I'm at a bakery. There's a big food competition and show at the weekend. My boss — Geraint — it's his bakery — has had to look after his wife. She's gone into labour a bit early. I'm here on my own and I need help. It's more than one man can do — '

Philly's heart soared to think he thought she was the one who could save him. But she wasn't a baker! Her cakes weren't even that good. And this was professional baking he wanted help with. She couldn't do it. 'Oh, Lucien, I'd come in a heartbeat, of course I would, but isn't there someone who can actually bake who could help?'

'No — that's the thing. It's a competition. Only the professional bakers whose names are on the form can bake, or it's cheating. But I've checked with Geraint. I can bring in unqualified help.'

'I'm certainly that. Though how you'd prove that unless the judges come in and watch me do it — '

'I'll sort that out. I think you have to sign a form or something.' She could hear the excitement and delight in his voice. 'But you'll be perfect. I know you're not a baker, but you can light fires and we're using old-fashioned wood ovens. I can teach you the rest.'

Philly didn't argue any further. Lucien was such an optimist. She doubted if he'd be able to teach her to bake in the time but she didn't care. She just wanted to be with him.

'I'll have to sort a few things here, then I'll set off. Give me the postcode . . . '

★ ★ ★

When she'd said goodbye to Lucien she looked at her watch. It was only seven fifteen. She decided to go to Lorna's house. If Lorna wasn't up she'd email and not disturb her sleep. She knew that Lorna was throwing herself into this project as if her life depended on it, which meant very early starts and long days. She sympathised. Although they hadn't talked about it much they knew they were both distracting themselves from the aching heartbreak they were both going through.

But now Philly was walking several feet above the ground because she was going to see Lucien, that very day! She tried to keep her happiness under control as she got into her van and set off to Lorna's house.

Lorna was outside, putting something into her car.

'Hey!' said Lorna as she saw Philly. 'What are you doing here so early?'

'Hi!' said Philly, unable to conceal her

274

excitement. 'I've got a confession. I had an email from Lucien. He needs me so I'm bunking off. It's a bit complicated and I think he needs a baker, but apparently his bakery is up for a competition and he can only have help from unqualified people. Anyway, I don't care. I'm going. I hope you don't hate me for leaving you all in the lurch.'

'Don't worry about that.' Lorna summoned a smile. 'We'll manage. But what about your market stall? I know Seamus is still baking up a storm but doesn't he need someone to sell his cakes for him?'

Philly shrugged. 'He'll be able to find someone else quite easily.'

'So would you like me to make your posies?'

'Will you have time? With the garden still needing so much work?'

Lorna nodded. 'It'll do me good to take a break. I'll do as many as I can and then add them to Seamus's cakes.'

Philly turned to go. 'Keep an eye on the nursery — there are things coming on. Just take what you need. Oh — and I've got quite a lot of pelargoniums coming. I forgot to say. They were grown for a big show but didn't flower in time. They were a bargain. I hope Anthea won't be snooty about them — '

'She said she wanted colour at any price,' said Lorna. 'Leave that to me. You go and find your boy!'

Philly set off, but almost immediately skidded to a halt and turned back. 'Just had an idea. If you need anything, here's my notebook. It's got all my contacts in it. Just in case.'

Lorna took it. 'It's really kind of you to trust me with this, Philly.'

'I know you won't lose it and you might need someone in it — you never know. I'm so sorry to be leaving you just when you need me most.'

'That's fine. Off you go!' said Lorna. 'Do what you need to do to help Lucien.'

Then Philly shot home to pack and to tell her grandfather what was going on.

They didn't talk long before she bounded upstairs to throw some things into a rucksack. He just said, 'You go for it, girl. And if you come back being able to make a decent loaf, that's all to the good.'

★ ★ ★

Philly wasn't expecting an industrial estate but the satnav said she was in the right postcode. Rather than drive round and round trying to find the right unit, she parked and then sent Lucien a text.

Stay there, he commanded. *I'll find you.*

Two minutes later she was in his arms, being hugged so hard she thought she'd suffocate. The long embrace was ended by a short but very determined kiss, full of intent. It took Philly a while to get her breathing regular again.

Lucien took her hand. 'The van will be fine here,' he said. 'Come on. There's no time to lose.'

When they arrived in the unit, Philly's first

276

thought was that she'd been expecting something rustic and attractive and it all seemed very stainless-steel and factory-like, and her second was that Lucien looked awful.

'Don't they let you have time off to eat?' she said. 'You're so pale and thin.'

He laughed. 'I just don't seem to go out in daylight much. We start work in the middle of the night so all the bread is fresh for the shop.'

'There's a shop? I thought you said something about a competition?'

He nodded. 'There is. We're doing 'heritage bread' that's cooked in wood-burning ovens. We're practising for that. Do you mind if we work as we talk? Put your bag in one of those lockers and then put on some whites and a cap. I need you to get going on lighting the fire.'

'This is not quite what I imagined, I must say,' she said, looking about her. 'I thought you said it was a wood-burning oven?'

'It is. It's there.' He indicated a huge cast-iron oven. 'And there's the wood.' He flung a hand towards a crate packed with evenly sized logs. 'It's all kiln-dried.'

'So, easy to light,' said Philly, tucking her hair into a black cap.

'Yes, but I can't be lighting fires all the time.' Lucien seemed rueful. 'Seriously, I can't do this single-handed.'

'I'm sure,' said Philly, 'and I'm totally thrilled to be here, but although I know you can only have an amateur, don't you know anyone who's better at this than I am? I'm a plantsperson, not a cook.'

He grinned. 'Indeed. But you're also the woman of my heart, which is mostly why you're here.'

Feeling ridiculously happy, Philly opened the huge heavy door to the oven and looked into the cave-like space. 'Not sure this is a job for someone happier with a trowel or a dibber.'

He shrugged. 'Rules are rules. The food fair and competition — did I mention it's on Saturday? — say that professionals have to be declared on entry.'

Philly listening, thought Lucien looked younger and yet more professional in his own black cap.

'Geraint and I are the names on the form. He can't do it, but if I get professional help and we win, the baker who helped me would share the award. With untrained help — someone will come and make you fill in a different form and declare you're not a master baker in disguise — '

Philly giggled at the thought.

' — then I can win it and I really want to — for Geraint. He's been so good to me — taught me a hell of a lot. Very tough, but fair. I probably *won't* win, but I'm going to do my damnedest.'

The way he looked at her made Philly determined to do her absolute best for him. 'Tell me about Geraint.'

'He's some sort of connection of Dad's. I think Dad thought he'd work me so hard I'd give the whole thing up. And to be fair to Dad, he worked my — well, never mind. But I loved it. I do love it. It's what I want to do, to be, so I

278

wasn't going to be put off by hard work.'

Philly felt a burst of pride for him. 'Of course not.'

Lucien grinned. 'Of course, if Geraint had been a bastard I might have been put off, but he works just as hard. I've lost nearly a stone since working for him.'

'And you weren't exactly a porker before.'

Lucien shrugged. 'It would mean so much for his bakery to win this. We have to do everything we can.'

'Can we win the prize? With me as your assistant? I really respect your ambition, Lucien, but don't bet your wages on it.'

'Don't worry, I've given up gambling. We'll work hard and do our best. That's all we can do really. Now, you get the fire lit and, while it's heating, I'll give you a few basic bakery lessons. I've kept some dough back so you can practise. We have a lot of rolls to make. This is a sourdough — '

'I remember, with the mother.'

'That's right. Now, you need to do it two-handed . . . '

★ ★ ★

'I know it sounds crazy but we don't leave the ovens on their own,' said Lucien. 'We have to keep checking the temperature so we can get the bread in when the right temperature is reached.'

'I totally get that. They have to be kept an eye on,' said Philly. 'So don't you sleep at all?'

279

'Shifts,' said Lucien. 'You sleep first. Then I'll catch some zeds.'

Philly shook her head. 'You and your slang — what would your nanny think?'

'Oh!' he said, enthusiastic. 'Let's tell her all about this. It would finish her off!'

'That's not kind,' said Philly.

'*She's* not kind,' said Lucien. 'She was horrible to you.'

'But I wish her no harm. Bad karma.'

'OK, I won't.' He looked at her, his eyes glazed with something — it could have been lack of sleep or passion. 'I don't suppose you're on the pill, are you, Philly?'

'No, Lucien. I'm an Irish Catholic. Why would I be on the pill?'

He sighed deeply. 'If I'd thought properly about what I was asking you to do, I'd have nipped down to the shop and got some condoms. But I didn't. So — '

'We could just take the risk,' said Philly, suddenly desperate for him.

'No we couldn't. Supposing you got pregnant? We'd have to get married in a hurry — '

'Not these days,' said Philly insistently.

'With your parents? With my parents? They'd be livid!'

'And they wouldn't give you the money for the bakery — '

'It's not that, it's all the other stuff. They'd always accuse you of trapping me. No, we won't start.'

Philly felt a pang of disappointment even though she knew he was right. 'OK.'

Philly felt slightly dizzy. She had slept a little in the three days since she'd been in the bakery, but not much. It was now five a.m. on the morning of the food competition. They had to get the van loaded and drive it across the country to the fair.

But what Philly had lacked in sleep she'd made up for in learning. She'd learnt how to just flick the flour across the work surface so not too much was added to the dough. She'd learnt to knead bread, holding it down with the heel of her hand, pushing it away from her, reshaping it, over and over until the gluten strands had been created. She'd learnt to test for this by stretching a sample between her fingers. She'd learnt to make rolls two at a time, one in each hand, and she'd nearly learnt to cut off a lump of dough of exactly the right weight first time. She felt she'd had a personality transplant. She'd started off as someone who sowed seeds and brought them up to grow strong and healthy, and now she was a baker. It had been a baptism of fire — wood fire — hot as hell but producing amazing loaves of all shapes and sizes, rolls, and enriched doughs making iced buns, fruit breads and brioches.

'Are you ready? We need to load up,' said Lucien. He looked even worse than he had when Philly had arrived, but also exhilarated. The adrenalin was keeping him on a high. Seeing his excitement, Philly prayed that even if they didn't win, they would do well. He deserved it so much.

'Think so. To be honest, I'd drop if I had to do

281

more than just sell the stuff,' said Philly.

'I've exhausted you. I'm so sorry.'

She laughed. 'You've done worse than exhaust me these last days. You've shouted, you've nagged, you've bullied — '

He looked stricken. 'Darling, I — '

'It's fine. I've loved it. And I've learnt so much. I might even fancy becoming a baker myself!'

'Well, that's good. And there's something else I'm going to do to you — '

'Lucien, much as I want to, I don't think I've the energy to have passionate sex with you right now.'

He laughed ruefully. 'Don't tempt me. What I have to confess is that my parents are coming.'

Philly was so short of sleep, she panicked. 'Oh my God! I can't go. They mustn't see me.'

He shook his head. 'No. We've done this together. If they disown me because I broke my promise, too bad. We're a team, Philly, and if I've learnt nothing else the past few days it's that I'm not ever going to be separated from you again. Whatever happens.'

'But, Lucien, apart from them cutting you off without a shilling or whatever it is, I'm terrified of them. They think I'm a bogtrotter.'

Lucien was distracted for a moment. 'What's a bogtrotter?'

'Never mind.' This wasn't the time to explain obscure derogatory expressions applied to the Irish over the centuries. 'Haven't I got enough to cope with without your parents turning up their noses at me? Making a huge scene? Is that what we want in a public place?'

Lucien thought this was funny 'My parents are far too British to make a scene in public. Anyway I've told them to come once the judging is over so it won't matter what they do then.' He paused. 'Let's get this show on the road!'

★ ★ ★

The stall looked beautiful when they had finally finished setting it out. There were several sorts of bread made with different flours and different shapes. There were round loaves with their tops cut like a chequerboard; long loaves slashed three times; shorter bloomers; and square tin loaves. Then there were many different rolls. Philly felt so proud to have been part of creating such a wonderful display.

Then they put on their baker's caps. 'You look seriously cute in your hat,' said Lucien.

'And you look ever so slightly ridiculous in yours,' she said. It was true, but he still looked incredibly handsome.

The show started slowly and Philly suggested they buy some butter from a nearby stall and cut up some bread so people could try it. The butter went so well with the wood-fired baked bread that the cheese and butter stall bought a couple of loaves so people could sample their butter.

Soon after this came the judging, a dreadfully tense time. Lucien was questioned; Philly was tested for lack of experience prior to this event; both seemed to pass. But the judges gave nothing away. They picked up loaves and

283

knocked them, examined the crust, cut into them and examined the crumb. They ate samples — quite big samples that, to Philly, looked more like lunch. Eventually they moved on and Lucien and Philly relaxed.

As ten o'clock came so did more people and soon Philly and Lucien were really busy. Philly's experience on the market stall she shared with her grandfather, though far slower paced, came in very handy. But it was her barmaiding that made her so quick at dealing with money and giving change. It was a transferable skill and she was far faster and more efficient at selling the bread than Lucien was. But he was brilliant at chatting, telling people about the wood-fired oven and why it made such amazing bread.

'We're doing this for Geraint really, and for his bakery,' he reiterated to Philly. 'This business is so important to him. If he can't be here to tell people about it, I have to. And that last man is quite a famous food writer!' he added proudly.

'Oh, excellent!' said Philly.

'Actually, Phil, as you're so good at the change and stuff, would you mind if I went for a walk round? Chat to some people? Networking is so important and I think maybe we should think about starting an online ordering system, with a catalogue, so people can get these great products without having to live near the producers.'

'Sounds a good idea. You go off. I'll be fine here.'

She *was* fine and really enjoyed selling a product people really loved. She directed people across to the dairy stall and received people they

284

had directed to her. They were nearly sold out of bread and she was thinking what a good entrepreneur Lucien was, as well as a brilliant baker, when she looked up and saw a familiar face.

She just said, 'Next, please? How can I help you?' hoping the woman in front of her would somehow stop being Lucien's mother, and stop looking at her as if she were Eliza Doolittle before she'd had the Professor Higgins make-over.

'You!' said Camilla. 'What are you doing here?'

'Selling bread. For Lucien,' said Philly. She was nervous but defiant. She had nothing whatever to be ashamed of. Maybe she and Lucien had gone against his parents' wishes but she was proud of what they'd produced. 'What can I get you?' she added politely.

'I don't want — '

'Here!' Philly produced a sample of one of the few remaining loaves with a deftness that impressed even her. 'Try this. It's a sourdough but we like to think that while we've got the texture, it doesn't taste too sour. And fermented foods are very good for you,' she added, hoping this revealed her as a caring person and so not entirely unsuitable for Lucien.

Camilla's hand responded automatically to the offered plate of bread and butter. She took a piece.

'Hi, Ma!' Lucien appeared from behind, put his arm round his mother and kissed her robustly on the cheek.

285

Camilla jumped. She had been chewing and was taken completely by surprise. Philly, momentarily sorry for her, hoped she wouldn't choke.

No sooner had she swallowed her mouthful than Camilla was attacked again, this time by a bear of a man, who picked her up and hugged her as if she were a small baguette. 'Camilla, your son is a bloody genius baker!'

'Geraint,' said Camilla. 'I thought you were with your wife?'

'I was,' stated Geraint, who had a voice to rival Brian Blessed's. 'But we have a lovely boy now. They're both doing fine and I had to come and find out if we'd got our gold medal.'

'And we did!' said Lucien, going to scoop Philly out from behind the stall and hugging her. 'We did it, Philly.'

'Your boy's been a bloody star, Camilla. Worked like a slave for me, and it seems like his girl is the same — a bloody hard worker.'

'You won a prize?' asked Camilla.

'Bloomin' gold medal for our heritage bread!' boomed Geraint.

'I couldn't have done it without Philly,' said Lucien triumphantly. 'Dad can — '

Philly trod on his foot. This was no time to sound like a rebellious teenager. Fortunately he understood her message.

As if summoned, 'Dad' appeared. 'Lucien?' His eyes flicked towards Philly. 'Isn't that — '

'Darling?' Camilla warned. 'Geraint's here.'

Geraint enveloped Jasper in his arms and then punched his shoulder, causing him to stagger

286

slightly 'Lucien's done you proud. Done me proud. Took everything I threw at him and then ran with the ball. Best apprentice I've ever had or will have. You should definitely back him, man! He's the business!'

Lucien, who'd had his arm round Philly, squeezed her to him. 'I couldn't have done any of this without Philly. She's been brilliant too.'

It was Philly's turn to be caught up in a giant's embrace, squeezed briefly and set back down again. 'With a woman like that beside him, a man can do anything,' said Geraint. 'Like my Myfanwy. And now I've got my medal I'll go back to the hospital and tell her all about it. But, Jasper, mate, your son is the real deal. You should be incredibly proud of him!'

Philly watched Geraint move through the crowds, people parting before him, and then she looked at Lucien's parents.

'Well,' said Jasper. 'Maybe we'd better go out for a meal and get to know each other a bit better.'

'Love to, Dad,' said Lucien. 'But when we've finished up here, we need a bit of sleep.'

His father looked at his vintage Rolex. 'OK, shall we make it tomorrow? Call me.'

'Yes, darling,' said Camilla and then turned to Philly, hesitant but gracious. 'And thank you, dear. You've obviously worked very hard for our son.'

Philly suddenly felt a bit tearful at this volte face. 'I didn't do it because he's your son.'

'Of course you didn't,' said Camilla, 'but I'm grateful anyway. And very, very proud of the pair of you.' She paused. 'So, where are you staying?'

'We've been sleeping on the floor at the bakery,' Philly said.

'I have a key to Geraint's house,' said Lucien. 'We're staying there.'

★   ★   ★

They had just drawn up outside Geraint and Myfanwy's house when Lucien's phone whistled. It was a text.

'Oh!' he said. 'It's from Geraint. He says we should go to the Mowl House Hotel. There's a suite booked and paid for. It's a thank-you present.'

'Wow!' said Philly. 'How amazing. But could I shower and change first, do you think?'

'Nonsense. If we shower and change we'll never get there.' And he turned round to Philly. 'And if I don't show you exactly how much I love you, very soon, I think I'll go crazy!'

25

Lorna sat back on her heels and put down the hand brush. She moved the camping lantern nearer to the shells so she could see them more clearly and then she ran her hand lightly over them. She smiled. The pattern was clear and the shells on the walls of the grotto all felt secure.

There were a few more sections that she needed to clean before she could put off the inevitable no longer. In other words, before she had to replace the missing shells on the ceiling.

She had all the shells she needed. The chest she had found in Burthen House had been brought down and she had already sorted them out. She knew which ones she needed to replace the missing ones, to make the stars, spirals, triangles and parallelograms.

She knew she was too emotionally involved in what she was doing and also she knew why she was hesitating: she wasn't sure what material she should use to fix the shells although it was obvious whom she should ask. Jack. And she could not ask Jack.

She gathered up her things and went out from the cool dampness of the grotto into the garden. At least there she was confident that she knew what she was doing.

★　★　★

It was late afternoon, and Lorna was tying in a rambling rose, trying to persuade it that its supporting arch had always been there and hadn't just been put in the previous day, when she saw Philly approaching.

'Hello,' she called anxiously, studying Philly carefully. 'Oh!' she exclaimed when Philly reached her. 'You look — well!' What she meant was 'loved up', but she didn't want to embarrass Philly, who really seemed to be walking on air.

'Hi! We just got back. Seamus suggested I should come over immediately and see what you've done here.' She looked around. 'It looks — utterly amazing!'

Philly was looking even prettier than usual, Lorna thought; her skin was glowing and her eyes were sparkling. 'It was good of you to leave Lucien to come back here.'

'Oh, he came back with me. His apprenticeship with Geraint — that's the baker — is over. He's passed. His father is going to back him.' She looked around eagerly. 'I can't believe how much you've done. I've not been away a week! It looks like a proper mature garden. How has that happened?'

Lorna smiled, slightly guilty. 'Mostly thanks to your amazing contacts book and I'm afraid your polytunnels are practically empty. I'm really glad to see you before you went in them, but don't worry too much. We've gone very Chelsea. Most of the things are still in their pots.'

Philly looked at her. 'But you've done so much. You must have worked night and day?'

Lorna laughed. 'Well, most of the daylight

hours have been spent here.' Not only was she determined to get the garden as near to finished as she could, given that things took time to grow, but she didn't want to have any time or energy to think about Jack. Although she did think about him, all the time.

'So, give me the tour,' said Philly. 'As if I haven't seen it before, which actually I haven't really. It's changed so much!'

'OK.' Lorna was pleased that Philly seemed so relaxed about having had her plant stock hijacked. 'But shall we get a cup of tea to take round with us? We've got a camping stove in the shed. All mod cons.'

'I wouldn't call it a shed.' Philly gestured to the building shaped like a dovecote. 'It's far too pretty, with roses climbing up it and all! What is that one?'

'It's a Rambling Rector,' said Lorna. 'I got the shed from the same people I got most of the mature ramblers. They'd done a show and were very happy to sell me them. But before we get too involved with the garden, tell me about you and Lucien. Did you manage to see Lucien without his parents finding out? Hang on, let me fill the kettle first.' Lorna nipped outside to the tap that was attached to the side of the dovecote, filled the kettle and went in again quickly.

Philly was admiring a noticeboard covered in vintage seed packets. 'This is lovely.'

'Isn't it fun? So pretty. I couldn't resist it. If Anthea doesn't want it I'll have it somewhere at home. Now: biscuits in that tin — and tell me everything.'

291

'Well, Lucien's parents have relented. They no longer think I'm horrendously unsuitable. I mean, they probably still do think that but they've had to come round to the thought of me. Lucien was so determined. They took us out to dinner and everything.'

Lorna shuddered. 'Oh, was that all right?'

'It was actually. Jasper kept filling my wine glass and they were so impressed with what Geraint, the baker who Lucien was working for, said about Lucien — us both really — they couldn't grumble about me having an Irish accent.'

'Wow! So how did you go from zero to hero?' Lorna held out the biscuit tin.

Philly perched on a stool opposite Lorna and took a bite of her biscuit. 'One of Grand's?'

Lorna nodded. 'He said they were too crumbly to sell. Now do get on!'

'Well, first thing: Lucien taught me how to bake. Which was really hard although I did enjoy it. We had three days to get ready for this show which was a competition.'

'Sounds tough.'

'It was — no sleep. But I picked it up quite quickly though I say so myself.'

'And?'

'We won a medal! It's for Geraint really — it's for his business. He makes heritage bread, which basically means he uses a wood-burning oven for it. Not all the time, but that's what we did for the competition.'

'Sounds lovely.'

Philly nodded. 'While I was selling the bread I

looked up and saw Lucien's mother.'

'Oh no!'

'But then we found out about the award, and Geraint said how amazing we'd been and they realised I wasn't the Irish girl on the make they'd thought I was.'

'Quite right too.'

'And Geraint booked us into a luxury spa for a couple of days.'

Philly said this fairly blandly but Lorna didn't miss the subtext. 'So I gather you and Lucien — '

'Oh yes!' Philly agreed. 'My mother never let on that sex was so lovely. And probably just as well. I'd have been at it years ago if she had.'

Lorna laughed. 'Only with the right person! As someone old enough to be your mother, it's my duty to emphasise that.'

'Lucien is absolutely the right person,' said Philly, twinkling. 'But we had dinner at the hotel with his parents and I was convinced they must have known . . . Anyway, they tried really hard to be nice. They ordered lovely wine and, as I said, Lucien's dad kept filling up my glass. And his mother gave me a bottle of really lovely perfume.' She paused. 'I think they were just worried about Lucien in the beginning. As they keep saying, we're very young.' She frowned. 'Young, but not stupid. And now Lucien's father will pay to set up a bakery in our outhouse. But I don't think we'll go entirely wood-fired. It's fun and the bread is fantastic but it's hard work. Even harder than baking is already.'

'It sounds as if you've become a baker. Are you giving up your nursery?'

'Oh no! I do love baking and we will have a pizza oven so we can do wood-fired some of the time. But I'm still a plantswoman.' She stood up. 'Let's go back into the garden so you can show me everything.'

Lorna ushered her through the door of the dovecote. 'I'm afraid, as you'll see, I raided your nursery pretty thoroughly, but I've written down everything I've taken. Anthea will pay you.'

Philly flapped a hand. 'Oh — well — '

'Come on, Philly,' said Lorna. 'You're running a business.'

'OK. If you've made a list I'll work it out.'

'Right. Oyster shell for the paths — pretty?'

'Lovely. The white sets off the flowers. And there are so many flowers!'

'Mostly because of your clever succession growing. We'll do it all in period next year, but for now, we just want colour and quick effect. That's what Anthea said, anyway.'

'But the roses will stay? I love this pergola — it's a tunnel of wonderful scent.'

'Oh yes, this will stay if the roses survive. I've put gallons and gallons of water on them every night. Anthea loves it. She loves that it's wide enough to walk through without being snagged by thorns. We measured very carefully and I hope when everything grows it'll still be OK. And if they don't survive, we'll replant, but not roses. We'll have another rose-covered pergola somewhere else. There is a spot.'

Philly nodded. 'Because of disease? Very wise.

And there are lots of things you could put in.'
She walked on a few paces. 'Oh! My dahlias!'

'Yes — don't they look fantastic? All those wonderful scarlet Bishops of Llandaff that worked so well in the Italian garden? Plus a lot of oranges and deep yellow.'

'It's so vivid.'

'I know. When it's historically accurate, and Anthea says she wants it to be, more or less, it'll be much more subtle, but it has been fun just going mad with the colour palette.'

Philly looked at her watch. 'I shouldn't be too long — '

Lorna recognised the symptoms of a woman in love, desperate to get back to her man. 'Just look at the grotto quickly. I've nearly finished it. I've got to redo some of it but I'm not sure what I should use to stick the shells to the wall.'

'You should ask — '

Fortunately for Lorna, before Philly could say she should ask Jack, Anthea appeared. 'Hello, darling,' she said to Philly. 'So glad you came back. I really want Lucien to do the food at my party. Do you think he would? Or is it too short notice?'

'He's got nearly a week so I'm sure that's plenty of time. Why don't I pop back and ask him? He's at home.'

After Philly had said her farewells, Anthea turned to Lorna. 'Lorna, darling, there's something I want to talk to you about.'

Wondering what on earth it could be, given how much time they'd both spent in the garden recently, Lorna felt a frisson of anxiety.

'What is it, Anthea?'

'It's the statues — '

'I thought we'd agreed,' said Lorna, sharply. 'We're not going to use them. They're damaged. With bits missing.'

'Come and look at them with me.'

Anthea sounded placatory, which was unusual for Anthea. Lorna followed her to her garage which, to her certain knowledge, hadn't been used to keep a car in since Anthea had moved into the Dower House. Anthea opened the side door and they both went in. The statues, minus their mid-sections, were lying on sheets of tarpaulin.

'There they are,' said Anthea. 'Don't you think they're rather lovely?'

Lorna suddenly felt very tired and wanted to go home. She looked at a jigsaw of marble pieces roughly depicting three female figures. She didn't see beauty, she saw brokenness and it seemed to mirror the feeling in her heart. She didn't want statues that would remind her of Jack every time she saw them in a garden she felt very personally about. It wasn't her garden but it was her creation, which was almost more important.

'They're missing their torsos and that does spoil their beauty somewhat. And it would take months and months to restore them.' She fought not to sound snappy. What Anthea was suggesting wasn't unreasonable.

'To restore them properly would take ages,' Anthea agreed. 'But they're not that badly damaged. What about — '

'But there's still lots to do with this garden before your party. We haven't time to fiddle about with bits of broken marble. Now if you don't mind, I'm going home now. I've got a headache.'

'You need to take a couple of painkillers with a good slug of whisky,' suggested Anthea.

But Lorna's ache wasn't one that could be cured by painkillers and strong drink. She wasn't sure there was a cure for it, really.

★　★　★

It was the day before the party. Lorna had put replacing the shells in the grotto to the back of her mind until it was nearly too late. There'd been so much else to do and she was still unsure of what she should use to attach them to the wall. Finally, and only now, did she use the cement that Seamus had found for her. And once she'd gained confidence working with the shells and ammonites she'd enjoyed it. But then, annoyingly, the cement had run out just when she got to the ceiling.

She'd gone to tell Anthea she was going to the DIY shop to get some more cement when Anthea had produced some domestic filler. 'It'll be fine. Don't fuss, Lorna,' she had said when Lorna had protested. She had thrust the dusty packet into her hands, obviously keen to be rid of her.

So she'd used it and, to be fair to Anthea, it did seem to be fine, and so when Peter arrived, inviting her to Burthen House for a drink, she had stopped worrying and gone back to the house with him.

The moon was well up as Lorna set off afterwards, having rejected Peter and Kirstie's offers of first dinner and then a lift. She had had enough social life for the moment and just wanted to get home.

But she couldn't be lured there until she had checked the grotto even if she'd be doing it by torchlight.

The minute she was in the garden, and the fragrance of it reached her, she forgot about the minor details, and little anxieties about tasks left undone. Her cares slipped away. Everything was even more beautiful by moonlight and the scent was extraordinary.

The sweet peas, phlox, old-fashioned pinks and lilies added their fragrance to the roses and tobacco plants. It was just the effect she'd wanted, to create a garden full of mystery and sensuality.

She was just looking around her and breathing in the perfumed air when movement caught her eye and made her jump violently.

'Sorry I didn't mean to frighten you,' said Jack, coming out of the shadows.

Lorna managed not to scream but only just. She forced moisture into her suddenly dry mouth. 'What are you doing here?'

'Anthea asked me to set up the statues after you'd gone home. She said I had to do them when you weren't around.'

Conflicting emotions meant that Lorna was unable to reply. Shock, betrayal and — insanely

— happiness swirled in her mind. She realised she was pleased to see him because it meant he was still alive, and that made her happy. But confusion was uppermost.

'But I thought Anthea had given up on the statues. She just had the pieces lying in her garage.'

'She found the missing torsos and rang me. She said she didn't mind ignoring them when they were just heads and bodies but she couldn't waste them when they were more or less complete.'

'Oh.'

'She didn't want to upset you. And now you've caught me.' He paused, alert and attentive. 'Are you upset?'

Lorna shook her head. 'I don't know. I'm very surprised. I thought after I walked out of your flat that you'd dropped off the planet.'

'There are good reasons why you thought that. Can you put up with me telling you what happened? Or do you just want to forget you ever met me?'

At least this was a question she knew the answer to. She gave a shuddering sigh. 'Tell me what happened.'

'A whole chain of things. When I was in France I had a call from a neighbour to say my father had had a fall. My parents had me very late in life so I've always had to look out for them — well, for a few years now anyway. My father was ninety . . . '

She noted the past tense. 'And your mother?'

'Still with us but very frail.'

'Go on.'

'I rushed back and managed to lose my phone with all my contacts somewhere along the way. I think it fell out of my bag.'

That would explain his not returning her text or email. 'I see.'

'It meant I couldn't reassure you — do anything really — '

'And you had your parents to worry about.' Lorna could imagine it. She'd had difficulties with her own parents several years previously trying to work out what was best for them — or the best that was possible, anyway.

'They hadn't got a computer and I had no time to find one so I couldn't track you down through a website or anything.'

'Tell me about your parents.'

'Oh, well, it was grim. Dad had broken his hip and was in hospital. I realised that he'd actually been losing his marbles but Mum hadn't said anything.' He paused. 'I'm an only child, apple of their eye — spoilt rotten, I expect — so she'd protected me, told me they were fine whenever I rang. I should have gone home more often.'

'I understand about the only child, apple of their eye, spoilt rotten,' she said. 'I have one of those. I was an only child too. If circumstances permit, I think it's better to have more than one child. But go on.'

'Dad died in hospital and I had to find a home for Mum, which I did, and actually she's happy there. She'd been isolated when she was looking after Dad and now she has company. So finally, finally, I felt I could come back to work.'

A rush of sympathy welled up in her: for him, for his parents, for the unkindness of old age. 'But everything's sort of all right now?'

'Yes. It is. Lorna, why didn't you answer my letter?'

Lorna felt suddenly faint. 'What letter? I didn't get a letter.'

'I wrote to you — on my mother's ancient Basildon Bond paper — an old-fashioned letter. I did have to make up the address rather and didn't have a postcode, but I thought it would have reached you.'

Lorna shook her head. 'There's another house in the village with a very similar address. It's a holiday home so the people are hardly ever there.'

Jack groaned. 'So it's probably lying on a doorstep in among all the curry-house menus and DIY store adverts.'

She couldn't help smiling. 'It probably is.' Just knowing he'd written, really tried to get in touch, made a huge difference.

'I didn't think you ever wanted to see me again. Anthea said I wasn't to worry, she'd sort it out, but I wasn't convinced. Especially when she was so insistent on keeping it a secret that I was repairing the statues.'

Lorna didn't answer straightaway. 'I probably did give her the impression that I never wanted to see you again.' She looked up at him, unable to read his expression with the moon behind him. 'I felt so desperately embarrassed about you having that drawing. And when I'd had time to get over it a bit I sent you a text. And then an email.'

'Which I didn't get —'

'And then I went to your workshop to ask about you. They said you'd been to France and were on leave. They didn't know when you'd be back. I was resigned never to seeing you again.'

'So you wanted to see me then,' he said eagerly. 'What about now?'

She found she couldn't speak.

'I'm rushing you,' said Jack. 'You need to get used to the idea of me again.' He gestured to the garden. 'This garden is amazing. I couldn't believe it when Anthea told me how you'd discovered it, and how you'd done all this, starting from a jungle. It's almost unbelievable.'

She laughed ruefully. 'Everything looks better in moonlight.'

'I expect that's what you'll say if I tell you that you look amazing, too.'

She nodded. She felt very self-conscious. The sensuousness of her surroundings had rather gone to her head. As he didn't speak, but just looked at her, she felt obliged to go on. 'Shall I give you a tour? And you can show me the statues.'

Together they walked along the oyster-shell paths, which shone white in the moonlight, between flowers bleached of their colour, matching the paths.

By the time they reached the grotto Lorna felt almost drunk with it all. She imagined the creator of this garden coming out on her own at night, to indulge herself in the loveliness, secret and special.

'Let's look at the grotto,' she said, bringing herself back down to earth. She was finding the combination of the garden and Jack's presence almost too much for her.

She got out her torch for although the moonlight had been enough outside, it wouldn't penetrate the stone walls of the grotto.

'Just a minute. Before we go inside, I have to do this,' said Jack, and took her into her arms. 'I hope you don't mind.'

After a moment's awkwardness she relaxed. She felt herself melt into him, like wax pouring into a mould. She sighed: at last she was where she belonged.

He seemed to feel the same because it was only when a pheasant squawked in the hedge nearby that they broke apart.

Lorna held on to him to steady herself. 'Come on, just a quick look.'

'We can do that tomorrow, surely?' said Jack.

'No, I must check it. Then I can really relax.' She gave him a look she was half glad he couldn't properly see. She knew it was full of desire and invitation and she wasn't quite ready for him to know how much she wanted him. Not just yet.

The entrance to the grotto was dark and she shone her torch into it. There was no door, just an arch of shells. Over the entrance were initials picked out in ammonites: 'A' and 'S', the letters entwined. Lorna shone her torch at them, proud of the work and time she had put into them.

'We needn't be long,' she said, 'I just want to be sure it's OK.' She was still worried about using that domestic filler. 'I want to see the statues too.'

'They are very beautiful, I must say. Now — '

Lorna stepped across the threshold and gasped in horror. All the shells she had so painstakingly placed on the ceiling had fallen and there was a pile of them on the floor of the grotto. 'Oh no! I can't bear it. I spent so long, took so much trouble copying the design from the plan Anthea and I found.' She put her hands up to her face but then allowed Jack to take her into his arms, hugging her to him. Tiredness, emotion, disappointment and shock meant she started to weep.

'Come on,' Jack breathed into her hair. 'I know it's awful when your work gets damaged but it's not the end of the world. Come on now, let me take you home. We'll sort this out in the morning.'

She stopped crying. It went so against the grain with her to cry on the chest of a man. She pulled herself together. 'I need a cup of tea.'

'You need something far stronger than that. And a bath. Let me look after you. I've had a lot of practice at looking after people lately. Let me show off my skills.'

He led her gently to his car.

'I can't believe I've been so pathetic,' she said. 'I'm not a crier — not over things like that. I'm just very tired.'

'And a bit shocked, maybe. Having me jump out at you from behind a tree.'

This made her laugh and feel a bit better. 'That too! I'm sorry to miss the statues — do you think we should go back and look now?'

'Certainly not. You can see them in the morning.'

'You don't think they'll look better by moonlight? Like everything else?'

He nudged her to acknowledge her attempt at a joke. 'No. Although actually they do look wonderful in moonlight. You can see them by moonlight another time.'

'Maybe not a moon as wonderful as this.'

'A harvest moon. It'll still be beautiful tomorrow night though. Now, I'm taking you home.'

26

By chance, Lorna had left a table lamp on so the cottage wasn't in complete darkness when they got back. A couple more lamps and it looked cosy again. She collapsed on to a chair at the kitchen table.

'I do want tea,' said Lorna as Jack filled the kettle, 'but you're right, something stronger as well. I think we've earned it.' She got up and went to her old corner cupboard and found a bottle of brandy and some glasses.

'Oh — nice,' said Jack, when he saw the bottle.

'It is. A present from Peter. I make brandy butter for the pudding at Christmas and he supplies the brandy. He doesn't want the rest of the bottle back.'

'My mother just has brandy butter and no pudding. She says it's either that or the pudding and she prefers the butter.'

Lorna laughed. 'I think I'm with her there!'

'I'd like to take you to see her.'

Lorna was horrified. 'Don't do that! She'll think you've taken up with a cougar.'

'No she won't. She'd think: At last, Jack's found the right woman.' He paused. 'Anyway I've already told her about you. How do you like your tea?'

Lorna was floundering. 'Oh, fairly strong, not much milk. But, Jack . . . '

'Lorna — I was broken-hearted. I'd lost you.

306

Mum and I had a lot of time together. It was natural I should tell her my problems.' He paused. 'She was quite encouraging.'

'Oh?'

'She said if I was really clever and attentive I might get you back. She saw your point about the drawing, a hundred per cent, but thought you might be able to get over it if I played my cards right.'

Lorna sipped her brandy and laughed gently. 'I do think I'd like to meet her.'

Jack gazed at her for a few moments and then said, 'You haven't got anything to eat, have you? I'm starving.'

Lorna nodded, still smiling. She got to her feet. 'I have cake. Seamus is making Anthea's birthday cake and he made some trial versions. Eventually Anthea went for a chocolate cake, so he gave me the fruit one.'

'It really is quite like Christmas, isn't it?' said Jack. 'Brandy and fruit cake?'

'Mm.' Lorna yawned hugely. 'And feeling impossibly tired. When Leo was little, and it was just us sometimes, if we weren't seeing my parents, I used to gather up other families and we'd do it together. It was huge fun but then suddenly I'd feel exhausted.'

'Right. Finish your drink. I'm going to run you a bath.'

Lorna left one lamp on and followed him up the stairs. She could hear water running into the bath and wondered if he was about to see her naked. She wished they could have made love in the garden, when the moonlight and the

307

fragrance were so potent. Now she would be facing electric light unless Jack spotted the candles that were dotted about the bathroom. He probably wouldn't. On the whole men didn't notice things like that.

'It's ready!' said Jack. 'Come and see if it's too hot.'

She'd put on her best dressing gown, vintage silk and one of her favourite items of clothing. The one she usually wore was a bit stained with hair colour and not terribly flattering.

She went into the bathroom and was delighted to see that Jack *had* spotted the candles, so instead of harsh but economical LEDs the room was softly lit. She went to the bath and put her hand in it. 'That's the perfect temperature,' she said. 'Just slightly too hot for comfort so it'll be a little while before it gets cold.' She cleared her throat. 'Are you going to join me? It's a big old bath.'

He shook his head and looked a bit embarrassed. 'Oh, Lorna — I'm afraid I can't. I'm so sorry but I have to go.'

Immediately she felt abandoned. She'd been nervous about taking off her dressing gown — just as she'd felt nervous taking it off all those years ago when she'd done nude modelling for art students — but she'd been prepared to do it. Now he was leaving her. Well, she wasn't going to ask twice.

'Oh, OK. Just close the front door on the way out. I'll go down and bolt it later.'

He didn't move. He seemed to be looking for the right words and then he sighed. 'I'm sorry,' he said eventually. 'I really am. I'll see you tomorrow.' He leant in to kiss her cheek but she turned away so he got her hair instead.

'Bye!' she said. She waited until she'd heard the front door close before she went back downstairs and added more brandy to her glass. Then she bolted the door and went back to her bath. At least the combination of tiredness, alcohol and hot water would make sure she slept. At least for a while.

★ ★ ★

She awoke at five. The moon was still visible but it was some time before dawn. She knew she wouldn't go back to sleep — she had far too much on her mind. She got up and, after a quick breakfast, set off for the secret garden.

She didn't take the car. She wanted to walk through the main garden, get some exercise, get her blood pumping, so she could face the day.

It wasn't going to be easy. First, she had to clear up the mess in the grotto and then replace the missing shells, although she couldn't do that until she could get hold of some cement. But also she had to face Jack. Somehow, after their passionate kissing his rejection of her seemed a hundred times worse. It was so confusing — he'd wanted to introduce her to his mother, which did indicate some sort of serious intent. But then he'd walked away, left her, just as she was about to take off her dressing gown. Maybe the thought of her naked body put him off at the last minute. It was like a knife stabbing at her.

A sparrow cheeped from somewhere as she arrived at Anthea's and in spite of everything her heart lifted a little as she opened the gate to the secret garden.

It wasn't quite as sensuous as it had been last night but it was still glorious. It was lovely being in it alone. She imagined once again the woman who had created it. She imagined her wanting to get away from the claims of a household, a demanding husband or brother who wanted her to devote her life to his needs or his family's needs. Here was where she could escape them all.

Lorna was only escaping them for a relatively short time. In a couple of hours other people would start appearing, she'd have to face the grotto, explain to Anthea about the disaster. If she couldn't repair it, and make sure it was safe, they may have to tell people they couldn't go in. There would have to be tape and notices about it. It would spoil the whole effect and be desperately disappointing. She couldn't even start until she had some cement.

To distract herself for a little while, she went first to see the statues, the ones she'd been going to see with Jack.

Whatever else in her life might be confusing, the statues were beautiful. When she'd last seen them they'd been lying in sections on a bit of tarpaulin, like bodies at a crime scene. Now they were complete, and if the joins were obvious, their beauty was too. Jack had done a brilliant job with them.

Someone, probably for the sake of the party

guests, had written cards with their titles. There was Flora, holding a garland of flowers, Ceres, with a cornucopia for flowers and fruit, and then Pomona, with a basket of apples.

She took out the torch she always had with her and inspected them closely. From a distance they looked perfect but with the aid of the torch and the fading moonlight she could see lines where broken pieces had been cemented together. The softly curving limbs, the drapery, the expressions on the beautiful faces: all were as near to how they must have looked originally as possible.

Although she had thought she was fully in control, tears started to trickle down her cheeks as she looked. Then, unexpectedly, a robin began to sing from somewhere and the sound jolted her and she moved away, heading for the grotto and the mess that awaited her.

She switched on her torch and went in, and thought she'd made a mistake. Where last night there'd been a heap of shells and ammonites, some of them broken, all of them jumbled, there was now a beautifully patterned roof. It wasn't quite the same as it had been but it was complete. The elves had been in the night!

Feeling tearful all over again, she went back out and looked to see if the elf in question was still there. He was looking into the ornamental pond. She came up behind him but he saw her reflection in the water. Turning, he put his arm round her waist and pulled her into his side.

'You did that,' she said. 'You redid the grotto's ceiling.'

'Yup.'

'You didn't use Polyfilla, did you? I think that was my mistake. Anthea made me use it when I ran out of cement.'

She felt his laugh rumble. 'I used lime mortar. Luckily I had some at the yard.' He paused. 'I knew you must have felt it was odd me leaving you like that, but I knew it would take a long time to put those shells back up. If I'd said I was going to do it you'd have insisted on helping, and you were so tired.'

'So you've been up all night?'

'More or less. Well, yes, actually. I put a fine gauze over the ceiling because of course it's still wet and I can't be a hundred per cent sure the shells will stay up. They should do but — '

'Well, mine didn't,' said Lorna. 'That ceiling has previous.'

'I know.' He was silent for a few seconds and then sighed. 'This garden is so beautiful.'

'I'm very pleased with it. Lots of the plants are still in their pots because I got them from contacts of Philly's — nurseries who'd provided material for flower shows and things.'

'Give me the tour now it's nearly light and then I must get some sleep.'

'You can come back to mine, if you like,' said Lorna, sounding casual, feeling bold.

'Can I? That would be great — and very kind of you for many, many reasons.'

'You can come, I've invited you, but I want to know why you were so intent on redoing the ceiling. I was going to try and do it today — it was why I came so early. Or it could even just have been tidied up.'

'I wanted to do it to prove I wasn't a useless so-and-so who just disappeared out of your life at a very bad time.' He paused and took her into his arms again. 'I love you, Lorna. And I wanted to prove it. Actions speak louder than words, and all that.'

'That's . . . I don't know what to say.'

'It's too much to hope that you feel the same way but give me time and I'll try to win you round, to convince you . . . '

Lorna didn't feel this would be too difficult for him but didn't say it out loud. 'Come on,' she said instead, 'let's go home.'

★ ★ ★

After they'd got to the cottage, Lorna left Jack having a shower while she went to the shop for bacon, mushrooms, tomatoes and a loaf of fresh bread.

When she got back he was looking fresh-faced and happy, not at all like someone who'd been up all night. 'I've put some coffee on,' he said. 'I hope you don't mind.'

'Of course not. I'll make breakfast.'

Sometime during the process of frying and keeping things warm and making toast, a tissue-wrapped parcel appeared on her plate.

He removed it so she could put her plate down. 'It's a present,' he explained.

'When did you have time to go and buy a present?' she asked, pleased and mystified.

He laughed and handed it to her. 'I didn't buy it! I made it — them. See what you think.' He

313

turned his attention to his breakfast, feigning a relaxed attitude to her reaction to his gift.

She unwrapped the tissue and two carved wooden spoons fell out.

'They're Welsh love spoons — copies of, anyway,' he explained. 'I made them and, although I'm not Welsh, they're a love token. They also have them in Scandinavia. While I was sitting by my father's bed, or talking to my mother, I carved them. Kept my hands busy and you in my thoughts in a practical way.'

'They're beautiful.' She examined the pair of spoons, carved with hearts, angels, chains and an anchor. 'Does everything mean something?'

'It all means I love you.'

She realised she was crying again, so she didn't speak for a while. 'I don't know what to say!'

'Just say, 'Let's go upstairs to bed.''

She laughed. She had never felt so loved or so loving before. 'Finish your breakfast first.'

★ ★ ★

It didn't take long before Jack took her hand and led her to the bedroom. The curtains were still half drawn from the previous night and she was grateful that there wasn't sunshine streaming in. She hadn't had a relationship for a long time and while she loved him and believed he loved her, she was shy.

She needn't have been. He took control of the situation completely. First he pushed her hair gently away from her face and kissed her. Then he took off her clothes one by one and looked at her.

His look told her everything she needed to know but he said it anyway. 'You were very lovely when you were eighteen but so much more beautiful now.'

After that, no one said anything else for quite a long time.

27

Philly was helping Lucien in Anthea's kitchen. It was large with plenty of work surface, especially as the table, usually a repository of all kinds of things, had been cleared. Now it was covered in large platters filled with food. A couple were green and silver with flecks of scarlet, laden with vast salads topped with chopped mint and parsley. Another brilliantly painted pair of dishes offered finely sliced tomatoes with onion and green peppers with walnuts. Everything was a delight to the eye and desperately tempting and the kitchen was full of the smell of aubergines and pomegranate.

However, something was not right with Lucien, Philly thought. He seemed surprisingly edgy. She was observing him as she worked through the mountain of parsley he wanted her to chop.

'What's up?' she said eventually, wiping her hands.

He turned to her and she frowned. He'd looked less nervous than when they'd been about to open their bread stall to a critical judging panel and this meal, according to him when he'd told her the menu, was fairly straightforward. 'Trouble is, I'm not very good at this!' he said, looking down at her.

'Good at what? Surely you're not worried

about the meal? You said it was easy. Besides, you're brilliant — '

'No, it's not the food!' He was indignant.

'What then? If you gave me a clue, maybe I could help you?'

He swallowed. 'OK, I'll just do it.' He put one hand on her shoulder and with the other he groped in his back pocket and produced an envelope. 'The thing is — ' He was clutching her shoulder. 'Philly?'

'What!' Philly was really worried now. Why was he holding on to her so tightly? He was usually so confident and good with words but now he seemed incapable of finishing a sentence.

'I went shopping earlier,' he said.

She was none the wiser. Had he forgotten something? 'I know. You needed pomegranate molasses. Do you need me to get something else? I don't mind.'

He ignored this. 'Oh God, this is terrifying!' He fumbled with the envelope and got it open. 'I got you this.' He produced a tiny gold envelope from the larger one. 'Philly? Will you marry me?'

It took her a moment to work out what he'd said. 'Marry you?'

'Yes! Philly, I love you. I want you to be my wife. Will you?' he added, quiet but urgent. He swallowed. 'Wait a minute. You need to see the ring. Of course you can change it — '

She looked up at him. He was her hero; she hadn't seen him like this before: diffident, lacking in confidence. 'Oh, Lucien! Of course I'll marry you!'

He gave a great sigh and took her in his arms,

burying his head in her shoulder. 'Thank goodness. I don't know what I'd have done if you'd said no.'

She had to clear her throat before she could speak. 'Of course I wouldn't have said no. I love you.' She had wanted to say this to him for such a long time. It was something she knew in every fibre of her body.

'Oh, Philly! Now let me show you the ring. I've kept the receipt and the shop said we can change it if you don't like it.' He opened the little gold envelope that somehow he'd managed to keep hold of; then he took Philly's hand and slid something into it.

She gasped. It was a plain solitaire diamond ring but the stone seemed quite large.

'Lucien!' Her eyes were wide. She didn't know if she was delighted or horrified at the amount of money it must have cost.

'Try it on. Do you like it?' Without waiting for her to reply, he took her hand and slid the ring on to her finger.

'I've never seen such a beautiful ring!' she breathed. 'It must have cost a fortune!'

'Don't worry. I had a quick flutter when you weren't looking. I did well! So tell me: what do you think about it?'

Philly looked at the slim gold band with the diamond that now graced her finger and thought it was the most wonderful ring she had ever seen. 'I love it. But promise me you'll never gamble again!'

'Anything!' Then he kissed her.

They were disturbed by someone coughing.

'Sorry to interrupt — ' Seamus began.

'Seamus! We're engaged,' said Lucien. 'I asked Philly to marry me and she said yes. I'm so happy!'

'So am I!' said Philly feeling slightly embarrassed at having been caught in such a passionate kiss.

'Well, congratulations, the both of you.' Seamus was obviously delighted. 'Philly, I've never seen you look so pretty Your eyes are sparkling like sunbeams on the water. And you, young fella, you look as if you've won the lottery.'

'He did win some money on a horse,' said Philly, 'and he bought me this.' She held out her hand so her grandfather could admire the ring.

'You didn't get that out of a Christmas cracker!' said Seamus.

'I certainly didn't,' agreed Lucien, looking, Philly thought, terribly pleased with himself.

'Come and give your grandfather a hug,' said Seamus and, after she had done this, Philly took a good look at him.

'Now I look at you properly, you're looking very grand, Grand,' said Philly. 'You've got a new suit. I swear you haven't bought one of those since I've been alive.'

'Well,' said Seamus, slightly awkwardly. 'Your mother's been on to me to buy one for years. She'll be thrilled when she sees it.'

'So, will you wear it at Christmas?' Philly was surprised. They only really saw her parents at Christmas these days and, traditionally, her grandfather always wore the sweater that someone had given him.

'No. She'll see it when she gets here in an hour.'

Philly felt faint with shock. 'What do you mean? She's coming to the party?'

Seamus nodded. 'They all are. Your parents and the boys. Now isn't that handy? You can tell them you're engaged.'

'But why are they coming? It can't be anything to do with me, we've only just got engaged.'

'Anthea invited them and they said yes.'

'But why? She doesn't even know them.' Philly had had a couple of shocks in the past half-hour; she could do without this one. The thought of having to deal with her family, whom she found quite hard work, at the same time as she wanted to help Lucien in the kitchen with the food, was horrific. Then she realised. 'Oh God. They've come to have a look at Lucien, haven't they?'

Seamus shrugged. 'Maybe. It's fair enough, after all. You are engaged.'

'Not until twenty minutes ago!'

'You have been walking out, or dating, or whatever the current expression is, for some time though.'

Philly sighed. 'I suppose so. We were planning to visit them in Ireland — when we're not so busy.'

Seamus looked wise. 'That will be the reason they accepted Anthea's invitation. They knew you'd never find time to go and see them at home.'

'Come on, Philly,' said Lucien bracingly. 'It is a bit of a surprise but the timing's perfect.'

Her grandfather smiled gratefully. 'I would have told you before but you've only just got back and I didn't want you to be worrying about it.'

Another worry came into Philly's head she couldn't ask her grandfather about. She wanted to know if her mother would be able to tell that she and Lucien had been having sex — a lot. Then she remembered Lorna's reaction to her. She blushed at the thought of her mother coming to the conclusion she was sure Lorna had arrived at. Still, there was nothing she could do about it now. And at least she and Lucien were engaged.

'C'mon now, Philly,' said her grandfather. 'With a ring like that, at least you won't have your mother asking Lucien if he's serious about you.'

'I knew it was an investment,' said Lucien, who'd gone to check something in the oven.

'To be sure,' said Seamus. 'He's a grand young man, your family will see that.'

★ ★ ★

Later, when Philly had been sent into the garden to see if there was any rosemary, she reflected that, like almost everyone, she'd thought about the man she might fall in love with on and off since she was a teenager, what getting married would be like, how she'd cope, all the normal stuff. But what she'd never imagined was how ecstatically happy it made her, how proud she was of him, and how certain and confident she was that he was the one.

Her mother might comment on her youth, but as her mother had been a child bride too, she could hardly complain if her daughter followed suit. But she was fairly sure, because her mother had always insisted it was the case, that Marion had walked down the aisle a virgin.

She caught up with Seamus a little later. 'I wonder what I should wear for the party?' she said to him as he retied his tie in the hall mirror.

'Something pretty. A dress. Something to honour the beautiful garden,' he said.

Philly was slightly surprised that her grandfather had such a definite opinion. It had been a more or less rhetorical question, and she hadn't expected him to actually give an answer. 'I'll find something,' she said. 'At least we've a lovely day for it.'

'We have been blessed,' said her grandfather, oddly serious.

★ ★ ★

After Philly had been home to change she went back to the garden and spotted Lorna straight away. She was standing on a stepladder, tying in a rose. She was wearing a flame-coloured dress and her dark red hair was pinned back with one of the roses she was tying. Jack was holding the ladder. Seeing him look up at her, Philly recognised that he felt about Lorna as she felt about Lucien. Though to be fair, Lucien looked at her like that too. She couldn't help smiling.

She was so glad. Anthea had told her about getting Jack to repair the statues secretly and how she hoped Lorna would, in Anthea's words, 'Stop being so silly about him.' Now it seemed to Philly that Lorna was being silly about Jack, but in a way that Anthea would very much approve of.

'Hi,' she called up to Lorna. 'You look lovely. You both do.' Jack did look quite lovely, Philly thought, in his linen suit, crumpled in the right way.

'So do you,' said Lorna, having come back down the ladder. 'We don't often see you in a dress.'

Philly looked down at the rather faded flowery dress she'd found in the back of her wardrobe, bought for some occasion years ago. Its much-washed appearance did give it a faded, vintage look, she realised, appropriate for a period garden. 'I know. I quite like this one. Grand was insistent I dressed up. I think it's because my parents and both brothers are coming — oh and Lorna, we're engaged! Me and Lucien!'

'Wow!' said Lorna. She gave Philly a massive hug. 'I'm so thrilled.'

'Lucien is a very lucky man,' said Jack.

Philly rolled her eyes. 'What? With my family coming to inspect him?'

Lorna laughed. 'Yes! And is that a ring I see?'

Philly held it out to be admired.

'That is a very serious piece of jewellery,' said Jack.

'It's gorgeous,' said Lorna. 'I'm impressed.'

'So they don't know you're engaged?' said Jack.

'We hardly know ourselves!' said Philly, giving a little skip.

Lorna looked at Jack. 'We need to tell Leo,' she said to him.

'Tell him what?' asked Philly although she thought she knew.

'That we're together,' said Lorna firmly. 'He might find it a bit of a shock, his mother having a boyfriend.'

Jack frowned slightly. 'I think he's with Kirstie, checking that all the gazebos and things are up. I might go and have a word, get him on my side.'

'Good idea,' said Lorna.

While Lorna was watching Jack walk away, rather longingly, Philly thought, Philly allowed herself to think about her own mother having a boyfriend, if her father were no longer alive, and the thought was fairly gulp-making. Except her mother was nowhere near as glamorous as Lorna. 'Haven't you been out with anyone since you had Leo?'

'Not while he's been around and not many people. I'm very fussy' She laughed. 'I've had to go for a younger model.'

Her use of the word reminded Philly. 'So are you OK about it now? Him having a picture of you naked?'

'I am now,' said Lorna. 'Now I know that the real, grown-up me isn't a horrible disappointment.'

Philly laughed. 'Of course it isn't!' But she did understand Lorna's anxieties. Then she remembered her own.

'So, are you worried about your family meeting Lucien?'

She nodded. 'A bit. He's so different from

anyone they've ever met. He's posh, he's a chef, he never keeps still.'

'But he's a lovely boy — they'll see that straight away. If they look like not taking to him, I'll give him a reference. Anyway, you won his parents round. You were just as exotic to them.'

'I had to half kill myself to do it though.'

'And they saw what a good woman you are.'

Philly laughed. 'Anyway I'd better go and see how Lucien's getting on and warn him to keep the van revved up ready in case we have to make a quick getaway.'

'A horse would be more romantic,' said Lorna.

Philly shook her head. 'I'd fall off. It would end in disaster.'

⋆   ⋆   ⋆

'This looks and smells sensational,' said Philly back in the kitchen, having made a quick survey of the finished dishes that were now laid out waiting to be put in the gazebo. 'Is Anthea pleased?'

'Anthea is very pleased,' said the woman in question, who had appeared. 'But not as pleased as I am about you young things getting engaged. You're going to make a wonderful couple, a real team.'

Lucien, who was looking, in Philly's opinion, incredibly sexy in his chef's whites, nodded in agreement. 'I never thought I'd find a woman I wanted to be with for the rest of my life,' he said. 'I never thought I'd find one who matched me. But Philly does.'

Philly coughed away the tears that had suddenly gathered.

'You're very lucky,' said Anthea. 'Not only is she a hard worker, she is extremely pretty. And I like that dress. It's very suitable.'

She turned her attention to Lucien. 'You, dear boy, will have to get changed, devastating as you may look in those clothes.'

'But I'm staff,' he objected. 'I'm catering.'

'When it's done, you're a guest,' said Anthea firmly. 'I insist upon it.'

When Anthea insisted, others complied. Lucien sighed. 'OK, but not until I'm happy. What's happening with the puddings? I haven't done any.'

'All organized,' said Anthea. 'Kirstie has produced the usual Eton mess, strawberries and cream, chocolate roulade, and I'm making trifle.'

'Surely not,' said Philly. 'You're the birthday girl — you should be getting ready.'

'It's the work of moments, darling. I don't use jelly.'

She pulled a very dirty apron down from behind the door and put it on.

'If you don't mind my saying,' said Lucien, 'have you got a cleaner apron? That one is fairly disgusting.'

Philly realised she'd never have had the nerve to say anything like that to Anthea. Was it the confidence of his class that made him able to do it? Or his interest in kitchen hygiene?

Anthea looked down. 'Oh, I suppose it is a bit grubby. And of course I've got dozens more. It's just a matter of finding them.' She opened a drawer with difficulty and produced an apron.

'I must get on with my flatbreads,' said Lucien.

'What do you want me to do?' asked Philly.

'If you could clean down — ' he said.

Philly helped herself to an apron from the drawer as Anthea, pouring sherry on to trifle sponges, shook her head. 'We cleared up in my day.'

★   ★   ★

Annoyingly for Philly, she couldn't help in the kitchen and keep an eye out for the family. She was sprinkling flaked almonds over Anthea's trifles when her mother came and found her.

'Darling!' said her mother. 'How are you?' She crushed Philly to her as if they hadn't seen each other for years. 'And what's all this your grandfather told me about you being engaged? To a boy I've never even met?'

Philly's heart sank a little. She'd heard her mother's anger although she'd tried to disguise it. 'Come and meet him.'

Lucien was there before Philly could even call his name. 'Mrs Doyle. I'm Lucien. How do you do? I am so glad to meet you at last. Philly and I were coming over to visit you very soon.'

Philly observed her mother take a mental step back. She'd been fired up with indignation at her daughter getting engaged to someone she hadn't pre-approved but now he was before her, handsome, cultured and incredibly confident, she couldn't keep it up.

Mrs Doyle took the offered hand and studied

its owner briefly. 'Very nice to meet you, Lucien, if a little late in the day. Did you have to get engaged so quickly, Philly? Could you not have waited until your family had had time to meet your young man?'

'I'm afraid we couldn't wait,' said Lucien.

'And what do your parents think about it?' said Mrs Doyle, still fairly steely.

'They don't know yet,' said Lucien with a very endearing smile. 'And my parents — well — they're quite old-fashioned, but I think they'll be delighted.'

'I think you'll find that we're quite old-fashioned too,' said Mrs Doyle. 'And in my day it was usual for families to know each other a little before the young people got engaged.'

'Mum! That's because we come from a very small place. Most of my friends got together with boys they were at school with. Of course you knew the families.' Philly wondered if she'd feel quite so frustrated with her mother if they weren't in Anthea's kitchen, making food for a party. 'Will you look at the ring he's bought me?'

'Oh my God!' said Mrs Doyle before she could stop herself. 'It's like something Elizabeth Taylor would wear.'

'Who's she?' said Philly and Lucien together.

Just then, Seamus came in. 'I'm just looking for a beer for my son,' he explained. 'Oh, and you will have an opportunity to meet Lucien's family. They'll be here later.'

'What?' said Philly and Lucien in unison. 'And why?' added Philly.

'It's a party' said Seamus. 'Sure, why wouldn't

Anthea invite them?'

There seemed no answer to that. 'I'd better go and get tidy' said Philly, to get herself out of the kitchen. 'I need my party shoes.'

'And you had too, Lucien,' said Seamus. 'The party is due to start in an hour. Though the rate my grandsons are hitting the champagne, it's started already.'

★ ★ ★

By leaving Anthea's house via the back door and a hole in the hedge, they managed to get into Lucien's van without being caught by any of their relations — or indeed anyone. Pulling away in the van like fugitives made Philly giggle and she was still laughing when they reached home.

'I really want to see your parents meet mine,' she said as they raced up the stairs, 'but I kind of don't want to be there when it happens.'

'I know. But they're really just the same as each other. Concerned for us, and thinking we're too young to make such an important decision,' said Lucien. 'Although my parents do know what a wonderful woman you are and if they hadn't worked it out for themselves, Geraint would have pointed it out again.'

'And mine will love you when they stop being terrified,' said Philly, not quite as convinced. 'But they might think you're style over substance, until they realise what a hard worker you are.'

'It'll be fine,' said Lucien. 'Should I wear a suit?'

Philly loved the idea of Lucien in a suit. 'Have

you got one with you?'

'Dad brought one over when we had dinner with them, remember?'

Philly frowned. 'But you didn't wear it?'

'No. I was rebelling at the time. I'm happy to wear a suit for Anthea, though. And to honour you, beautiful girl.'

A little while later, Lucien, smart in his suit, and Philly, her old dress enhanced by flowers in her hair and her fabulous engagement ring on her finger, appeared in the garden. Lucien was desperate to go to the kitchen but Philly clung on to him. 'Kirstie's got all sorts of people in to do the serving. We must do the parent-meeting thing. Before the bulk of the guests come. Or it'll be hanging over me.'

'You're not worried about seeing my parents, are you? They love you.'

'They might have changed their minds. At least you've met my mother already. She's the tough one. Come and meet Da.' She took his hand and led him.

'Da!' She gave him a long hug. 'This is Lucien.' Philly's father wasn't one given to hugging members of the opposite sex, but he offered his hand in a friendly way. 'Lucien. How are you? I gather you've taken on my daughter?'

'And she's taken me on, I'm glad to say,' said Lucien.

'And these are my brothers,' said Philly, seeing them through Lucien's eyes as tall, bulky men in shiny suits.

But he didn't seem to see them like that. 'Hi, guys. What do I have to do to show you I'm

330

worthy of your sister? I'm not much in the fighting line but my bread rolls are outstanding!'

After a second, Liam, the eldest, laughed and clapped Lucien on the shoulder. 'You're as mad as she is. You'll get along fine.'

Philly was just celebrating that having gone well when they spotted Lucien's parents approaching. Briefly she considered rushing to the loo to escape but realised both sets of parents would be convinced she was pregnant. No, she would have to go through with the introductions.

'Um — Mr and Mrs — ' she began.

'Mum and Dad,' said Lucien, earning her undying love only he had it already. 'Meet Philly's parents and brothers.' He performed the introductions as if he'd been doing it all his life. Philly realised he probably had. 'We're so thrilled you could all come,' he finished.

'Yes,' Philly managed, smiling and blushing.

'You must call me Camilla. And this is Jasper,' said Lucien's mother to Philly's. 'And I have to tell you we adore Philly.'

'They're very young — ' began Marion.

'I know,' agreed Camilla, 'but very committed. Philly was absolutely marvellous helping out with Lucien's bakery.'

Marion frowned. 'A bakery? But Philly's never cooked in her life!'

'You should try her sourdough onion rolls,' said Lucien with a wink. 'Now, let me organise drinks for everyone.'

28

Lorna was in the little glade behind the grotto, decorating Jack's statues with garlands. It was partly for fun, and partly so she wouldn't have to help Anthea with the meet-and-greet of the people who would shortly be arriving. Mostly though, it was a tribute to Jack.

Ceres, goddess of agriculture, who had a cornucopia, now had a garland of poppies, daisies, various grasses and anemones and cornflowers. Flora was already wearing a stone wreath, and now had real roses, little pansies and some very historically inaccurate dahlias, which looked gorgeous. Pomona, who only had a wreath of flowers, had real tiny apples and pears in her stone basket, stuck there with Blu-Tack.

Lorna was just contemplating nipping back to Anthea's fruit garden for some undersized plums when her son found her.

'There you are,' said Leo.

He was, she thought again, incredibly handsome. His hair was clean and floppy, his cream linen suit (which she hadn't seen before) was only slightly crumpled, and the panama hat he was holding in his hand appeared more of a prop than sun protection. To his mother he seemed to resemble a character out of *Brideshead Revisited*. He was also looking sulky.

'Were you looking for me? You look wonderful, darling.'

'I *was* looking for you. Philly told me you were here. I wanted to know if it was true.'

'What was true?' Although she knew perfectly well.

'About you and Jack? Are you back together again?'

'Yes. Yes we are.'

'But you didn't see him for weeks and weeks. You never heard from him, did you?'

Lorna considered lying but only briefly. Part of her wanted to tell Leo it was none of his business but she understood his anxiety. And she was a bit worried about him. He spent so much time with Kirstie (she'd suddenly realised Kirstie must have provided the linen suit and panama hat) she was worried that he might be in love with her. And it was unlikely that Kirstie would leave Peter for Leo, even if she was fond of him. As always, honesty was best.

'There were communication problems but since — '

'Since when?' Leo was indignant.

Lorna was sympathetic. 'Listen, I know it must all seem a bit rushed to you. One minute we have no contact, the next we're a couple. But things change, settle, sort themselves out.'

'It's just not very dignified, Mum. He leaves you broken-hearted then swans back into your life — and you just let him.'

'It wasn't quite like that.' Although she could see it must appear so from his perspective.

'Well, what was it like, then?' Leo demanded, sounding worryingly parental.

To Lorna's enormous relief, Jack appeared

333

from behind the shrubbery. 'Hi, Leo.' He came and put his arm round Lorna's waist, hugging her possessively to him. 'I do understand how it must look. And you're right, we weren't in touch for weeks and it was agony. I won't bore you with the technicalities but the fact that Lorna realised the reasons I wasn't in touch with her were true was amazing.' He paused. 'I love your mother very much. I won't ever be your stepdad or anything scary like that, but I hope you will come to think of me as a friend, someone you can turn to for advice, stuff like that.' He seemed a bit embarrassed. 'I can't believe I just said all that. It's true but it sounds — '

Lorna, who was blushing after his public announcement, said, 'It sounds a bit of a cliché but clichés only become clichés because they're true.'

Jack went on: 'But when I said I wouldn't ever be your stepdad, I didn't mean I didn't want to marry your mother. I do, very much.'

Leo regained his sense of humour and started to laugh. 'You're not asking permission to marry my mother, are you?'

'Oh my God!' said Lorna, appalled for many reasons.

Jack frowned a little. 'Well, no, I'm not. But I want you to know my intentions. I need to talk to Lorna first.'

'Bit late now!' said Leo. 'You've made it public. It's like one of those flashmob proposals, when fifty people break into song — '

'Hardly' said Lorna.

'So, will you marry me?' asked Jack, turning to her.

'I'm not going to be proposed to with my son present,' said Lorna firmly, but laughing as well.

'I'd better run along then,' said Leo, but before he could leave, Philly appeared.

'Anthea's trying to gather people. Ordinary guests are arriving and she wants us all there together,' she said.

'Have you any idea why?' asked Lorna.

Philly shrugged. 'Not really. But frankly, I don't understand anything that's going on today.'

'Me neither,' agreed Leo. 'But I think I need a drink.'

'What a good idea!' said Lorna. But as she made to follow Philly and Leo into the main garden, Jack caught her arm.

'So, will you? Will you marry me?'

In the months when they'd been apart and every waking and unwaking thought was of Jack, Lorna hadn't thought about marriage. But now, when he was looking at her so urgently, so ardently, with his restored statues as witnesses, she knew she wanted it too: she wanted to plight their troth in public, to tell the world they loved each other and were truly committed. 'Yes,' she said. 'Yes I will.'

He crushed her to him, and they stayed there until one of Philly's brothers came to find them.

★ ★ ★

'Ladies and gentlemen,' said Peter to the assembled guests standing in front of the grotto,

335

'as you know, we are here to celebrate my mother's birthday. Kirstie and I, on my mother's behalf, are delighted to welcome so many of you to this occasion, which is also to celebrate this recreation of a garden, lost for many years, and now rediscovered and restored.'

'Not completely restored,' muttered Lorna to Jack. 'There's loads more to be done.'

Peter hadn't finished. He had cue cards in his hand. 'I think you'll agree, if you've had a chance to look already, that the highlight of the garden is the grotto. This has been restored by the wonderful Lorna, who painstakingly, shell by shell, restored it, including my mother's initials: 'A' and 'S'.'

Lorna was forced to interrupt. 'Actually, it was ammonites for the initials and Jack did the — '

But no one heard as Seamus had come forward. 'If you don't mind, Peter, could I say a few words?'

Peter looked disconcerted for a few moments and then said, 'Well, I was just going to thank everyone — '

'I'll do that,' said Seamus firmly. Anthea, at his side, smiled at the assembled company.

She was wearing a beautifully cut dress in silver-grey. The bottom half was embroidered with exotic birds and plants and her low-heeled shoes were embroidered to match. Her hair, which was swept into a chignon, had a clip with real flowers that matched those on her dress.

Lorna had never seen Anthea look so beautiful or so groomed, and as she admired her friend she remembered seeing a young woman in a smart uniform slip into the house. Anthea must have had help doing her hair and make-up. All was now clear. Today was Anthea's birthday and she wanted to celebrate by looking sensational.

'Well now, everyone,' said Seamus, who also looked extremely smart. 'Peter here has welcomed you, and Anthea and I also want to welcome you, but we're not here because it's Anthea's birthday.'

There was a murmur of disappointment.

'Although it is her birthday, it's not a *significant* birthday. At least . . . ' He paused, obviously relishing having an audience. ' . . . not significant in the way you think it is.'

'Well, it is her seventy-fifth!' said Peter loudly.

Kirstie, who was looking like a WAG at Ascot, slightly inappropriate but very decorative, hushed him.

'Why you're all here, including my family from Ireland, who up until now haven't had the pleasure of meeting Anthea, is because we're here to celebrate something quite different.'

Lorna suddenly felt slightly dizzy. Surely not!

'We are here to celebrate our marriage!' said Seamus.

There was a shocked silence before Lorna, closely followed by Jack, began to applaud. Everyone else joined in and there were whoops and cheers from the Irish boys, drowning out the sharp intakes of breath uttered by their mother.

'We've actually been married for a few days now but have kept it secret until we could announce it to our families, all together,' Seamus went on.

Then Anthea stepped forward. 'We thought you'd make a fuss if we told you before we did it, so that's why we didn't say anything until now. And although my initials are A. S., those ammonites that Lorna and Jack placed so carefully aren't for Anthea Susannah, but for Anthea and Seamus. But that's it as far as drama is concerned, so now please do go and get another drink or two before the food is ready. Lucien has done a splendid job.'

Seamus embraced his wife in a bear hug to more applause and Lorna realised she was slightly relieved they didn't go for a full-on kiss. Somehow it would have been undignified.

Peter was looking a bit shaken. Kirstie had hurried away, possibly to get him a glass of champagne. Lorna went over to him and drew him away from the throng to a little seat that was screened by roses. The news hadn't come as a huge shock to her, and probably wouldn't surprise Philly, because they'd both seen how close Anthea and Seamus were getting. But Peter hadn't spent time on the garden, or noticed how often Anthea turned to Seamus for support. He probably saw Seamus as the motor mechanic he was proud to be, not as a potential husband for his aristocratic mother.

'Peter? Are you OK?' He had been her friend for so long that she was probably the best one to reassure him now.

'I don't know,' said Peter. 'I mean, I like Seamus, but it never occurred to me that there was anything going on between him and my mother. I mean — she's always been such a snob! He has an Irish accent! And don't say it's a brogue, that always says 'shoes' to me.'

'It's a charming accent,' said Lorna. 'I love an Irish accent myself. And he's a dear man. He'll look after her and they have fun together.'

'Did you know?' he asked accusingly.

'No, but I've seen them together and so I'm not surprised they love each other.'

'But, Lorna — I don't want to seem snobbish now but really — '

'Now, Peter, they are both quite old enough to know their own minds. It obviously wasn't a spur-of-the-moment decision — she's clearly been planning it for months. I think part of the reason she wanted to restore this garden is so they could celebrate their marriage here. I think it's absolutely lovely!' She paused. 'You're going out with a woman you found on the internet, after all.'

'Nothing wrong with that!'

'I know. And there's nothing wrong with people meeting each other in the ordinary course of events and getting married either. Even if they didn't ask permission from their families first.'

'She might have consulted me! I mean, she's my mother. As far as I know, she hasn't had anyone since my father died.'

'Only as far as you know, Peter. Maybe she has had flings with other people, but this time it's serious. Now go and congratulate her. Be happy for them both!'

'Oh, very well,' he said reluctantly. 'But would you get married without telling Leo first?'

Lorna laughed. Peter and Leo were both being indignant in exactly the same way. 'Well, as it happens, no.'

Peter turned to her sharply. 'What do you mean 'as it happens' — you haven't got married, have you? You and that stonemason chap?' He found her left hand and inspected her fingers.

'No!' said Lorna, who was laughing a lot by now. 'Although Jack and I are engaged — but only just, so I haven't got a ring yet.'

Jack appeared, holding two glasses of champagne. He gave one to Lorna. 'I only asked her about half an hour ago,' he explained. Gallantly, he handed the second glass to Peter.

'You can be the first to drink to us,' said Lorna.

Peter sighed, but then smiled and raised his glass. 'I wish you both very happy' He turned to Jack. 'But if you treat her badly you'll have me to answer to. She was mine first!'

'No I wasn't,' said Lorna. 'We've been friends for years, certainly, but — '

'Well, that's what I meant, of course.'

But Lorna was aware that his gaze was lingering a little. Maybe, she thought, when I was still in love with him, I should have dressed up a bit more often. That might have done the trick. But she was very glad that she hadn't, she decided.

'There you are!' said Kirstie, also holding glasses. 'I've been looking for you everywhere. Oh, you've got a drink.'

'I haven't,' said Jack, taking a glass from Kirstie's hand.

'Lorna and Jack are engaged,' said Peter. 'We must toast them.'

'I don't see a ring,' said Kirstie sharply.

'It's too recent for a ring,' explained Jack.

'Well, honestly,' said Kirstie. 'First it's Philly and Lucien, then Anthea and Seamus, now Lorna and Jack. When is it going to be my turn?'

Lorna and Jack looked at each other. 'I think we should leave you to get on with it, Peter,' said Lorna, catching Jack's arm.

When they were out of earshot she said to Jack, 'Do you think Peter will propose?'

He shrugged. 'I expect so. This secret garden that you created is a very magical place.'

Lorna gave a deep sigh of satisfaction. 'It is enchanted. I really think it is.'

'Maybe we should have our wedding party here,' he said when he'd kissed her.

'That's an excellent idea,' she said. 'It brought us together and made me so happy.'

'Me too,' he said. 'Now let's not tell people straight-away. It's Anthea and Seamus's day, after all.'

Lorna smiled. 'It's lovely to know that you can fall in love at any time in your life, or at any age.'

'Exactly so, my darling,' said Jack.

We do hope that you have enjoyed reading this large print book.

Did you know that all of our titles are available for purchase?

We publish a wide range of high quality large print books including:
Romances, Mysteries, Classics
General Fiction
Non Fiction and Westerns

Special interest titles available in large print are:
The Little Oxford Dictionary
Music Book
Song Book
Hymn Book
Service Book

Also available from us courtesy of Oxford University Press:
Young Readers' Dictionary
(large print edition)
Young Readers' Thesaurus
(large print edition)

For further information or a free brochure, please contact us at:
Ulverscroft Large Print Books Ltd.,
The Green, Bradgate Road, Anstey,
Leicester, LE7 7FU, England.
Tel: (00 44) 0116 236 4325
Fax: (00 44) 0116 234 0205